BRIDE TAKES A SCOT

Highland Vows & Vengeance
Book 1

by Kara Griffin

ARE YOU SIGNED UP FOR DRAGONBLADE'S BLOG?

You'll get the latest news and information on exclusive giveaways, exclusive excerpts, coming releases, sales, free books, cover reveals and more.

Check out our complete list of authors, too!

No spam, no junk. That's a promise!

Sign Up Here

www.dragonbladepublishing.com

Dearest Reader;

Thank you for your support of a small press. At Dragonblade Publishing, we strive to bring you the highest quality Historical Romance from some of the best authors in the business. Without your support, there is no 'us', so we sincerely hope you adore these stories and find some new favorite authors along the way.

Happy Reading!

CEO, Dragonblade Publishing

About the Book

Laird Declan MacKendrick, falsely imprisoned in King Alexander's dungeon, is offered his freedom with one stipulation—that he marry a border baron's daughter. Accused of murdering his neighbor, a Campbell, Declan means to prove his innocence and find his enemy. If he must marry to do so, then so be it. But Declan doesn't expect his new bride to be as beautiful or beguiling as Lady Isabella.

Isabella Forrester isn't pleased by the king's edict that she marry a man of his choosing. She doesn't believe in marriage for love and always knew she'd marry a man for political alliance. Marriage to a Highlander means that not only must she adjust to a husband, but a whole new way of life amongst people who won't trust her for her Sassenach ways. Then she meets Declan MacKendrick who introduces her to a life she never could have imagined as a wife to a laird.

Her days are spent in loneliness and isolation, but the nights in his sultry embraces might win her heart's surrender. She cannot help but be won over by the noble, seductive Scot. Isabella meets her new husband's son, a lad of tender years who cannot hear. The poor lad is ignored by all in the clan, even his father. Isabella makes it her responsibility to see to his caring and hopes the clan eventually accepts them both.

Declan wants nothing more than to find his accuser to enact his vengeance. He suspects the Campbells are behind the claims that induced his imprisonment. Someone wants to destroy and weaken his clan. But could his enemy be closer than he thinks? When Isabella's life is threatened, Declan must confront a trusted ally to carry out his vengeance.

Will these Highland vows and vengeance hold the promise of love and redemption for Declan and Isabella?

Character List

MacKendrick Clan
Declan MacKendrick – Hero
Leona – Wife (deceased)
Noah – Son
Claude – Brother
Rhona – Sister
Marian – Grandmother
Helena – Stepmother
Silas – Stepbrother
Anse – Cousin, Commander-in-arms
Trevor, Slone, Lorcan – Soldiers
Rolly – Steward
Edith – Maid Servant
Lillith – Healer

Heroine
Isabella Forrester – Heroine
Adam – Father
Joan – Mother
Christopher – Brother
Bedelia – Healer

Other Notables
Robbie Campbell – Rival
Micah – Campbell commander-in-arms
Dermot Murray – Ally

Faelan – Friar

Willeli – Rhona's beau

King Alexander

Queen Margaret

CHAPTER ONE

Castle Dungeons
Edinburgh, Scotland
March 1260

CLANKS FROM IRON bars, shouts from the prisoners, and pleas for help from the dying alerted Declan MacKendrick that the warden was making his rounds. For nearly three months, he'd been imprisoned in Edinburgh's dreadful dungeons for the murder of his former father-in-law, clan leader, Alan Campbell, but it was a crime he hadn't committed. During that time, he became accustomed to the stench of rotten food, and death, and God only knew what else existed in the dungeons beneath Edinburgh's impenetrable fortress.

He awaited the opportunity to profess his innocence, but no one came to retrieve him for his sentencing. Declan expected the chancellor's curia to tell him what the court had decided. He knew well enough that getting a fair trial was laughable and that his fate would probably be death by hanging. The sentence would be his cross to bear because murder was a heinous crime punishable by death. If someone wanted to imprison you or end your life, all they had to do was make an accusation. Bent sheriffs ruled lawless areas of Scotland and subjected anyone, even lairds, to their unlawful will. One of his enemies must have paid handsomely to have him detained. Yet he could think of no enemy or situation that would warrant such provocation besides the Campbells, whose laird he'd been accused of murdering.

Footsteps came closer and reverberated in the small corridor. The warder stopped before his cell and motioned to the other men standing behind him. "Bring him."

The rattle and clinking of keys and creak of the door as it opened echoed off the long narrow hallway. Noise from the guards caused the other inmates to shake their chains and they shouted blasphemous words when they passed. Declan wanted to cover his ears as the noise jarred him but when they stopped outside his cell door, he shrank back against the wall.

He didn't move when the men entered and approached. Given barely enough food to sustain him, and even less water, he'd weakened and couldn't stand on his own. The jailers unlocked his fetters at his wrists and ankles and tossed them aside to land with a clank on the damp stone floor. They reached for him and forced him to stand, but his knees buckled, and he pitched forward. The men grabbed his arms and practically dragged him from the cell.

"The king wishes to see you," the warder said. To his underlings, he clipped, "He is not to be harmed. Have a care because the king commanded that he not be injured."

Why the king had sent for him perplexed Declan. Perhaps he wanted to hand down his sentence himself. Declan tensed at that. Would his life be ended on this day? If that was so, he had no regrets. His maker knew the truth. He lived with a wee bit of piety, and although his sins were many, he had not committed outright murder. If only he could convince Chancellor Inverkeithing of his innocence, he could save his neck from the noose. Yet he had no proof to sway justice to his favor.

Thoughts of his family entered his mind. Anguish filled him that he wouldn't see his young son again, his siblings whom he practically raised, and his clan. Declan prayed his clan wouldn't mourn him long or be in chaos after learning of his death. But he relied on good men to keep order whenever he was away from his lands. Anse, his cousin, and commander-in-arms, would ensure all maintained order. His most seasoned soldiers, Trevor, Slone, and Lorcan, would see that the men protected their lands and clan. Silas, his stepbrother, would most likely be elected to lead the clan upon his death. That appeased him somewhat and reassured him that his clan was in good hands.

Corridors of stone walls and walkways led to the upper floors of the castle, where King Alexander made his residence. Although the young king still had two years before he reached his majority, he ruled over much of the kingdom with the aid of advisors. At a large wooden door that showed its age with cracking and discoloration, the warder knocked and waited. Someone shouted to enter, and he opened the door and motioned to his men to amble forward. The warder's men held tightly to his arms and dragged him forward, into the king's private domain.

A page holding a flagon stood at the end of a scarred wooden table flanked by more chairs similar to the one he'd been directed to sit in. At each place was an empty goblet, just waiting to be filled by that page, who stood staring at Declan with wide, rapidly blinking blue eyes.

Declan imagined he probably looked dirty and disheveled, and very much like the murderer he was accused of being. He wondered what would happen if he spoke to the lad and then decided not to in case he spooked him even more. Instead, he let his gaze travel around the room, taking in the faded tapestries lining the walls, the large hearth with its smoking embers, and the side table holding parchments, ink, and quills.

As he sat in wait for Alexander, he eyed a plain goblet that sat before him and wished it was full as a deep thirst taunted him. But he wouldn't be so forward to ask the page to fill it and risk possibly irking the king even more.

Declan took a deep breath to settle himself. What he wouldn't do to see his beloved Highlands again. He missed its frigid climate, barren stretches of land and hills, pristine lochs, and forests of towering pines. Most of all, he'd missed the fresh air and the solitary cottage he'd stolen away to when he needed a wee bit of respite from his needful clan. He didn't have time to ruminate further because the king himself entered the room.

Alexander strode into the chamber a moment later and approached the table where he waited. The page hastened to fill Alexander's goblet, which sat next to a stack of parchments on the tabletop. The tall king reached his place at the table with a quick stride, and as he sat, he pressed back the wavy reddish locks of his hair and then rubbed his eyes. Alexander appeared as weary as Declan felt. The page moved to stand by the king's chair and waited for his master's direction, but Alexander shooed the lad away. Declan was astounded when the king reached across the table and handed him the goblet.

"Drink, you must be thirsty."

Declan's hand shook as he held the goblet to his mouth. He didn't want to appear weakened to his king, but his health had deteriorated in the last month. The ale tasted sour, so he only took a few small sips, enough to wet his throat. With nothing in his stomach, he was sure he'd retch if he swallowed a gulp like he wanted.

"MacKendrick," Alexander said and leaned to grab a stack of missives from the table behind his chair. He tossed them onto the table in front of him and they spread across the wood. "These are proclamations from your clansmen and women declaring your innocence and demanding your release. Their pleas arrive daily. I'm inclined to believe them, but I must hear from your mouth that you did not murder Allan Campbell."

"I did not murder him." Declan's voice rasped from disuse. "He was my wife's father. Why would I kill him?"

The king nodded. "I know not how you came to be in the dungeon or who accused you of his murder, but you will not return. When I heard you resided there, I disbelieved what you were accused of because I know you to be an honorable man. I am aware of your troubles with the Campbells, but I find it hard to believe you would murder your dead wife's father. This matter is closed as far as I'm concerned."

That was a great relief, and Declan let the tenseness of his shoulders ebb. He had many questions, but it was best he allowed the king to speak and not cause his affront by being too forward.

"Your freedom, though, will come at a cost."

Declan should have known the king would demand recompense. He considered what the man wanted in return for his freedom, what had happened in recent months, and how his aid might benefit his sovereign. But he hadn't been privy to political matters since being behind bars, and what wealth he had he wasn't about to share with the king unless he had no other recourse.

"I am innocent, and of course, Sire, I wouldst gladly repay ye for your benevolence. Ye have only to state your need." He waited for the king's demand.

Alexander stood and rounded his table, striding to the window casement with his hands clasped behind his back. He peered out where Declan could see the castle grounds that butted the courtyard, and the two large turrets flanked the gatehouse before turning back to him. The king appeared apprehensive. Whatever Alexander wanted certainly caused his uneasiness.

"As you know, I am not on good terms with the Highland clans. I mean to change that, and so I would like you to marry a woman from the south. It has long been my hope to unite our lands and marriage will afford me to bring my people together."

Bollocks, Declan thought, there it was, the price of his freedom. Alexander had no care about the unity of his people. There was something greater that he hoped to achieve. Declan wasn't dim-witted and could almost smell the pile of cosh Alexander was dishing out. He suspected Alexander hoped to infuse his army with Highlanders and Lowlanders.

But it mattered not to him because Declan was loyal to Scotland, and if his king needed additional men with swords, he certainly had the wherewithal to supply him with such. He would be free and if the king needed him to marry a woman from the southern region as well as the use of his army, he wouldn't gainsay him.

"Do ye have a specific lady in mind, Sire?"

Alexander turned from the window and smiled at his acquiescence. Declan noted the widening of his lips behind his reddish, straggly beard. "You are not the only groom. There are four women who I mean to betroth."

Declan grunted. "Do I get to choose from these lassies? Who are the other grooms?"

"Lairds Cameron, Buchanan, and MacKintosh."

He shifted forward on his chair and scowled. His discord showed on his face because he couldn't hide his outrage at hearing the names of the other clans involved in Alexander's ploy. Though he wasn't on good terms with those clans, neighbors whose lands butted his, they weren't particularly rivals either. At least the king hadn't included the Campbells, his most hated enemy of late. The Campbells had befriended many clans in the Highlands, but Declan was unaware of any alliance with the Camerons, Buchanans, or MacKintoshs.

"Before you balk at being in their company, MacKendrick, you should know that I have asked those lairds because they, like you, are unmarried. They also have fierce armies, which I will call upon when needed. King Haakon cares more about Norway's piety than he does about keeping his lands. If he cares not for them, then those lands are there for the taking. I want to stretch my kingdom as far north and west as I can. With the Highland clans' aid, I mean to do just that."

His suspicions came to fruition because the king wanted something more from him than to unite his subjects. He wanted his army, but Alexander would need skilled soldiers if he intended to go against Haakon and his invincible fleets. Haakon's fleets ruled the northern and westerly waterways which probably caused Alexander's grief.

If Declan's freedom wasn't in jeopardy, he would have

scoffed aloud at the man and told him to find another milksop to do his bidding. It was enough that he paid a handsome levy to the king for his vast lands, but now he wanted his soldiers to fight for his gain as well. Being far north, he and his brethren could easily give their fealty to Haakon, the king of Norway, or they could give it to Alexander. Declan gave his loyalty to Scotland's sovereignty because he would rather serve a demanding king than an absent one.

"Your scowl tells me you're in disagreement, but before you say nay, I would tell you that there are other important incentives to consider. You will wed a woman from the border, and shall offer your army when in need, and in return, I shall forgo the tithe on your lands for one year."

The inducement of Alexander's offer raised his brows because the king practically offered a fortune in the dispensation of tax for his acquiescence. Of course, he wasn't about to turn Alexander down, regardless. Gaining his freedom and the opportunity to wreak vengeance on his enemy was enough to gain his favor. It mattered not who the king insisted he marry, nor that he wanted his army to fight for his causes. But the exemption of paying the tithe was of great interest. With more coins in his coffers, he'd be able to use them to secure his clan and enrich his farmers, something which greatly mattered to him. Clan MacKendrick's future was looking brighter by the minute.

"There is one further benefit to your accord."

He shifted back in the chair and focused on the king's face. Alexander appeared sincere in his offer and so Declan decided to give him his full attention. "Aye, Sire, and that is?"

"I am aware of the rivalries in the north and that you often fight amongst yourselves. You are not on friendly terms with the Camerons, Buchanans, or MacKintoshs, I take it?"

"We are not on friendly terms, nay, but we are not warring at the moment."

The king chuckled. "Aye? You're all a bunch of misbehaved bairns—aye, like children—there in the north fighting amongst yourselves over a mile here and a mile there of land. Fortunately, you are all far enough away and I rarely have to contend with your squabbles."

"We do appreciate a good fracas once in a while." Declan almost smiled at the king's banter.

"I have decided to hold a hand-to-hand battle without weapons. This shall settle the matter of the first choice of bride. I will select the matches. The winner of each match will choose his bride until all the lassies are selected."

Declan wanted to bellow with laughter. The king wanted entertainment, and he used his ploy to bring him a show of their strength. Yet Declan was in no condition to fight anyone, though perhaps in three months or possibly more, he would regain enough vigor to be effective enough. He wasn't about to lose to his fellow Highlanders, but he wouldn't say so to his overlord.

"I understand you have been kept in the dungeon for months and are in no condition for such a melee," Alexander said as if reading his thoughts. He returned to his chair but didn't sit.

"Aye, without a trial," Declan said with angst.

"I cannot speak to that, MacKendrick, because I only just found out that you were there. This matter must be settled at the soonest because I am leaving after the weddings and am taking my wife to see her family in England."

"Ye are traveling to England, Sire?"

Alexander scowled as if he wasn't thrilled with the prospect of visiting England. Declan suspected that had more to do with Alexander's relatives, the King of England himself, Henry, Queen Margaret's father.

"Aye, my wife wishes to have our bairn there amongst her family and I promised I would take her for a visit. Be warned, MacKendrick, always follow through on your promises to your wife. For if you do not, it will make for a hellish life, especially when your wife's father is a damned king."

Declan resisted chuckling at Alexander's disgruntlement. He'd heard there had been discord between Alexander and his wife, which appeared to have been settled since he was taking her to England for a visit with her family.

"I shall remember that, Sire, and will follow your advice."

Alexander leaned on the edge of his chair and nodded. "You'll need a wee bit of time and so I will allow you a month to heal and to settle your clan matters. You will return here on the first of April, and we shall have the battle, the wedding, and your signed accord. You may bring family with you if you wish, for it is your wedding and a time for joyous celebration." The king chuckled under his breath, albeit sarcastically.

His hanging was sounding better with each passing moment, but Declan wasn't about to declare that to Alexander. "Ye have my accord, Sire." That wasn't much time, but Declan would have to make do.

"Good...Good. Then I shall have you taken to a chamber where you can bathe, eat, and rest before your journey home on the morrow."

"My thanks, Sire."

Alexander raised an auburn eyebrow and Declan thought he might have winked at him. He shook his head and disbelieved the king was being amiable because it was well known that Alexander was temperamental and had an unpleasant nature. Though he was young, he handled the country's parliamentary lords and gained many of their respect. Yet he hadn't won over the clans of the Highlands yet.

"I should tell you, MacKendrick, before you leave...You won't be disappointed with the ladies I have selected as the brides. I have found the bonniest women in Scotland, and I bid you to remember that when the time comes to take your vows. You'll have a hard decision to make, choosing one of the brides."

CHAPTER TWO

Corstorphine Village
Midlothian, Scotland
March 1260

ISABELLA FORRESTER SPENT all morning toiling over various pots and tying herbs to hang about Madam Bedelia's cottage. Most of her mornings were spent learning the healing methods Madam was renowned for. As a close friend to her grandmother, the aged, white-haired woman offered to teach her the correct methods of dispensing medicinals and stitching wounds to avoid infection. She'd learned how to ease the pain from broken bones to the minor discomfort of an ailing stomach. A stern teacher, over time Madam's blue eyes now more often softened when Isabella answered her questions accurately.

She was proud to possess such skills, mainly because her mother objected to the pursuit of healing. Mother often remarked that healing was an improper skill for a wife and that it was best left to the servants or others. If only her mother knew the lengths she'd gone to gain such wisdom, she'd probably scold her for days. But Isabella disregarded Mother and she learned the healing practices mainly to aid her father or his men, who often returned home injured from a night of revelry.

Isabella first began her lessons at the age of five and for nearly fifteen years, she'd surpassed most of Madam's tests. Unbeknownst to her mother, Isabella only stayed in the village until the sun rose high enough to indicate it neared midday. That's when her mother typically rose and left her bedchamber.

Still, it was easy to lose track of time when she was intently listening to Madam's instruction. Midday had passed, and in haste, Isabella bade Madam farewell and sprinted toward home. She had to get inside the manor before her mother noticed her absence.

Fortunately, her mother hadn't risen yet and she rushed up the steps to her bedchamber. There, she changed her garments because she was certain she smelled like the herbs she'd tied in bundles most of the morning.

Men's shouts came from the great hall on the lower level of her home. Isabella derided the cheers and scoffed at their blatant sinful behavior. The hunting party had returned early and with apparent success, evidenced by the men's mirthful mood. Isabella hoped they hadn't harmed anyone whilst raiding their neighbors. Though her father had told her he'd gone hunting, she was well aware that really, he'd been thieving. Stolen sheep, cattle, and other valuables were one thing, but harming or taking the life of a person was an entirely different matter. She had spent her first waking moments in the chapel, praying for God's forgiveness for her father and his men's wretched behavior. Had it all been for naught?

As quickly as she could, Isabella re-garbed herself and ran a comb through the soft waves of her blond hair. She slipped on her boots and tugged a shawl around her shoulders. In her haste to join her family in the hall, she had forgotten to grab her satchel of medicinals. Surely one of her father's followers needed aid. It was unlikely they'd returned unscathed from their dubious mission.

Isabella snatched the pouch from the side table in her bedchamber and tucked it under her arm. With quick steps, she left her room to march through the keep until she reached the hall and found the trestle table filled with her father's closest men, all of whom thieved. She set the pouch on a side table and moved farther into the great hall.

"Look at the lot of you," she said accusingly with a waggle of her finger. "You're all sotted already and have only returned. Supper hasn't even been put on the table and you're well into your cups. What did you take this time?"

Her father, Lord Adam Forrester, laughed garishly. "Be not hostile, my dearest daughter…"

"Your *only* daughter, I remind you. And do not 'dearest daughter' me. Just tell me this: did you hurt or kill anyone? Have I wasted time on my knees in the chapel for naught?" She set her hands on her hips and glared at her father in wait for his answer.

"Now, now, sweet lass, we only took a cart full of sheep. None were harmed, I vow."

"But it was a merry time," Joseph, her father's steward, said with a grin.

Isabella scowled harshly at Joseph and then at her father. Her father's short dark hair stuck out and it appeared he hadn't bathed in days, given the smudges of dirt on his lightly whiskered cheek. Along with that, her father's garments were filthy and smelled of sheep excrement and Lord knew what else. To her relief though, he appeared uninjured, as well as his followers. She wouldn't have need of her medicines or skills today, praise God. As usual, however, she needed to remind her father of the perils of his entertainment.

"One day you're going to get caught. I worry that you will be hurt or worse, imprisoned. You'll all be swinging from the gallows one day for your thievery. I would beg ye to cease, but you are all too bull-headed to listen."

Her father thought she was jesting and bellowed a laugh as did the rest of his men.

Isabella wished her brother wasn't off fighting at the behest of the English king because he might help to sway their father from his sinful thievery. When Christopher had heard that King Henry of England would send more men on a crusade, her brother left home to join the cause. If only King Louis of France hadn't lost the battle in Levant. Now her brother was off fighting a noble war on behalf of the Pope. Christopher was extremely devout and sided with her on the matter of their father's thievery.

At the thought of Christopher her heart ached because she doubted that she'd ever see her brother again. Few returned from the crusades, and many had perished in the battles against the infidels. To her, though, warring against anyone was sinful regardless of their beliefs.

"Isabella, you know we like to raid, and no one ever holds us to account for it. It is just our way, daughter. Our neighbors expect a little thievery from time to time, just as we do. Cease nagging me about it. It's all respectable."

"Respectable? You should all be praying to God for His forgiveness. Thievery is sinful, Father, and I remind you to seek the confessional soon. I cannot believe Mother allows you to steal from our neighbors." Isabella ambled across the hall and poured herself a small cup of wine. She was about to sit next to her father when her mother made her way into the hall.

Lady Joan Forrester's beauty was renowned, and her father had said he'd fallen in love with her the moment he had set eyes on her. Isabella didn't believe such a thing was possible. There was no such thing as love at first sight or even love, for that matter. That people professed such nonsense humored her. She was more pragmatic in her view of marriage and courtship.

"Darling, sit up straight. You shouldn't hold your cup like that. It's unladylike." Her mother pressed a hand over the strands of her blond hair. "You must take better care of your hair. My maid should fix it for you. And why in heaven's name would you wear that wretched old gown?"

Isabella didn't answer because her mother didn't expect her to do so. Instead, she set her cup down and sighed at her mother's reprimand. The "old gown" was a favorite of hers and she wore it as soon as it was laundered. She didn't care to put her hair in coifs, braids, or even pull it up. Instead, she preferred to let her hair flow down her back. So what if it got tangled and straggly by day's end?

Her mother constantly berated her for her unladylike behavior and even the most minuscule matters. But Isabella knew it was better to stay silent because talking back meant even more criticism. She'd never hear the end of it and had learned that doing so certainly wasn't worth the lecture she'd receive. But this day Isabella's hackles were up, and she meant to reproach her father for his behavior and her mother for her harassment as well.

"Should you not speak to Father about his stealing? He and his men went on another raid and stole our neighbor's sheep again." She glared at her father, who seemed impervious to her scolding.

Her mother laughed lightly. "Oh, darling, they do like to raid. This matter doesn't concern you, for it is a man's nature to thieve and you shouldn't involve yourself in matters of men. Now cease this unbecoming talk at once. Have a little decorum and set your mind to matters of the home."

The discussion was closed. Isabella sighed and snatched her cup from the table. She held it in her fisted hand and drank down the contents until it was gone. As much as she cared for her parents, they could be a tad bit overbearing. Her mother had the most ridiculous rules concerning what a lady should and shouldn't do, which mostly had to do with the keeping of one's home. But Lady Joan wasn't one to follow her own rules and only enforced them on Isabella. How tedious it became, day in and day out, trying to please her mother while keeping her father from the gallows.

The gate watchman marched into the hall and continued until he reached her father. His heavy steps thundered across the floorboards. He held a missive which he handed to her father. "My lord, this was just delivered from the king's messenger. He said it is a matter of urgency."

"Well now, is this not shockingly delightful? I wonder what

the king wants. Probably my attendance at an important meeting of the lords." Her father sounded gleeful.

She would have laughed at that because he wasn't on the best of terms with the king at present. Only the month before, King Alexander had sent a writ declaring her father had to return the four horses he had stolen from Lord Heatherington's fields. The only reason the king didn't have him tried for the crime was that Alexander detested Heatherington more than he disliked her father. But she wouldn't remind him of that minor detail.

Her father opened the missive and read silently. His expression gave no hint as to what the message contained. When he finished reading, he set the missive on the table in front of him and cleared his throat. Isabella was about to demand to know what the king wanted of him, but then her father finally spoke.

"'Tis the most grievous news. I vow my heart is heavy." His eyes sought her mother's and then hers.

When she noticed his gaze linger on her, a cold shiver wound its way up her back. Whatever was in that missive had to do with her. She held onto the table as her heart raced, and a light-headedness overtook her. Her father spoke to her mother, but she couldn't hear him over the pounding of her pulse in her ears. Isabella prayed that it wasn't news relating that Christopher had died. Her brother had only left a month before and hadn't arrived yet in the Holy Land. Surely the news couldn't be about her brother. She swallowed and bade herself to be calm so she could hear.

"But how can this be?" her mother asked in a clipped tone. "Is it a punishment after all, for the horses? Has Heatherington come forward to demand you be tried? The nerve of the man. He's the vilest of men and deserved to have his horses taken."

Her father shook his head. "Nay, 'tis not about Heatherington or his horses. I disbelieve what the king has demanded of us."

Her mother set her hand on his arm and nodded. "Speak it, my dear. How dreadful can it be?"

"The king orders me to send Isabella to Edinburgh at once.

Alexander has betrothed her. She is to wed a man of his choosing. Aye, he has indeed punished me and takes my baby from me." Her father's eyes shone with the beginning of tears.

Isabella hid her relief. The fact that her father hadn't betrothed her before now somewhat displeased her. Her father cared for her, and he'd boasted many times that he didn't want her to leave his home. He had turned down their neighbor Heatherington's appeals for her hand countless times. Isabella was grateful for that because she detested Heatherington. She'd thought that her father would eventually use her to gain an alliance or improve his political position. But he had professed that no alliance was worth losing her.

It wasn't that Isabella had hoped to find love because marriages were more contractual than that of matters of the heart. Nor did she wish to be under the rule of a husband. She had enough trouble adhering to her parents' rules, as it was. Yet at age twenty, she was past the age when a lass was offered to a man in marriage, only slightly. Still, she was not too old to make a good wife. She had many child-bearing years ahead of her.

Isabella admitted she had always longed for children and a family. This was her opportunity to make her way, which she had thought of so many times. The only thing that concerned her was to whom the king would marry her. She hoped he was a worthy chivalrous man or a knight who beheld honor. The last thing she wanted was to be married to an overbearing man or one as sinful as her father, or God forbid, a man like Heatherington.

A swirl of nerves trembled through her and her breath caught in her throat like an invisible hand had wrapped around it—and squeezed. She was trapped. Helpless. There was nothing she—or anyone could do because to do so would be treason. "He cannot take my baby from us," her father said and pounded his fist on the table. "I won't allow it. She's but a lass."

Mother put a restraining hand on his arm, stopping him from slamming his fist against the table again. "'Tis time, my dear. Isabella is past the age when a girl takes a husband. It's time to let her go." She spoke in a soft, soothing tone. "I have taught her how to be a lady and now it is her time to shine. Besides, my dear, you have no say and cannot refuse King Alexander. Think about it...We will not have to incur the expense of a wedding since the king demands she wed. Surely, he wouldn't ask for a dowry. We pay enough tax to appease him."

Her father looked as though he would weep into his tankard. Isabella kept her expression devoid of humor, but the situation was somewhat comical. She raised her eyes heavenward and gave thanks to God that she would finally be free of her meddling parents.

Her mother didn't share his emotions. Instead, she seemed elated. "Dearest daughter, go and ready yourself. We shall journey on the morrow. Worry not about your father, for I shall see to him and ease his discontent. Be sure to pack your finest garments, for we wish you to look your best when you are presented to the king."

Without a retort to her mother, Isabella covertly grabbed her medicinal pouch from the side table on her way out of the hall and hurried to her chamber. There, a maidservant entered behind her, placed a valise on the bed, and began placing items inside. Without her seeing, Isabella placed the pouch under a pillow.

As the maid readied for her departure, Isabella sat woefully on the bed. She'd hoped to marry eventually, but the news received this day was definitely unexpected. She assumed a marriage contract would be made without her input, but to have such a choice made for her by the king unsettled her. Would he marry her well or would she be forever tied to an unworthy man? She'd always coveted an amiable marriage to a man who treated her with respect. Now who knew what kind of man she'd marry? Such thoughts tightened her chest.

The maid drew her from her musings when she spoke, "Mistress, I placed your favorite gowns and garments in the baggage but left the tattered gowns. Is there anything else you wish to take?"

Isabella had few possessions that she held dear. She opened a small chest where she kept a collection of pamphlets, parchments with written poetry, and a small booklet of stories her father had brought to her on his return from travels. Isabella cherished them and now she tucked them inside the valise before the maid closed it.

After the maid left, Isabella retrieved the hidden medicinal pouch and stowed it inside the valise between a few gowns where it would be hidden. Then she readied for bed. Sleepless, she tossed and turned and thought of her future husband and her hope that her life would be bettered by a marriage. Tears gathered in her eyes as she considered she'd leave her home for an unknown place with unknown people. What would her husband's people be like? More importantly, what would her husband be like? Would he be kind or mean-spirited? The thought of being married to a contemptible man caused her tears to fall. At least she would no longer have to contend with her parents' unrelenting squabbles, nitpicking, and thievery. Would she come to regret that notion?

IN THE MORNING, she hastened to get ready for her departure. Outside, her father's men waited to ride sentry on their journey. A small carriage afforded enough room for her, her mother, and her father. During the ride, she barely spoke a word. To do so would have caused her father grief and gained another reminder from her mother of all the things she needed to remember when in the king's presence. Her mother had already berated her to sit up straight, keep her hands folded on her lap, how to eat in the presence of others, and not to look overlong at any man in the king's hall.

The journey took almost a full day and near the end of the trek, rain fell heavily. She hoped they weren't delayed by it, but the rains lightened when the castle came into view. At Edinburgh Castle, the sentry admitted their party at the entrance. They rode up a small rise, which took them between the two tall stone turrets and through the gatehouse. When they reached the courtyard, six men approached to assist them and removed their baggage from the rear of the carriage. One man grabbed her valise and her parents' satchels and retreated with their belongings into the castle.

"Welcome Lord and Lady Forrester, and Mistress Isabella. I am Edmund, our great king's chamberlain. Come and I shall get you settled. Mistress Isabella, the king wants to speak to you privately before the festivities begin. I'm to take you to his private chamber."

Her mother and father dared not protest. Isabella followed them inside. Her nerves made her jumpy and bangs from somewhere down the hallway caused her to flinch. She wasn't sure why the king wanted to meet with her privately, but she wouldn't cower before him.

After her parents were whisked away down one corridor by servants, the chamberlain led her down another, walking beside her. They went up and down a randomly placed set of stone steps, passing empty, narrow tables set here and there along the walls, and sconces set high above her. Their open flames did little to eliminate the darkness in the windowless corridor, though it pushed it back a bit. Indeed, Edinburgh Castle was the most luxurious keep she'd ever seen.

The chamberlain smiled at a passing servant woman and then motioned Isabella forward. Not knowing what to say, Isabella remained quiet.

"I suppose you might be a wee bit anxious, meeting the king?" The chamberlain read her mind. Or maybe he could feel the nervousness radiating from her in spite of the fact that she was trying so hard to emanate calm.

"Aye, perhaps," she granted. Her throat was dry, and her voice came out in a raspy sound. She frowned and reminded herself not to show anything but bravery, in a ladylike way, of course.

They reached a door at the end of the long hallway, and he stopped and turned to her. "There is no need to fear our king, Mistress. Our king is noble, especially when it concerns bonny lassies like yourself. I have heard he has selected a few other maidens to give to several Highlanders in marriage. I deem you shall be pleased by his reward."

Reward? Was the chamberlain maddened? He had to be if he considered marriage to a Highlander a reward.

Besides, the king's missive had said nothing about Highlanders. Surely their sovereign understood how the people by the border felt about those who lived in the Highlands. Isabella had heard the most outlandish tales about the men who lived in the far north from their old stablemaster. He'd said that they were primitive, still lived in tribes, dug out trenches on the side of hills, and worshiped pagan gods. Lord help her, was she about to marry such a man, a confounded heathen?

If King Alexander forced her to marry a barbarian, Isabella would have to object. He couldn't make her agree before a priest. Somehow, she thought that probably wouldn't matter, her objection. No one dared to defy an order from the king, least of all an insignificant woman like herself.

Edmund opened the door and waved her forward. Isabella swallowed hard, then entered. She stood in wait and wonderment. Inside the cozy, warm, private chamber of King Alexander stood a group of people. Her heart began to pound. The Highlanders! She noted right off how tall they were, how muscular, and how intimidating they appeared. The men wore tartans over yellowish tunics that reached their knees, and their boots were well-made. Most wore their hair cut to the base of their necks but some had long tresses that fell upon their shoulders—sinfully barbaric. They might have been primitive-looking, but by her faith, they were exceedingly handsome…and looked strong. They seemed displeased to be standing together, given the hostility in their glares and the harsh grimaces on their bearded faces.

The king, with his wife Margaret, entered the chamber by way of a side door and murmured to the men before he and the queen proceeded to the dais. She smiled at them. Margaret was a young queen, perhaps only a year or two younger than Isabella. The king appeared younger than the men being offered as husbands. He stood as tall but was not as muscular or intimidating as the Highlanders.

The women, she suspected, who were also brides, stood cloistered together by the row of window casements. Isabella joined them because she didn't want to stand out. She didn't introduce herself to the ladies but smiled.

"This is a day of import, and I am pleased to see you here," the king said. "This evening, we shall have a feast with dancing and merriment. I will give you this time to greet each other and become familiar. Before the night ends, the selections will be discussed, and finalized on the morrow. I bid you to eat and drink."

Isabella was somewhat relieved to receive confirmation that the women there were also offered as brides. She wasn't alone. Amongst the eight of them, there would be four weddings. Given that, she couldn't bring herself to glance back at the men because each man was as intimidating as the next.

At once, servants bustled into the room and opened double-wide doors that led into the great hall. The hall's splendor held Isabella breathless. There had to be hundreds of candles sending a glow throughout the chamber. Tables were ladened with all kinds of foodstuff and lined the wall from one end of the hall to the other. A group of musicians sat at the far end and began to play soft music appropriate for mealtime. Soon, parents and other relatives joined them, and the hall filled with people.

Isabella didn't know what to do. She dared not eat because her stomach was filled with flutters. Her parents, she noticed, had entered the hall but mingled with the other elders. Isabella stood by the windows and waited to see what the night would bring. The men appeared rooted to the floorboards too and none moved about the chamber.

She turned and peered through the windows in hopes of avoiding the men as much as possible. Brazenness, her mother had once professed, ran in her blood. Isabella was often outspoken and usually being in the company of others didn't bother her, but that was at home. She didn't want to make a bloody fool of herself at the king's castle in front of so many strangers, so she kept to herself.

The women coyly strode forward and drew the men from their perches. Soon after, conversation flowed within the chamber and some danced to the music which rose in tempo. The first man to approach her smiled and asked her who she was, where she was from, and other nonsensical questions. She answered as best she could. Isabella detested how he felt free to interview for the position of his wife. It felt cold, unfeeling, and utterly humiliating.

After that, each of the men sought her in turn, and she spent a short time with each of them. That was certainly not enough for any one of them to gauge an opinion of her, but it mattered not because she had no say in whom she would marry.

All she learned was that the Highlanders were something to behold. One of the men had a charming disposition and seemed honorable. The next man wore such a scowl and had a fearsome warrior mien about him, he certainly wouldn't do as her husband. Another professed to care about his clan and that being a laird took up most of his time. She got the subtle idea that the last thing he wanted was a bride, which was fine with her as she wasn't truly interested in a groom. Yet here they were, all forced to marry by their sovereign's order.

The last man had yet to approach her. He stood by the large hearth with his arms folded at his chest, surveying the chamber with piercing golden eyes. He hadn't spoken to anyone. When his eyes met hers, Isabella's breath caught slightly. After that, he kept his gaze fastened on hers and did not glance elsewhere. The man was tall, broad-shouldered, thickly legged, and wore his hair far too long. It was his eyes, though, that she noticed the most. They were golden-brown and rich like honey, but his gaze gave little away. She couldn't tell if he was pleased or displeased at being there, or what he thought of her.

His garments were tidy, his tannish-colored tunic stretched across his manly chest. Covering most of it was a woolen tartan of blue with a green plaid. Her eyes scrunched at the belt holding his lower garment in place; beneath the hem, his bronzed knees led to low, well-made boots that barely reached his calves. In her opinion, he showed a little too much skin. But all that wasn't what held her attention. Instead, it was that he had the largest sword strapped to his side that she'd ever beheld. Isabella was surprised he hadn't removed his weapon when he'd entered the king's castle, but Highlanders were known to be stubborn, and he probably refused to leave his weapon at the door.

She stepped back when she noticed he'd begun stepping toward her. Isabella wanted to flee, but she smiled instead, gathered her courage, and waited for him to join her. His height wasn't exaggerated because she barely reached his shoulders. As small framed as she was, he could crush her with little effort. Never, in all the years she thought of her future husband, had she ever envisioned marrying a man such as the man now towering above her. Lord help her if she had to marry the Highlander.

"Are ye as appalled as I am to be here?" His voice was gruff but entirely masculine, with a deep burr to his words.

Isabella let out a small nervous laugh, but then she realized he was quite serious. She moistened her lips and tried to shake away the overwhelming sense he brought forth. She hoped he'd reveal a little about himself because there was a kindness in his eyes but perhaps a little sadness too. His size intimidated her but she admired his relaxed manner as he stood next to her. The fact that he was appalled alluded to the fact that he was displeased by the marriage he would soon undertake.

"I cannot say I'm too outraged to be here. I am Isabella. My father is Lord Adam Forrester." She curtseyed to him and when she raised her face, she couldn't help but smile. Lord, he was handsome, even if he somewhat frightened her. The men at home would probably run for their lives if they ever encountered him, whether in the light of day or dark of night.

He bowed slightly. "I am Declan, Laird MacKendrick of Inveraray."

"I suppose you will want to question me now about what kind of wife I shall be, how many children I'll give you, and how pious I am. I fear that I shall probably disappoint you with my answers." She raised her chin, even if she knew it made her appear defiant. With any luck, she realized, her attitude would frighten this lord—and any other—away.

"Ye do not wish to marry, lass?" He sounded stunned that she would speak so openly. Within an instant, he changed his expression. His scowl disappeared and he almost smiled. At least, the edges of his manly lips turned upward. Still, Isabella saw the brief sparkle of outrage, or perhaps it was mirth, in his eyes.

"It's not that. I just don't wish to be questioned about things that do not matter."

"You think it matters not what kind of wife ye will be, or how many children ye will have, or how God-fearing ye are?"

Isabella sighed with consternation. "How can such decisions be made when I hardly know the man I am to marry? What if I wed someone who eventually displeased me? I wouldn't want to have children with such a man. And I shan't sing my praises of how good a wife I'll be. I will let my husband judge for himself after he marries me."

His laughter lightened her. "Well, lass, ye have God-given sense. 'Tis meaningless, is it not—this meeting. We will choose our brides and it will not matter what your answers were or why."

"Exactly my thoughts. And what, pray tell, are your requirements for a wife? Do you care to share them with me?" She had meant to tease him, but he raised a dark brow at her bluntness.

He gazed at her solemnly, leaned toward her, and said in a low voice, "All I require in a wife is a lass who is kind and is not too much of a harridan."

"You dislike harridans then?" What was wrong with her? She further teased the giant and then berated herself for being so forthright.

"I might be able to suffer a harridan if she is good in bed," he teased back. His grin attested to the fact that he was being wicked, baiting her so.

Isabella gasped and her cheeks heated a little because it seemed he meant to encourage her. Perhaps he was jesting. It was true that his jest—if that's what it was—made her chuckle, and she had to withhold the urge to playfully swat his arm. "You are a knave, Laird MacKendrick. At least you don't expect much from your wife. But I wouldn't be too brash because the weddings will be over by this time on the morrow, and you shall be married to one of us. Is Inveraray far north?"

"Far enough, lass." He leaned against the wall, and it appeared as if their discussion disinterested him. "I detest being this far south, near the border, near England."

"I understand. Being north, I expect you wouldn't get on with people by the border."

"Too many of them side with the Sassenach, and I detest England more than I detest the border barons. They are weak and easily manipulated by the Sassenach king."

She lowered her face at his bluntness. If that was true, then he was indeed displeased at having to marry one of the women here. Isabella had heard their introductions and the instructions to the men. All the maidens were from the border and all the grooms from the Highlands. She had to wonder if the Highlanders were being punished for something which caused the king to force their hands in marriage to women from a place they disdained.

"Then I shall leave you, Laird MacKendrick, for I am from the border, and I don't wish to waste your time." Isabella did a half-curtsey and tried to make her escape.

Laird MacKendrick stopped her by catching her arm. His hold on her elbow forced her to turn back toward him. His touch heated her through the fabric of her overdress sleeve. Isabella withdrew her arm and raised her chin far enough back to look him in the eyes.

"Lass, I said I detested the border barons, but I did not say I detested their daughters."

Isabella almost laughed at his banter. He had a mischievous shine to his eyes.

"Well, my lord, that's a good thing since you are set to marry one of us on the morrow. You are fortunate because you get to choose your bride." She had already shown him her rebellious, un-wifely attitude, so there was no point in playing submissive now. Since she had no choice of who to marry, she decided it was better to give him a show of her spirit beforehand. At least, he'd be aware of it—if he did, indeed, choose her to be his bride. "The king bids me to marry, and I have no say in the matter. But you men do, I suppose. What do you think? Do any of the ladies suit you?"

His eyes raked over her briefly and sent a rush of tingles through her body. It was as if he'd reached out and caressed her with his eyes. Did he notice the adoring look in her gaze because surely it was there? There was much more to this man than she'd initially thought. She was surprised to discover that she hoped he liked what he saw in her.

He didn't smile. "Aye, there is one."

CHAPTER THREE

T HE NIGHT'S REVELRY was lost on Declan. He wasn't much of
a reveler and wasn't in the mood to celebrate or rejoice at a
forced marriage. At home, he had too many pressing duties
calling him that took up most of his time. Rarely did he partake of
entertainment or revelry. He needed to ensure his soldiers were
well-trained for the oncoming war with the Campbells. Being at
the king's castle, in the adorned hall, did little to brighten his
spirit. Declan wasn't much for talk either, and usually, he just
gave orders and had them followed.

It hadn't escaped him that the lass to whom he'd spoken
looked as out of place as he felt. She didn't appear to want to join
in the revelry either.

Declan took a short walk outside to escape the crush of the
revelers and glaring mamas inside the hall and needed to get
some air. He found the king standing in the courtyard and
approached. "Good eve, Sire."

"MacKendrick, what are you doing out here?"

"I thought to take in a wee bit of air."

"Aye, 'tis a fine brisk night. I say, MacKendrick, you are causing affront."

Declan frowned and shook his head. "I am here, am I not?
How am I causing you affront?"

"You have yet to dance with any of the ladies. Aye, you are

being difficult. Have you met any of them yet? On the morrow, I remind you, you will need to choose one of them."

He blanched at that—the thought of dancing. Declan wasn't much of a dancer either. The bride, he didn't mind so much. Once married and back home, he could set her aside and continue on with his duties to his clan. Whoever she was didn't have to change his life that much, though his king would be satisfied.

To appease his sovereign, he said, "I shall see to the matter posthaste then. And aye, there is one particular lass who interests me. I just might choose her for my bride if she does not get snatched up before I might name her."

The king leaned closer. "Who is she?"

Declan chuckled. He wouldn't say and would leave the king to wonder. "You shall see on the morrow, will ye not?"

Alexander hooted a laugh and rubbed his hands together. "There's a nip in the air. Let us get inside before we freeze to death. I'll see you on the dance floor. My wife has been pecking at me all eve to join her in a dance. I promised her only one go around."

Declan followed the king back inside the hall. The music had just ended. Before the next ballad was played, he approached the woman he sought. "Milady Isabella, will ye join me?" He stood still, his shoulders stiffened while he waited for her reply.

Isabella curtseyed to him. "Of course, I will."

He waved her onward to the dance floor where other couples, including the king and queen, awaited the first chords of the music. Declan faced Isabella and kept his gaze on her face. She was exquisitely beautiful with her blondish locks flowing over her shoulders. Her eyes, the bonniest blue, shone with merriment. What was it about her that affected him? He supposed he was attracted to her, but there was more to the attraction that held his gaze. She was brazen enough to look him in the eye, and she didn't cower away. He appreciated a woman who stood her ground.

Declan hadn't been with a woman in some time. It wasn't

because he had no interest in sex or courtship, but because clan matters took up most of his time. Since his wife had died, he hadn't given much thought to the opposite sex or wooing a woman. At first, mourning prevented him from the interest, and since, he had too many pressing matters on his mind besides women or his needs.

Isabella stood out amongst the other women on the opposite side of the men. Again, he noticed her air of confidence and that boldness that drew him. With his lack of experience with women, especially of late, he wasn't sure how to approach her. Would she be amiable to marry him? He hoped so because she was the only woman in the selection of lassies whom he wanted to pursue.

It was decided. One way or another, he'd take her home with him.

The music began and the troubadours played a slower song. Declan lifted his arm and moved with single steps toward Isabella. The moment his hand touched hers, she raised her chin and her eyes bore into his. Her touch brought awareness to his body as if he'd awakened from a long sleep and he was struck with desire. He circled her and turned back with double steps, keeping his eyes fastened on hers.

Each time he returned to her, his body came alive with sensations he hadn't felt in a long time. Aye, he wanted her, and the fact that it was within his means to obtain her made him grin. All he had to do was beat his brethren in hand-to-hand combat to win her. Yet he was not well-versed in wooing a woman of her quality. At least he didn't have to attend normal courtship rituals to win her hand.

As he mused about the tournament scheduled for the next day, they moved in unison in a variety of spatial floor patterns and repeated the movement to the beat of the music.

Isabella strode forward and clasped his hands as they took two more steps toward one another and then encircled each other. She moved easily, her body swaying and swinging to the music. Declan couldn't help but notice the swell of her bosom above her modest bodice, and he swallowed hard at the sight of her creamy-colored skin. The dance continued, and with each step, his body heated and stiffened. Yet, her gaze never wavered from his and Declan felt as though only the two of them danced around the floor in the king's large hall. He was unaware both the king and queen watched him and his dance partner until he turned to face them.

On the last turn about, he stepped forward and raised his arm again. Her palm touched his and sent even more riveting twinges through him. He would make her his wife, he decided, because there was no way he would allow another man to have her. Now, if only he had the ability to court her as she deserved, and to show her that he deserved her.

The musicians ended the song and the dancers ceased and disbanded. Declan bowed to Isabella and when he raised his face to look at hers, she smiled with shining eyes.

"You surprise me, Laird MacKendrick. I didn't think you knew how to dance." Isabella curtseyed to him and clasped his hand. "My thanks."

He didn't want to release her hand and held fast. "I usually do not entertain a dance, but I did not want to displease Alexander. He insisted I take to the floor."

"It would do well to appease the king."

Declan led her from the center of the room. "May I… Do ye wish for a refreshment?"

"I would like that," she said and released his hand.

He was disappointed and wanted to continue to touch her, but he wouldn't be so forward. Declan left her and retreated to the refreshment table, where he'd intended to get a drink for her. Her father approached and stepped in front of him, stopping him in his tracks.

"I take it you're interested in my daughter?" Forrester glared at him.

Declan had never had a father to answer to before. His first wife was given to him by a neighboring laird, his daughter, for the safety and alliance their marriage would bring. He bowed slightly to the older man. "If I must choose a bride, I wouldst that it be your daughter."

"You'll treat her right?" her father asked.

"I will, Lord Forrester. Ye need not worry about her. I am an honorable man." Declan spoke the truth because he'd never harmed a woman or mistreated her. Isabella wouldn't need to worry about her safety.

"You will allow her mother and me to visit and to send messages? I heard that you northerners stay to yourselves and don't allow outsiders," Forrester said.

Declan didn't know how to answer the man. His clan normally didn't allow visitors or outsiders, and he was unsure if he should agree to visits from her family. "We shall see. But ye may send missives if you wish to stay in touch."

"I suppose that is more than what I expected. We care greatly about our daughter, MacKendrick. If you do, by chance, win her hand, you will gain a great prize. Fair warning. She is a spirited lass and not easily tamed."

Declan bowed to him, snatched a cup of wine from the table, hurried away, and retreated to where Isabella awaited him. The strum of a harp and the melody of a lute announced the next dance. Couples took to the dance floor. Isabella stood alone, watching the dancers. How lovely she appeared, but out of place too. She wasn't a woman who frequented Alexander's court given her amiable, yet demure, attitude.

On his approach, he regarded her. Aye, she was spirited, though. He had gotten that sense during his first conversation with her. She'd had the courage to tease him, and he admitted that he hadn't minded so much. Only a few people had the bollocks or dared to jest with him. What he wouldn't give to be the man to tame her.

When he reached her side, he handed her the cup. "Milady."

"My thanks, Laird MacKendrick. Did I see you speaking with my father?"

"Aye, he wanted to warn me about you." He'd meant to tease her, but she didn't take his comment in jest. Before he could explain further, she stepped toward him.

Her dainty eyebrows furrowed. "In my defense, my lord, my father is a difficult man and quite emotional. I might be a bit outspoken with him, but I—"

"Ye need not explain, Milady. I was but teasing you." Declan didn't know what to say to her. He'd upset her and he was uncertain how to defuse the situation. So, he said nothing more and stood there in chagrin.

"Laird MacKendrick," she said softly.

He turned to her. "Milady, please call me Declan."

Isabella smiled sweetly and set her hand on his arm. "Declan, I must apologize because I misjudged you when we first met. Will you try to win my hand on the morrow? I heard the lairds discussing the matter and I wondered..."

"Do ye wish me to try to win your hand?" Declan didn't want her to see the hopefulness in his gaze and instead of turning away from her, he stood his ground. Under his scrutiny, she lowered her eyes but not before he recognized the glint of an answer in her gaze. Her shoulders moved from a slow sigh, and she raised her bright-blue gaze to him. There was no coyness in Isabella— something he admired about her. She didn't play him for a fool and he appreciated that.

"I don't believe the other lairds would suit me. If you won my hand, I wouldn't be abashed by it." Her warm fingers slid over the bared skin on his forearm, warming every part of him.

Declan drew in a breath, certain his heart skipped several beats. His reaction to her quite puzzled him because he hadn't ever experienced such longing, not even with his first wife. Before she stepped away from him, he grabbed her hand to stop her from leaving. "I would not be abashed either."

She said nothing more to him but pulled away to cross the hall where, he assumed, her parents sat. Isabella spoke briefly to a woman whom he took as her mother and then she was approached by one of the other grooms. Isabella and her partner made their way to the dance floor. Declan took the opportunity to dance with the other offered brides but none of them sparked any fervor in him like Isabella had.

During the dances, he couldn't cease watching Isabella. Their eyes met more than once and each time, she smiled at him. On the morrow, Declan decided, he would do what it took to win her hand.

CHAPTER FOUR

THE CASTLE WAS buzzing with activity. Servants bustled about and set out the morning fare for all the guests. Isabella sat at the trestle table with the other brides and waited anxiously for the announcement of the commencement of the bouts. That the men had to fight in a brawl to claim one of the women was barbaric. Surely the king could have settled the matter in a more civilized manner.

The woman next to her leaned toward her and whispered, "I cannot eat a thing. Just think, by day's end we shall know who our husbands will be." Isabella peered at the woman whom she knew to be Eva Scott, the youngest of the brides. Her enthusiasm was misplaced. Eva smeared a piece of bread with fruit and shoved it in her mouth. "You should eat something."

The lass was a contradiction. "Have you a favorite? Is there a man who you hope to win the bout and claim you?" Isabella asked her but left her food untouched.

Eva's dark blue eyes shimmered from the candlelight in the dim hall. The long tresses of her dark hair fell over her shoulder as she leaned closer. "I spoke with all of them for some time, except for Laird MacKendrick. He wasn't very forthcoming, but still, he did dance with me. If I had to select one of the men, it would be a difficult decision for they're all handsome," she said. "What about you? Do you have your heart set on any of the men?"

How could she answer? She almost asked Declan last eve to claim her but then he teased her, and her subtlety was lost on him. There was another man who interested her, Laird Shaw MacIntosh, who was indeed charming. He courted her with sweet words when she'd danced with him and said that she was near the top of his list. At the same time, the man certainly made himself available to the other ladies and mingled with them all evening. Isabella glanced across the room and spotted Declan standing with Shaw. They appeared to be having an intimate conversation and she wondered what they were saying.

Eva picked up her cup and took a small sip before she asked her again, "Do you? Perhaps it's one of those two?" She pointed to Declan and Shaw. "They seem to be staring at us."

"Since I have no say, it really doesn't matter. Besides, my heart will not be affected. Marriage is nothing but a contract between a man and a woman. The man is the master and the woman his property. It is the way it is done." Isabella reiterated her mother's words, the adage she'd been told since she'd begun her training to be a wife. She sighed because deep down, she believed a woman should be a partner and respected for her views.

She was saved from their conversation when the chamberlain entered and announced the bouts would soon begin and to make their way to the courtyard. Isabella followed the women outside and stood near the dais that was erected for the king and queen.

All hushed when Alexander and Margaret appeared and approached the dais.

The king spoke to the chamberlain and Margaret left her husband's side. She ambled toward them and stopped in front of them. Dressed regally in an elegant overdress, the queen wore her garments well and fitted to accentuate her body. Her mousy brown hair was pulled back in braids and was tucked beneath a simple wimple. "Ladies, worry not for you will not be displeased with any of these men as your husband. I took great care to notice your interactions last eve. If you—" Before she could continue, the trumpeter called everyone's attention. The queen left them and returned to her husband's side.

The grooms strolled through the mass of onlookers until they reached the dais. They bowed their heads to Alexander and gave firm nods. The king seemed pleased by this. The solemnity of the moment instilled a tenseness within Isabella. There was no turning back, no way to stop the events that would unfold on this day.

He announced, "The first battle will commence. Those fighting are MacKendrick and MacIntosh. There are to be no weapons, hand-to-hand combat only. You shall fight in the marked square to the finish. If for any reason you step out of the square, you will be declared the loser. If you call a truce, you shall forfeit the match. The winner of each match shall get to choose his bride." Alexander sat in his chair and waited for his chamberlain to start the tourney.

Isabella stood stock still with her breath a small rasp on her lips. Declan and Shaw stepped into the center of the square and faced each other. The fight began within a blink of an eye when Declan threw out his fist and hooked Shaw on the right side of his face. She winced at the sound of Declan's fist striking the man. Voices rose, instructing and encouraging the combatants. She couldn't move a muscle or cheer on the melee.

Shaw jabbed Declan until he rolled his shoulder and tucked his chin to his chest to avoid the punches. Regardless, Declan's nose seeped blood. He began to use his upper shoulder to catch the punches Shaw threw at him and grunted from the onslaught. Isabella's breath just about ceased altogether as she witnessed Declan's downfall. Her eyes moistened with the beginning of tears, but she willed herself not to weep. She wanted to shout at Declan to strike back, to do something to help himself, but the brutality of the fight held her silent. Shaw appeared to be winning. God help her.

But then, before Shaw could cut away, Declan began to

throw uppercuts and landed his fist repeatedly on the side of Shaw's head. Isabella's heart clashed languidly as she watched in awe of Declan's powerful jabs. The crowd's reaction rose in a meshing of *oohs*, *bahs*, and *ahhs* which sounded as they stood afar from them. Shaw grabbed hold of Declan in a chokehold to keep him from striking him, but Declan kept throwing punch after punch, hitting Shaw's face, upper body, and head. She'd never seen men fight in such a way and the savagery of it held her enthralled and somewhat sickened.

Shaw's knees shook, and finally, he ended up on the ground. He had no choice but to concede to Declan and call a truce when he failed to stand. Both men rasped from their exertion. Declan wiped the blood from his nose with the edge of his tartan and bowed over Shaw who continued to lay on his back, groaning. But in a sign of gallantry, he helped Shaw to rise.

Oddly, Shaw wore a smile on his face. Though they both bore the marks of the fight, the crowd seemed somehow slighted. It was as if the men purposely ended the fight sooner than they should have. Isabella was glad it had ended, and she had to keep herself from celebrating Declan's victory because it would be unseemly and a slight to Shaw.

The queen, on the other hand, squealed with delight and clapped her hands. "I knew MacKendrick would win this bout. Is this not wonderful, Alexander?"

The king muttered, "I am gladdened you are enjoying yourself, My Lady."

Edmund shouted and called, "The battle is finished. The winner is Laird MacKendrick. Come forward to claim your bride."

Isabella squeezed her hands together and closed her eyes briefly. The moment was at hand when he'd declare who he chose for his wife. Would her name cross his lips? She prayed silently that he would select her and opened her eyes to view the proceedings.

Declan stood before the dais. He had a blackening eye and

swollen cheeks, but his face wasn't nearly as battered as Shaw's. Her fingers tightened in their clasp, and she just about breathed as she waited in anticipation, with her heart thrumming in her ears.

"MacKendrick, ye have your choice of bride. What say ye? Whom do you select?" Alexander asked in a booming voice.

With an unwavering voice, Declan declared, "I choose Isabella, Lord Adam Forrester's daughter."

"Very well, you shall wed directly after the midday meal," Alexander said. "The next bout will commence in a short moment. Three brides remain."

If she had to marry one of the Highlanders, she was gladdened it was Declan. She appreciated that he hadn't taken offense to her teasing and outspokenness. And at the very least, he seemed noble even if he was somewhat daunting in his appearance. His demeanor couldn't be mistaken with the slight frown he wore, his overly long hair cascading wavy blond locks over his manly shoulders. He didn't appear pleased to be marrying her in spite of the fact he'd fought to name her, given the scowl on his brow.

Still, if another had chosen her, Isabella had been told by the queen that she could reject the proposal until the man she wanted selected her. When the queen questioned her about her choice of husband, Isabella happily vowed that only MacKendrick would suit her. But she needn't have worried because there were whispers in the queen's antechamber that Margaret liked to meddle in her husband's affairs. Isabella suspected the queen took matters into her hands which was probably why Declan had won the bout so easily and especially had won her hand in marriage.

ISABELLA STILL REELED from the fight she'd witnessed. Supper ended much too soon for her liking. The trepidation of the wedding weighed on her and she couldn't eat a bite of the midday meal. As much as she wanted to abscond, she had little choice but to go forth. She stood in front of the dais with Declan MacKendrick by her side, her mind a whirl of events that happened since she'd arrived the day before. She wore her favorite of the gowns her mother had allowed her to bring with her.

Declan wore a bruised eye and a little swelling on the side of his face to the wedding. Other than that, she could hardly tell he'd been in a fight.

The king and queen sat in their chairs, avid onlookers to their nuptials. Only family and friends were permitted besides the king and queen in Alexander's private chamber for the taking of the vows. Isabella regarded her parents, especially her father, who appeared forlorn, but they bore it well in front of their sovereign. She had expected her father's emotional outburst, but he kept his sobs to a minimum. Declan, she noticed, had no family present.

The king's chancellor bespoke the sacramental rites and offered his marital advice. When he finished, he bade them to state their agreement to marry. It was all a blur to her, but before she knew it, the chancellor had instructed Declan to kiss her. He leaned forward and she waited in anticipation for him to set his lips on hers. Instead, he brushed her cheek with his nose and placed a chaste kiss there, leaving her surprised and disappointed. She'd expected the bold man to kiss her possessively, or at least with some kind of vigor. Instead, Declan pulled back and stepped to her side.

"I offer my congratulations to you both," the king said. "MacKendrick, you will consummate the marriage with all due haste. There will be no petitions for an annulment. You shall uphold your end of our agreement. Is that understood?"

"I give ye my accord, Sire." Declan nodded slightly and pulled her away. When they reached the entrance to the great hall, he stopped and pulled her aside. "Milady, we will leave in a moment. Make ready and say your farewells."

"Now? You wish to leave now? But it's after midday.

Shouldn't we await the morrow?" A heated sense wound its way up her neck, and she fanned herself with her hand, but it did no good to alleviate her panic. It wasn't that she was afraid to be alone with Declan, but the thought that she was leaving her life and going to an unknown place quite overwhelmed her.

"Aye, I will not stay another minute this close to the Sassenach. If ye wish to say your farewells to your parents, they await you." Declan bowed his head and set off.

Isabella turned and found her parents standing behind her. She called to him, "I shall meet you outside then, my lord." Then she waited for her parents to speak, but it was evident that her father was far too emotional to utter a word. "Worry not, Father, I shall fare well. Promise me that you'll not be saddened. I will write to you when I can. Take care when you go…hunting. I shall worry for your safety."

"Remember all that I have taught you. You have all the knowledge of how to be a good wife," her mother said. "In time, you shan't miss us at all. You'll be busy raising your babies."

Isabella nodded absently to her mother. "If Christopher returns, please tell him… Tell him to write to me." She worried so for her brother, but the likelihood that he would return from the crusade was slight. News arrived daily bringing the names of soldiers and regiments that had perished.

"We shall. Go on, dearest, your husband awaits," her mother said. "'Tis best not to keep him waiting. That is not a good way to begin a marriage. Remember your manners and tamper your temper. You do not want your husband thinking you a shrew."

"I will keep you both in my prayers." As Isabella turned to leave, her father bawled and carried on. Her mother consoled him, but all in the great hall, including the king and queen, witnessed his sorrowful behavior.

With brightened cheeks, Isabella left. She was completely humiliated by her father's manners. Still, it lightened her heart to think he, and maybe even her mother, though she always presented a strong sense of duty, would miss her.

She found their belongings along with others outside await-ing the footmen's handling of putting the trunks and baggage on the carriages. A manservant hastened forward, retrieved her valise, and walked toward the horses to secure it.

Isabella backed up and tried to find Declan among the men standing around. She gasped when she bumped into someone. He prevented her from falling to the ground. Isabella gazed behind her at Declan whose hands clasped her body just beneath her breasts on her upper waist. A rush of warmth shot through her.

"Milady, are ye ready?"

She shook her head and swallowed hard at having his hands intimately holding her. He continued to keep his hands firmly on her and she turned, set her hands on his chest, and wanted badly to lean into him and have him embrace her. All to be held in his strong arms, but he released her, and his arms shifted to his sides. He approached the horses all but ignoring her silent plea.

As she drew near to him, he finished tying her valise to a horse and held out his hand to assist her. "You have no others to protect you on the journey home?"

"I need no others," he replied boastfully.

"Oh," she replied, astounded by his prowess. He certainly appeared able-bodied enough to protect himself on the trek. She placed her hand in his and he helped her mount the horse. Once she was seated, she watched him curiously. "It shall be dark soon. How far do we travel?"

"We will ride a few leagues and shall stop at an inn that I frequent when I travel to Edinburgh. Do not look so dour, Wife, you will have a roof over your head this eve."

Declan was seated upon his horse before she blinked. He nudged the animal forward and didn't glance behind him to ensure she followed. Isabella watched his back as she trailed him. He had strong muscles evident by the way his tunic stretched over his shoulders. He was a well-built man and she had to admit that not only was he handsome, but also his body was definitely pleasing to look upon.

By late evening, they'd arrived at a small manor home. He jumped from his horse and assisted her to dismount. Her legs ached and a stiffness settled in her lower back from riding for so long. Isabella appreciated his aid. She purposely closed her eyes and leaned against him, delighted to be held by him but it also gave her time to adjust to standing. He steadied her and she wouldn't let him release her when she took hold of his tartan. After a few moments, he stepped away from her.

"Lass, we should get inside and get ye warm." He forced her to release him and handed the reins of the horses to a lad. "Stable them. We'll leave early in the morn."

The stable lad nodded and walked off, leading their mounts behind him.

Isabella followed Declan inside the stone building.

At the entrance, an older woman with short brown hair greeted them. Her face lit with a smile. The innkeeper yelled to her husband, but he didn't come at her call. "Laird Declan, 'tis good to see ye again. I'll ready your room for ye."

"We will need two rooms, Mistress," he said absently and followed her.

They took the stairs and the woman stopped at a door. She opened it and turned to the door across the hallway and opened that one as well.

"Enjoy your evening, Laird. If ye wish, I'll have food sent up. 'Tis well past the supper meal and our cook retired for the night. But I'm sure I can scrounge up some light fare."

"Aye, that would be kind of you, Mistress. We could use a wee bite to eat."

The woman left them.

Isabella grimaced at the thought that he wouldn't be sharing a room with her. Shouldn't she stay with her husband? It was their wedding night, after all, and she'd heard the king profess that Declan should consummate their marriage. How she looked forward to it, but he didn't seem to want her with him. That dejected her more than she realized. Isabella didn't enter her room. She stood staring at Declan and hoped he would change his mind and call to her, but he leaned against the door jamb, unsmiling.

"Get rest, Wife, we'll set out early."

"Wait," she said and stepped toward him. "Why? Why do you not wish to share a room?"

"I thought ye might appreciate sleeping in your own bed this night." He offered no further explanation.

"I wouldn't appreciate that at all." She stepped into his room and waited for him to close the door, but he didn't.

Declan seemed anchored to the floorboards but eventually, he entered and shut the door. He ambled toward her and said, "I do not expect ye to perform your wifely duties, especially after a day on horseback. We can wait until we get home. Ye should return to your bedchamber. I'll have a hot bath sent up for ye to soak in so that ye can rest more comfortably."

Isabella wanted to scream. She had no intention of leaving him. "Nay, I shall be quite comfortable here. Why do you wish to wait until we get home?" Her face heated with her question. She couldn't even put words to name what they'd do—if they ever got around to doing it.

"We have been riding all day. Surely you are tired and sore." He pulled the tartan covering his upper body loose and tossed it on a chair.

Her eyes followed him, taking in his every movement, his body, and the way he exuded confidence. "I am not tired at all or sore."

"Well, Wife, I am," his tone was a little testy. He removed the scabbard that held his sword and set it next to the chair. "If ye wish to stay here, I will not object, but ye shall be more comfortable in your own bedchamber."

He *wouldn't object*? What was wrong with her that he wouldn't take his husbandly rights? Thoroughly ashamed, Isabella lowered her head and hurried through the doorway. "I bid you a good night then."

Isabella retreated to her room across the hall and entered. She closed the door and sat on the bed with absolute consternation. Her husband was a perplexing man. What man wouldn't take his husbandly rights on his wedding night? She held doubt that he was tired because he certainly appeared as if he could ride through the night with little or no complaint.

A knock came at the door, and she hastened to it thinking Declan had changed his mind, but it was a servant, delivering a tray of light foodstuff. She took the tray and thanked her, noted that Declan's door remained closed, and used her hip to shut her door.

Though her mother explained what happened in the marriage bed, it had never appealed to her. She'd been told to do her duty and suffer through it. It all sounded rather ghastly to her, that is until she met Declan. Declan wasn't like other men. Most would claim ownership of their wife, but he hadn't. There seemed to be a sense of admiration in him. The thought of his touches, kisses, and his body against hers brought a sense of excitement to her. No other man had stirred such emotion and sensual yearning from her.

Every new wife needed a little encouragement, didn't they? In her case, she needed very little. She wanted his affection. If only he wasn't so noble, she could, at that very moment, enjoy being with him and sharing the intimacy.

Isabella ate a little of the food, washed herself thoroughly at the basin since a bath hadn't arrived, and readied for bed. After, she pulled back the coverings. She tossed and turned and couldn't fathom why Declan objected to being with her. Her pride was as dented as armor after a fierce battle. If he had no care for her, she wouldn't give him the satisfaction of letting it bother her either. But she contradicted herself with her next thought—he didn't want her.

Groggily, she arose when the sun streamed into the bedchamber. Isabella had gotten only a few winks of sleep since her mind turned all night. Grumpily, she hastened to the chamber pot. When she finished, she used the basin to wash and pulled her hair into a tie at her nape. She wanted to look her best. Not that it mattered because her clot-headed husband didn't care a whit about her and probably wouldn't notice. She dressed and left her bedchamber, moving down the stairs and into the common room.

"The laird is outside," the innkeeper's wife told her. "He's awaitin' for ye. He told me to give ye something quick-like to break your fast whilst he gets the horses ready."

She stood by the small trestle table ladened with various breads and fruit smears, fruit, small wedges of cheese, and a pitcher of mead. Isabella ate a few bites of fruit and cheese and only drank half a cup of mead. She didn't want to have to seek nature on the ride, at least until later in the day.

Isabella stepped outside and saw Declan standing in the sun-light holding the horses' reins. Her heart fluttered at the sight of him. *Lord,* she prayed, *help me to win his affection. Even the tiniest bit would appease me.*

"Good morn," she greeted him with a smile and hurried to mount the horse. "I hope I didn't keep you waiting long."

"Nay, I only just got here. Good morn, Wife."

Declan helped her by giving her a leg-up. Isabel purposely appeared too weak to put her leg over the horse's back so he would have to hold her. His hands immediately surrounded her and protected her from falling. She placed a hand on his lightly-whiskered cheek and smiled. His eyes stared into hers briefly before he shifted her back atop her horse's back. Isabella enjoyed the moment while it lasted.

Back on the trail, they rode for a few leagues before stopping. He didn't speak to her which left her to her maddening thoughts. Though he was somewhat reserved, she sensed there was something more that caused him not to want to bed her. Whatever it was probably had nothing to do with her. She felt much better about the situation when that thought entered her mind.

They rode until the sun was high overhead. Declan pulled his horse to a stop. "We'll let the horses rest a bit," he told her. "If ye need some privacy, that copse will do, lass. It'll be safe. There's no one about."

She wondered how he knew this, and suspected Declan must've traveled through the area on his treks to Edinburgh. She used the opportunity to stretch her legs and relieve her needs, trading places to hold the horses while he did the same. There was no other conversation. Declan was a man of scant words apparently, and she was getting to know him, what little he showed of himself.

After a brief respite from riding, they continued. Isabella turned her attention to the scenery and discovered she enjoyed the beauty of the land they traipsed. The woodland seemed to grow sparser the more north they rode. Hills and meadows lay before them and in the distance, mountainous peaks rose to touch the sky. Newly sprouted flowers sprinkled the open areas where the grass was beginning to take over the fields. Isabella had always enjoyed the rebirth of nature when spring came. At least she'd had something to view on the laborious journey.

Toward early evening, he sidled next to her. "We'll stop here for the night." He dismounted and approached her.

When his hands settled on her waist, he snatched her from her horse as if she weighed nothing and lowered her to the ground. Isabella gasped at his quick movement. She put her hands on his shoulders and sagged against him until she could support herself on her wobbly legs. Isabella took longer than necessary so she could enjoy the feel of his muscles pressed against her body and the tingles she'd experienced whenever he touched her. She breathed in his scent—horse, and man, and yet, it was appealing, making her want him all the more.

They had stopped by a stream, and she made use of a nearby bush for privacy. On her return, she found him resting by a tree. He had started a fire and wrapped his tartan over his body. Isabella sat across from him, disheartened that he hadn't offered to share the warmth of his tartan. She was cold and shivered at the thought of having to sleep outside. Her cloak offered a little protection from the cold, but she suspected her husband's body would be much warmer.

Declan unfastened his scabbard, pulled his sword free, and set it beside him. His sword was quite large and hefty given the thickness of the iron blade. She'd never seen a longsword akin to his. His sword had a cross-hilt with capped arms that ended in quatrefoils to protect his hands. There were no adornments to it such as jewels or embellishments on the blade. The wide blade didn't appear too sharp, but thick enough to cause great injury. Isabella shook her head at the image of him using it in battle or against a foe. He likely knew how to protect them given the size of his weapon and that he frequently traveled the area.

"Do ye wish to share my tartan? There's a wee bit of a nip this night."

A wee bit? It was bloody freezing. Before he might rescind his offer, Isabella hurried to sit with him. She was grateful he'd offered to share his tartan, but more pleased that she could cuddle next to him. Declan shimmied toward her and pulled the tartan over them.

"You are cold. Here," he said and wrapped his arm around her back and pulled her tighter against him. "Share my warmth."

She wanted to share more than that but refrained from saying so. "How is it you are warm and I'm cold?"

He grinned and with his free arm, poked at the fire. "I'm used to the temperatures here in the north. This is a mild evening. You'll get used to it, Wife."

Isabella relaxed against him. She was lulled by the fire and his warmth and snuggled against his hard body. As usual, a thrill swept over her body from the places they touched to her extremities. She tilted her head back and watched his face. He seemed oblivious to her subtle signals. So Isabella reached to touch his chin and turned his face to look at her. "Declan…"

"Aye, Wife?"

"Why do you keep calling me 'Wife'?"

"To remind myself that I'm married."

What an unfeeling thing to say. He was a cad. She took a breath to settle her temper because it was becoming more difficult to keep from being outspoken. Isabella wanted to tell him what she thought of his inane comment, but instead, she said, "I'm so insignificant that you need to remind yourself that you married me?"

Declan leaned forward and turned to peer at her. "Ah, nay, lass, I did not mean it like that."

"Then why won't you at least kiss me?"

"You want to be kissed?"

Lord above, she drew in a deep breath. The man needed to be hit over the head. "Never mind. It seems my wishes don't matter. And just so you know, I preferred to be called Isabella, not Wife."

Declan took hold of her face, and his large hand cupped her neck. He pressed his lips on hers and then yanked her body to his. Isabella's heart skipped several beats. His hard manly lips covered hers and he used his tongue to get her to open her mouth. She touched her tongue to his and moaned softly at the exquisite sensations swarming her body. Their kiss was much more affecting than the modest peck he'd given her after their vows. But it ended too soon when Declan pulled away.

"Now get some sleep, *Wife*. We will set out early."

She scrunched her eyes in objection to him calling her wife again. "How much farther do we need to travel, *Husband*?" Isabella couldn't help but pout at the thought of another long day's ride. She wasn't one to complain but she ached all over and was exhausted. A harrumph escaped her lips before she could stop herself.

He sighed a heavy breath and likely surmised her annoyance. "Another day or so. We should reach home by tomorrow night or mayhap the following morn. It depends on how fast we travel."

It was probably the most he'd ever spoken to her at once and she reveled in the sound of his voice. Isabella nodded. "I shall do my best to keep up."

She closed her eyes and relaxed, feeling protected. The sensations, the tastes, and the feeling of their kiss continued to fill her thoughts. If bedding Declan was as pleasurable as that kiss, then she was in for a passionate experience.

CHAPTER FIVE

ECLAN CLOSED HIS eyes but kept his ears alert for any noise in the nearby woods, falling into the fitful and light doze he'd perfected as a warrior. His sword lay beside him at the ready should anyone come upon them. He didn't like that they now rode through hostile territory and if it wasn't for his bonny but soft wife, he would have ridden through the night. The sooner he reached his land, the safer they'd be.

He wasn't concerned for himself but for Isabella. She was too bonny for her own good. Any man would be proud to have her as his wife, but her beauty also instilled the need in him to protect her. Some men could easily be swayed by the lust for such a beauty to kill a rival.

As the sky lightened, he remained still and gave Isabella a few more moments of sleep. She slept heavily given the dead weight of her body pressed against him. He wasn't immune to her soft curvy body cuddled by his side. She was a sensual woman and joining with her was sure to leave him reeling. But his confidence with women was lacking, and although he wanted to be with her, he didn't want to displease her either. Soon enough he'd have to face the consummation of their marriage. Declan wasn't about to take her though, not in the woods. Nay, he wanted to wait until they reached home. Once he had Isabella settled in his home—and his bed—he'd figure out how to put the past behind him and dispel his uncertainty.

Isabella stirred and pulled away from him. Declan couldn't fathom how a woman could appear so enchanting upon awakening. She was perfection, and there was no doubt in his mind that he was enamored.

He shook away his wayward thoughts and stood. On his approach to the horses, she sprinted toward the woods. He gave her a few minutes of privacy while he pulled out a roll of bread and a flask of ale, though he wasn't hungry. When she returned to the clearing and stood by the remains of their fire, he held out the items to her. She snatched the bread with a grumble, broke a piece off, and handed the rest back.

"Good morn. I apologize if I have kept you," she said groggily and nibbled on the bread.

He almost smiled at the tone of her voice. Though she woke looking bonny, morning Isabella was surly and appeared to dislike awakening early.

After she'd had a few sips and handed back the flask of ale, he finished it and shoved the empty flask into the saddlebag. "You did not keep me waiting, Isabella. We should get going, though, if we want to reach home before dark." He put the rest of the bread away and helped her to mount her horse, ignoring her groans and winces. Riding was hard, he agreed, though in time she would develop the muscles for it. Right now, he could only admire her stamina and the fact that she wasn't openly complaining as some fine ladies might. He mounted his steed and headed westerly.

Throughout the morning, they rode along silently. He remained focused and was thankful Isabella was a woman of few words. At his thought, however, she broke her silence.

"Declan, why are you so quiet? Do you dislike talking? We should get to know each other. Are there any questions you would like to ask me?"

He swallowed his mirth. He'd given her credit for her silence too quickly. "It's nay that I'm not inclined to talk, lass," he explained. "But I'm listening."

"To what?"

"Not to, but *for*. Sounds," he said in almost a whisper. "For foes or animals."

She pivoted her head this way and that as if she expected someone or something to jump out of the woods. She addressed him in a whisper, now, suddenly aware, apparently, that their voices would carry and alert others of their presence. "Is there danger?"

"There is always danger, *Wife*." He shrugged and signaled to her to be quiet.

Declan had thought he'd heard something, perhaps a boar or a wolf nearby before she'd spoken, and now he continued to focus on the sounds around them. But other than the songs of birds, the wind in the trees, and the sound of their own horses' hooves, there was nothing now to give him concern.

After another league of riding, he noticed Isabella pitching to the side. He slowed his horse's pace until she caught up to him.

"You are tired?"

She visibly sighed and nodded. "Is it all right to speak now?"

"Aye, Wife. I thought there might be danger, but whatever I'd heard is gone. We can make camp or continue riding if you're up for it."

"I want to stop, but I sense you wish to keep riding." She winced as she curved her back into a stretch, then straightened her legs to flex her ankles in circles. She was obviously feeling stiff and tired.

"Och, 'tis but a short ride farther. If it helps to know, you shall have a warm bed this night." Declan smiled at her agreeable nature. Most women would have complained at the wearisome ride, but she hadn't. His wife had grit, which pleased him.

She narrowed her eyes. "Say no more. We will keep riding then."

"Come closer," he said and waved her onward.

Isabella nudged her horse closer, and he snatched her from the mount. She gasped and gripped his tartan. "Hold on, lass."

Declan reached for her horse's reins and tied them to his saddle then made sure she was settled in front of him. She sagged in his arms, and within minutes, the heaviness of her body and steady breathing told him that she slept deeply.

Now he didn't need to go more slowly to accommodate her. He made better progress and before he knew it, he was closer to his land. There was only one more wide space to ride through. Isabella continued to hold on to him and he liked the way her arms settled around him. When the winds grew brisker, he shifted his tartan to cover her completely.

Sounds of horses' thundering hooves came to him. He waited a moment, certain that Clan Murray's sentry approached. It had to be them because Murray's men never allowed trespassers. Fortunately, their clans had somewhat of an arrangement in that they could cross Murray lands to save time, thereby taking a shortcut. Declan had stopped at the last steep hill that led toward the open field. At the crest, riders appeared from the woods, and cut him off. There were at least ten men riding with their leader. *Damn.*

Before he could offer a greeting, Murray's men surrounded him, and their leader flanked his side. The sentry's horses shifted, stomped, and snorted, and were as ornery as their riders. All remained silent but glared at him to make known their displeasure at seeing him. Murray's men might be accepting of their pact to allow them to ride through, but they definitely weren't pleased by it.

But then, Declan took in the sight of his longtime friend. Dermot's almost black hair rested on his shoulders. His beard thickened and covered most of his face and his dark eyes held no animosity.

Although he wanted to be on his way, Declan had to show his appreciation for allowing him through. "Dermot Murray."

"MacKendrick. I suspected that be ye riding through." His dark bearded face hid his smile but there was a shine to his eyes that alluded to the fact that he likely grinned.

Declan answered him in Gaelic. Dermot Murray, an ally, spoke little English; speaking in their mother tongue was an advantage since he'd rather Isabella not hear their conversation in case she'd awakened. "Aye, I need to get home, or I would have stopped at your keep to pass on the news from Edinburgh."

Dermot shrugged. "Must not be anything of importance then, if ye did not stop." He shifted his eyes to survey the field below before looking back at him with one eyebrow lifted. "I saw your brother Silas riding through the other day. He was heading toward Campbell land. I thought it strange."

Declan suspected his stepbrother was spying on the Campbells to aid in his quest to find out who'd accused him of murder. Silas would be brazen enough to try to oust the knave. "Aye? Silas is a loyal MacKendrick and doing me a kindness."

"I just thought it strange." Dermot motioned to Isabella. "Who do ye have there?"

"My wife."

Dermot hooted. "Och, 'tis the truth? You married? I did not think ye would, not after what happened to Leona…"

"Aye, it's the truth. Alexander forced me to wed the lass, but I am not complaining."

His comrade chuckled, motioned to his followers to go on ahead of him, and waited for his clansmen to ride through. "It's been four years since Leona's death. Gladdened I am to see ye finally putting that wretchedness behind ye and moving on. 'Tis about time, my friend."

"Aye, I need to put it behind me. I must go if I want to reach home before dark. Good to see ye, Dermot." Declan encouraged his horse forward and was about to take the hill when Dermot called out to him.

"Await, MacKendrick. Is your woman bonny? Why do ye hide her?"

He almost chuckled but withheld the urge. "She's unsightly as hell with moles and bulging eyes. I do not want anyone to see her."

"Now I know ye speak falsely because ye wouldst not marry an unsightly woman. I'll stop by after ye get settled and meet the lass for myself."

"Truly, ye'd be less likely to lose your stomach contents if ye did not. Farewell, Murray." Declan heard his comrade's bellow of laughter as he crested the hill and began riding down the other side.

The last thing Declan wanted was for Dermot to spread the tale amongst the Highlands that he had married a beautiful woman. He'd have every laird or Highland man paying him a visit. Declan suspected he might have to keep his gates closed for the foreseeable future.

Isabella's body pitched toward him, and he held her tightly. She opened her eyes and smiled. Lord, she had a bonny smile and the way her eyelashes fanned her cheeks when she blinked made him want to kiss her. He was about to tell her that she could see the smoke from his chimney when she reached to turn his face toward her with gentle fingers.

"I had a wonderful dream."

"Aye?" He slowed the horse and waited for her to tell him what was so wonderful about it. Her lips were so close. All he had to do was shift a wee bit closer and set his mouth on hers. Desire swarmed his body, sending heat and hardness through him. If he had more courage, he'd take the pleasure she offered and the kiss he so wanted.

"You were in my dream, and I heard you laugh. It sounded so joyful. Do you ever laugh?"

Declan tilted his head. "Of course I do. Now look yonder, Wife, there is our home."

She remained quiet for a moment and didn't look at him when she said, "The wall is…massive. Why do you need to surround your home with such a high wall?"

"We live amongst many clans here in the north and there is always the threat of danger. We protect ourselves." She held onto him as they crossed the expanse of the field that abutted his clan's fief.

She leaned back against him. "You're not on friendly terms with your neighbors then?"

He tried to ignore the way it felt and the way his body responded by focusing on her question. "Aye, some we are, some not. We have allies and rivals. Worry not, Wife, there are plenty of MacKendrick soldiers who protect those walls. You'll be safe enough." It occurred to him that her home was probably much grander than what she'd live in now. Her father had wealth and likely had a large manor home surrounded by lawns and manicured gardens, but not walls. He should have explained what her new home would be like, but she'd see for herself when they reached the cottage.

They rode toward the open wall and after he passed the gatehouse, the sentry closed the heavy iron gates. Men-at-arms waved to signal all's well. He guided his horse through a crowded lane of clansmen and women who either greeted him or nodded. Chickens scurried out of his way, and they got held up by a lazy cow that wasn't in a rush to move past the lane. Noise from people's chatter and those chopping wood outside their cottages brought to him the sense of home. Cottages lined the path, and most had their doors open. Children either attended to chores or played in the grassy spots near their homes. He wondered briefly if Isabella was used to such clamor or if her home was more peaceful.

He didn't stop until he reached the large structure that sat in the middle of the walled surround. His home was large, a one-floor structure with various rooms, and big enough to fit his extended family. The thatch was thick enough to ward off the cold in the winter and the rains in spring. The cottage itself wasn't bonny to look at, but it was home for now. Hopefully, soon, he would move into the home his men were erecting. He needed to check on its progress and ensure it was almost complete. It might make for a nice surprise for Isabella and he'd tell her about it later.

He dismounted and then reached up to help Isabella from the horse. She stood beside him and stared at the cottage without saying a word. Her eyes were round and large. He removed her heavy valise and set it on the ground next to her.

One of his stable lads approached and he handed the horses off to him before telling her, "This is where you'll live. My family also lives under my roof."

"Family? You didn't mention family." She turned to him, and her face was downcast. "Why didn't you tell me you had a family?"

Declan shrugged because he didn't have an answer. He supposed he should have told her about his family, but it hadn't crossed his mind. There was much they hadn't discussed on their ride.

"What about your parents? Do they live here?"

"My parents are both dead. My ma passed when I was a lad. My da remarried after my ma died, a handful of years later. My stepmother Helena lives here as does her son. There's also my younger brother and sister. There are a few servants who also reside within. Helena sees to the keeping of the home. I shall tell her that she no longer needs to—"

"Please, don't tell her that. Allow her to continue. I don't want to intrude on her life if it makes her feel needed. In time, I'll ask if she wants me to take over the role."

Declan picked up her valise, took her hand, and squeezed it. "You are kind to think of that. I had not considered that Helena might wish to be useful. Aye, we'll let it be for now."

"Does it matter to you?" Isabella asked and turned back toward the cottage.

"Nay, why should it? You are my wife now and the responsibility is yours if ye want it."

"I shall think about it," she said and released his hand and took the three steps that led to the door. "But I will not overstep and insult your stepmother."

He opened the door for her and motioned her inside. His

stepmother stood at the table, kneading dough. She glanced up. Declan thought he might have startled her because she wore a frown.

"Oh, Declan, I wish I knew you were returning. I wouldst have prepared a welcome home feast for you and called the clan together. Is this the new wife? She's a petite thing, is she not?"

Isabella curtseyed to his stepmother. "My lady."

Helena inclined her head in response.

Declan nodded but continued, "We had a long journey, Helena. I am sure Isabella wishes to rest. It was a tiresome trip."

With that, he guided Isabella out of the kitchen and to his bedchamber, where he opened the door. "This is where ye will sleep."

She entered the chamber and turned to him, her cheeks brightening. "Is it also where you will sleep?"

He set her valise next to the bed and turned to her. "Aye, but I doubt I shall return this night. I often sleep in the barracks when I am working with the soldiers so I will not disturb you." His offered explanation appeared to make his new wife grimace.

Isabella grabbed hold of his tunic sleeve. "Where are you going? You are not going to just leave me…here, alone, are you?"

He set his hand atop hers, taking a moment to marvel at the softness of her skin before gently lifting it away. She dropped her arm to her side. Her shoulders appeared to slump. Guilt nagged him a little, but he wasn't used to explaining his actions to anyone. To ease her, he said, "There are clan matters to see to. I need to get reports from my men and take care of problems that need my attention. I've been away for much longer than I had planned."

"Oh, I didn't realize… Of course, you have duties to attend to." She smoothed her hands over her skirt and appeared weary.

"You get rest, Wife, and I will see ye on the morrow. Helena shall bring ye a bite to eat shortly. I'll make sure she has a maid fetch a bath for ye so you can wash off the dust and horse before ye settle for the night." He smiled as she reached for her hair and blushed, probably realizing she was disheveled from their journey. "I know ye are probably weary and saddle sore." Declan placed his hands on her shoulders and shifted her to sit on the bed. His lovely wife frowned up at him.

"I am tired but more nervous about meeting your family. I worry that they might not like me." Isabella folded her hands, set them on her lap, and peered at him uneasily.

Declan flinched. She would be apprehensive about meeting his clan, but he didn't know what to say to relieve her concern. His clan might not welcome her with open arms, but once he told them she was his wife, they would respect her. He didn't want to leave her feeling vulnerable, but right now, the security of his clan outweighed the needs of his wife. Somehow, he had to find a way to balance his role of being a laird and that of being a husband. He hadn't realized what it appeared to her or how intrusive having a wife would be. Declan hadn't had anyone else to consider or answer to when he went about his duties for many a year. "I will be here, but outside. I rarely stay in this room so make it your own if ye wish."

"I will fare well…on my own." Isabella gripped her hands and averted her gaze.

He hesitated by the door. "If ye need any—"

"I won't need anything, Declan. Good eve to you."

Dismissed, Declan left and closed the door quietly behind him. He met Helena at the table. "See that my wife is given food and a bath. We have not eaten a good meal in days. I will be out amongst the clan if ye needs me." He didn't wait for Helena's acknowledgment but hastened outside.

With a whistle, he called his guardsmen and commander-in-arms to him.

Anse, his cousin, and commander-in-arms, reached him first. He punched his arm and then shoved him. "Damn, 'tis good to have ye back. I take it ye had no trouble on the way home?"

"Nay, I thought someone followed, but whoever it was never showed themselves. I saw no one on my travels except for the

Murrays when I crossed their land. All goes well?"

By then, Trevor, Slone, and Lorcan stood around him. His trusted guardsmen were the most skilled of all the MacKendrick soldiers. Brothers, the guardsmen resembled each other with their dark hair and eyes. Their skin likewise was dark, made even tanner by the sun because they often forwent the wearing of a tunic. There were rumors that their mother was a Spaniard, taken by their father as a slave, but he'd been so enamored, he'd kept her as his wife.

"Did ye not go through with it, Laird?" Lorcan asked, shaking his dark-haired head. "Do we now have a lady?"

"Aye, I did," Declan answered. "I had no choice. At least now, we owe no tax and can put our coins to good use."

"Then where she be?" Slone asked. "You got married, aye?"

"I put her to bed." Declan took a moment to glance around their home, noting the fortification he had commissioned was about halfway finished. Three stories had been erected so far. Soon, he'd move into the stone structure and hoped it would be finished by harvest time.

"She must be a looker then if ye already finished with her," Trevor said. "Could not hold out, eh? Did the poor lass get any pleasure at all?"

Declan scoffed at his soldier. "What business is it of yours? I would keep from making such lurid comments if I was ye, or mayhap you'd like to lift heavy stone for the rest of the week." He reprimanded his soldier and bade him to be quiet, but then he couldn't resist sticking up for his wife. "She is a looker, Trevor, but nay, we just rode a great distance, and she needs rest. It is not what ye are thinking."

"Does this woman have a name?" Anse asked.

"Isabella."

Slone chuckled. "Is she bonny, Laird? Or did ye get saddled with the ugliest of the lot?"

Declan scoffed at the soldier. "Truthfully, she was the most pleasing of the brides and I got the first choice so…" He shrugged.

"Now, tell me the news and be quick about it." He nodded as Anse gave him the latest happenings of the clan. There wasn't much to report. "The Campbells have been quiet? They haven't caused any issues whilst I was away?"

"Nay, they have not stepped foot on our land. I commanded the sentries to go out day and night and to make sure they did not trespass. There have been no reports of anything untoward by them either," Anse said. "They're keeping to themselves these days."

"Good. And my brother Claude? Has he been training as I bade him to?" Declan's gaze sought his younger brother amongst the fledgling soldiers who practiced arms on the adjacent field. Claude was at an age where he should have taken to arms already, but with the death of their father, his brother had balked at fighting. Most lads his age were overzealous to begin their training. Declan had given him time to mourn, but now his brother was more than ready to wield a sword for the clan.

"Claude comes daily and does his duty, but he does not like it," Anse said. "His heart is not in it."

Declan sighed and gathered that he would have to speak with his brother. "I do not give a cosh whether he likes it or not. He will take to arms akin to the rest of the MacKendricks. Aye, and what about Silas? What has he been up to lately?"

Anse waived his guardsmen away. "Be about your duties, men. I will speak to our laird." Once the soldiers left them, Anse grimaced. "'Tis the truth, I have not seen your stepbrother. He goes about his way without reporting in and avoids me. Mayhap I should have a word with him."

"It is my duty, and I will speak to him. He should not be going off without at least letting ye know where he's off to. Murray said he saw him heading toward Campbell land recently. I think my stepbrother is intent on finding my accuser. That is commendable but he shouldn't go outside the walls without letting someone know."

Anse grimaced. "Perhaps, Laird, but I like not that he is

sneaky about it."

"You worry about the soldiers, Anse, and I will worry about my brother."

"Stepbrother," Anse corrected him with a clip, "I remind ye he is not related by blood."

"It matters not. When my father married his mother, he became my brother. Now cease this senseless talk." Declan didn't know why Anse wasn't fond of Silas. His commander should take his brother in hand and guide him.

Declan had promised his stepmother that he would see to his training, but Silas wasn't very good at arms. He suspected Anse reproached Silas because the soldiers often followed his stepbrother's lead. There was a wee bit of a power struggle there. Declan wouldn't do anything about it until it became necessary. Perhaps in time, it would sort itself out.

Anse ambled away, slowly moving toward the fortification and he trailed him. "So tell me, Declan, what think ye of this wife? I assume she is bonny since ye are not complaining about her."

Declan shrugged.

"I suppose ye are being closemouthed for a reason?" Anse asked. "Is she a harpy? God, I hope ye were not saddled with such a woman. A shrew for a wife is the most horrible thing imaginable, a fate worse than death if ye ask me."

Declan chuckled. "If ye ever do marry, you'll probably end up with such a woman. I cannot see any woman being agreeable toward ye." He laughed at his jest, but his cousin stared at him intently and Declan knew he was waiting for an answer. "Isabella is...she is...ah..."

"Uh, the cat's got your tongue. She has got ye all tongue-tied and must be bonny then." Anse laughed and punched his upper arm. "Are ye blushing, laddie?"

Declan shoved Anse's shoulder hard and forced him back a step. "Nay, of course not. I do not blush. Isabella is bonny, intelligent, kind, and..."

"Worthy?"

"Aye, more than worthy. 'Tis just… I have not been with a woman for so long that I fear I will disappoint her. She seems amiable to do her wifely duty. What if I…" Declan's face heated with his explanation and couldn't continue his thought. He would only confess his most uneasy thoughts to Anse; his cousin was his closest comrade and never judged him.

"Ah, there it is. Ye are intimidated by her. Never thought I would see the day a lass would waylay ye. I shall tell ye a secret. 'Tis like riding a horse, Cousin. Once ye learn, you never forget. The longer ye wait to bed her, the harder it will be, and I mean that literally." Anse bellowed with laughter at his own jest.

"Aye, I know. After what happened to Leona, I never thought I would marry again, let alone find myself attracted to such a woman."

"Ahh, you're attracted. Saints be praised for I had not thought ye would ever seek pleasure again. Gladdened I am to hear it. Laird, ye deserve happiness. 'Twas not your fault your wife drowned. You could not have saved her. Are ye still blaming yourself?"

Declan shook his head. "Nay, of course not. What happened to Leona was an accident and I was not at fault. I do not hold guilt for her death. But I have not explained to Isabella… She does not even know about Noah yet."

"You have not told her ye have a son?"

He shook his head. "I have not spoken about Leona, my son, or even about what happened for so long, I do not wish to speak of it now. But I will do so because Isabella deserves an explanation."

Anse set his hand on his shoulder. "Aye, Laird, she does. Ye best get to it before she learns of it from someone else. That will not sit well. Then ye can focus on bedding your wife and gaining the happiness you deserve." He pounded his back with an encouraging thrashing.

"Happiness will not be had until I find out who accused me of murder and who murdered Leona's da. Och, now that I am home, I can focus on finding the traitor. There has been no word from the Campbells. If it was one of them, they will make a mistake, and someone shall speak of it. Secrets are hard to keep here in the north."

His cousin scoffed. "Och, we will probably never learn who it was…or the truth. Mayhap ye should just forget about it and move on."

"Nay, I will have vengeance, Anse. If not this day, then on the morrow. Nothing will stop me from finding out the truth," Declan said heatedly.

"Aye, ye have vengeance in your heart, Laird. Ye better make room for your wife in there," he said and tapped his chest. "Or ye shall regret it." Anse began to whistle as he walked away.

It was true. Vengeance filled him and there was nothing more important to him than seeking retaliation. Until Declan fulfilled that vow, he couldn't let his heart be filled with anything else.

CHAPTER SIX

ISABELLA ALMOST WISHED she had never been forced to take the vow to marry Declan. He wanted a wife as much as she wanted a husband. That was evident in the fact that he left her alone with strangers. An older woman she took as the maidservant bustled into her chamber and had a bath brought in. She didn't introduce herself and appeared to be in a rush and left as soon as water was poured into the tub by two other servants.

When the last of the water arrived, the maids left her. Isabella stripped and sank into the warm water. She leisurely washed and enjoyed the ease the heat brought to her aching muscles. When she finished, she dried herself and dressed in a linen cotte she pulled from her valise. A knock came at her door and a younger maid entered with a tray of food. She didn't speak to her but nodded her head before she vacated the room.

She spent the night and most of the day in the chamber. It was unlike her to cower and hide away, but she was hesitant to venture forth. What had she expected? For one thing, Declan would, at the very least, introduce her to his family. It wasn't too much to ask, but it appeared he hadn't considered how awkward it was for her.

Isabella dressed in a plain brown frock, not her favorite dress, but it was presentable enough. After taking care to comb her hair and tie it at the base of her neck, she slipped on her favorite boots and ensured she didn't appear bedraggled. She intended to go outside and grabbed her shawl in case it was chilly.

Now, she opened the door a little and listened. There didn't seem to be anyone in the passageway. Isabella ventured farther into the hallway, then made her way to the open area where it appeared the family conjugated. They were settled around the table and one of the men there spoke animatedly about finding a treasure while the other appeared to scoff. A pot sat at the center of the table and there was a basket of bread as well. Isabella lingered by the wall, listening, and waiting for them to notice her.

Finally, the woman Declan had indicated was his stepmother looked her way. "Oh, there ye be, Isabella. I thought you wouldst laze about your bed all day."

The conversation ceased as everyone turned to stare at her. "At last, ye got the courage to leave the room. Come, eat with us. We do not bite," Helena said.

Their gazes told her otherwise. Still, Isabella sat in the nearest chair, across from Declan's stepmother, and snatched a roll from a basket in the center of the table. She wasn't usually one to be reserved, but she didn't know his family and was uncomfortable with their inquisitive stares. Until she gained a better sense of them, Isabella decided she would try to remember her mother's guidance: the less she said, the better.

Helena had dark hair, almost black, and she wore it in a bun at the nape of her neck. She wasn't a large woman, but she wasn't slight either. The expression in her eyes wasn't warm or welcoming but appeared to hold disdain. Isabella couldn't account for the way the woman gazed at her with such loathing. She had done nothing to cause the woman's affront though she probably would, eventually. It occurred to Isabella that if Declan's stepmother was anything like her own mother, she would have a hard time impressing or pleasing her.

"Let me introduce you to the laird's family," Helena said with a scoff. "You of course know me, I am the laird's stepmother Helena, Lady MacKendrick to the likes of you. Next to me is my dear son, Silas. Your husband is fond of him, so it is best to be amiable toward him. On your other side is Rhona, the laird's sister, and beside her is his brother, Claude. All, this is Isabella, the laird's new wife. Now, eat your fill, lass, and do not dally. We do not waste time at the table."

"It is a pleasure to meet you all," she said and looked at her trencher when Lady MacKendrick slopped a heaping spoonful of pottage on it. It splattered over the rim and onto the table. Isabella picked up her spoon and set to eating. Surprisingly, the stew tasted good. She focused on the food and after a few moments of uncomfortable silence, the family seemed to accept her presence and continued their conversation.

"I tell ye, there's a treasure and I aim to find it," Claude said. "I found great-grandda's map, and the markings will lead to it, I just know it will. I have begun my hunt."

"You are wasting your time, Brother, and the map is but a useless bit of scrap. Grandda was having your leg because there's no treasure," Rhona said. "Do ye not have better things to do with your time than search for something that is not there?"

Isabella smiled at Declan's sister, but Rhona frowned and turned away, all but ignoring her. That disheartened Isabella further. She had hoped to befriend Declan's siblings, but they were as friendly as a hoard of boars. Claude scowled at her and returned his gaze to the parchment in front of him. He appeared as friendly as his sister. If she survived a day in their presence, it would come down to God's intervention because they were downright mean.

Isabella regarded Declan's siblings. They looked much like him with golden locks of hair, brown eyes, and similar facial features. It seemed they weren't keen to want to get to know her, so she didn't join in the conversation and remained quiet. Melancholy crept its way into her heart, and she was saddened that they disliked her.

"Have you gone yet to the field, Silas? Surely, his lairdship means to see ye there this day," Lady MacKendrick asked her son.

"Best ye make a showing of yourself. Appearances are important if ye wish to make your way in this clan."

Silas, she noticed, watched her closely but at least he smiled. He hadn't looked away from her since she sat at the table. Isabella returned his smile and was thankful at least one of Declan's family was happy with her presence. Silas was handsome with straight black hair, a lean body, and a bit of scruff on his face. Isabella thought he neared Declan's age, but he wasn't as brawny as her husband.

Still, his gaze hadn't wavered. His light blue eyes were mesmerizing. She'd never seen a man with such becoming eyes. His intense eyes seemed to peer through her.

Silas turned to look at his mother finally and answered her, "I have been at the training fields. Declan was not there so I left. 'Twas no sense in wasting my time if he was not there."

"Ye would do well to take more of a leadership role with the soldiers. One day it might become needful or prudent. If something awful were to happen to Declan, ye could be next in line to serve this clan. Best ye remember that." Lady MacKendrick smeared butter on a piece of bread and continued her conversation with her son.

"I cannot believe Declan married a bonny woman akin to ye, Milady Isabella," Silas said and leaned toward her, ignoring his mother. "Is it true the king forced ye to marry him?"

"I certainly did marry him and was fortunate to be given a choice. Declan was the most handsome, noble man offered," she said and tried to instill that her marriage to Declan was coveted by them both. Isabella didn't want his family to think he was forced to marry her.

Silas guffawed. "Ye chose him? Was there naught any others who were worthy? I wish I had been one of the men ye got to choose from. It would have made your decision easier."

Isabella smiled because it seemed Silas was jesting with her even though his tone might not have implied it. "I am certain you are right."

"If ye like, Milady, I would be gladdened to walk with ye this day, show ye around the keep's grounds. The grounds outside the walls are just as bonny. There's a loch close by that the clan frequently visits."

"I would enjoy that, but I like to walk by myself… Ah, to clear my head. I should do so now." Isabella disregarded Silas's frown. She finished her meal and wanted to get away from Declan's family at the soonest. Before she left the cottage, she offered to help clean up, but Lady MacKendrick scoffed at her.

"'Tis the maid's job, lass, to see to the cleaning up. Ah, here's Edith now."

The maid whom she'd seen briefly the night before was a kindly-looking woman with light brown hair tucked beneath a kerchief. She entered the main room and took up the trenchers and bowls. Isabella noted the harsh look on the maid's face when she gazed at Lady MacKendrick. She would introduce herself to the maid later when Lady MacKendrick wasn't around. Servants always knew what was going on in the home, and Isabella hoped to get some answers from Edith or at least win her favor.

With nothing keeping her there, Isabella wandered outside. She wanted to get away from Declan's unpleasant family. Silas stood at the cottage door and watched her leave. He wasn't a bad sort, but she reasoned he might be attracted to her. Isabella needed to dissuade him from any interest. She had dealt with overzealous suitors before and his attention was the last thing she needed now when all she wanted was to attract Declan. Silas looked at her fondly, but in a seemly way, as if he had thought to win her favor. It was obvious Declan's family didn't like outsiders and she, being from the Scottish border only instigated their disdain, except for Silas. Perhaps she could make a friend of him. Having him on her side might go a long way to winning her husband's notice.

The day was nice enough with only a slight chill in the air. Isabella gripped her shawl and walked around, taking in the scene of the MacKendrick clan's people. Ahead, the men appeared to be building a fortress by the look of it. The stone structure rose high. She'd seen a similar building when she was in Edinburgh. When finished, the fortification would be impenetrable and unsightly in her opinion, with heavy stone and starkness. The men who erected the building excluded window casements but had put enough balistrarias to let a little light within. At least there was that.

People strolled along the lane and reverted around a horse and cart. Men loaded bales of hay onto the cart and jested with each other. She smiled at them and continued on her way, crossing the lane and walking on. Soldiers stood in a group yonder and appeared to be discussing something humorous because they bellowed with laughter. Down aways, she noticed several carts set up which likely were for the sale of wares. Her interest was piqued in wonder of what they sold. Several women stood by the hawkers likely purchasing something to go with their supper.

A young lad ran forth with a long stick in his hand. He appeared to be about five or so years of age. The lad shouted and played at being a knight who set out to defeat his foes. Isabella smiled at the lad and his enthusiastic movements. His light hair fell past his shoulders in what appeared to be tangled strands. In fact, she noticed that he was unkempt overall, with smudges of dirt on his face, scraped knees below the hem of his tartan, and a gray tunic that was probably once another color.

The lad turned and shot across the lane right by her. He kept running and swung his makeshift sword. She heard a thundering sound and turned to see what the commotion was when she spotted an unmanned horse tethered to a cart careening toward them. Her breath caught in her throat because the horse had been frightened by something, probably by the lad swinging his sword. The animal gave no care where it ran and galloped straight at them.

The lad paid no attention to the noise. He shot out on the lane and raised his stick in the pretense of fighting a foe. Isabella dropped her shawl and sprinted toward him. She snatched the lad off his feet and hurried to step out of the way of the horse. The animal and cart thundered by them even as she wobbled under the child's weight and fell backward and landed with an *oomph* on the lane. She groaned as pain shot through her. The ground was hard, and she likely had a bruise or two to show for her gallantry.

"Lad, what were you thinking? You could have been hurt." Isabella set him on his feet and held onto his hand. She got on her knees to rise.

The lad jerked his hand from hers and glared at her with big eyes before he scrambled backward and ran off without a by-your-leave or even a thank you. That he hadn't even acknowledged that she'd saved him astounded her. He needed to be taught manners. Before Isabella got to her feet, a man threw his hand down at her. She peered at the large, calloused hand before her and reluctantly accepted his help.

"Milady, are ye hurt?" He scowled fiercely at the cart, which had been stopped by several men who were even now calming the animal and unhitching it. When he turned back to her, he smiled.

She shook her head and brushed a bit of hay from her over-dress that must've fallen from the cart. The lad was nowhere to be seen now and had scampered off. Isabella hoped to have a word with him about the perils of playing in the busy lane and that he should greet his elders properly—and thank people for saving his life, at the very least. She prayed that he was safe and unharmed.

"I am Anse MacKendrick, the clan's commander-in-arms, your husband's cousin. Here, Milady," he said and handed her the discarded shawl.

Isabella gaped at the man in awe as she took him in. Anse was a large man, muscular, broad-shouldered, and handsome. His dark hair swept by his face in long strands. He had kind dark eyes and a manicured beard that was trimmed short. She accepted the shawl from him and wrapped it around her shoulders. "Good day,

Anse. Thank you for your aid. I am well, truly, just a little bruised."

"Ye frightened me to death, Milady, when I saw the cart ready to run ye down, I all but lost my breath. My heart is still pounding. Ye be fortunate to be alive." Anse sounded a little winded and rambled in a deeply accented brogue.

Isabella's cheeks brightened to be the focus of the hardened soldier's attention. "I do apologize, sir, and hadn't meant to frighten you. I had to save the lad." She paused, unsure if she should point out the boy's lack of gratefulness, uncertain whether it would endear her to Anse or not. But then, she decided, it needed to be said. "Do you know, he did not even thank me for rescuing him?"

Anse smiled, his unruly dark hair blowing in the wind. "Och, that lad cannot hear and probably wasn't paying attention. He likely did not know ye were saving him."

No wonder. It all made sense, then. *He wasn't rude, he was...* "He cannot hear?"

"Nay, he's a deaf-mute. His grandma usually looks after him, but I do not see her about. I will have a word with her."

"Oh, please, don't get the lad in trouble. I am not hurt, and I was able to save him from being run over. I only hope someone looks after him."

"If that pleases ye, Milady, I will not speak of it to her. Och, ye can be sure I'll be telling his da." Anse smiled at her. "You are Declan's new wife?"

She curtseyed to him. "I am Isabella. Yes, his wife."

"He said ye were lovely, but I vow he understated your beauty." Anse held out his arm. "If ye would like, I can show ye around."

Isabella smiled and could have laughed at Anse when he told her that. It was unlikely Declan had spoken of her at all, let alone professed such compliments. "I would like that. You mentioned the lad's father... Who is he? Perhaps I can offer to..." She discontinued speaking because it wasn't her place to offer assistance to the lad or his family. Isabella didn't wish to overstep.

"His da is Declan. Did he not mention the lad to ye?" Anse smirked. "He said he was going to tell ye about him this day."

"Declan is his father? No, he failed to mention that he had a son." Isabella's heart ached to hear that. Her husband should have disclosed such information. But what saddened her more was that the lad ran amongst the clan without a care. His grandmother certainly *wasn't* watching him. "How old is the lad?"

Anse gripped his chin in thought. "Hmm. I'd say he be about six or seven. Aye, he's seven in years. Most of the clan avoids him because it's a bother trying to get him to understand what ye are saying to him."

"That poor lad. I should like to meet his grandmother."

"'Tis Declan's grandmother, the lad's great-grandmother. She is aged and has a wee bit of trouble looking after the lad. He is always running about inside the walls."

Isabella refrained from asking him why his father didn't look after him. She would have to put the question to her husband if he ever showed himself.

Anse stopped by the building being erected and motioned to it. "This will soon be your home. Is it not grand? The men tirelessly work on it. Declan wants it ready by harvest time."

"Oh, it's for… He didn't mention that either. It's certainly large and looks…secure." Isabella flinched because the building made of heavy stone looked more like a soldier's fortress than a family home.

"Aye, there is a need. It will be grander when 'tis finished. I see that gaze in your eye, Milady. It might appear stark at the present, but we have yet to finish it. The flourishes will be added toward the end of the build and make it more appealing."

She couldn't fathom that it would be grand even with the most becoming flourishes. A few well-placed gargoyles would be more apt to its decoration. Obviously, Declan felt the need to have such a fortification for his home. Isabella hadn't realized they would require protection. Was it possible they could be besieged by another clan or even a bloody army? Everything she learned about her new home and family made her realize how distant she was from where she'd grown up. None of Mother's lessons had prepared her for this, although, from time to time they had to secure their home against intruders or raiders.

They continued walking, past more cottages and villagers. Nearing the end of the lane, Anse gestured to the cluster of carts set up. The scent of cooking food rose to her nostrils, along with the smell of smoke. People chattered and called out all around her, moving about their business. Women carried market baskets of goods. Children raced underfoot. Men passed, nodding to Anse, eyeing her curiously. She lifted her chin and looked past them to the merchants selling their wares.

Anse gestured. "Here, there are hawkers who sell almost everything ye might need. Just tell them ye are Declan's wife, and he'll see to the payment for anything ye might need. If ye need any coins, ye can ask Rolly, our steward, and he will see to it."

They walked past what was obviously the blacksmith's shop where a burly, aproned man stood over a fire of coals and an anvil. He began hammering at a hot bit of metal with rhythmic, metallic clangs. She couldn't help but wince at the loud ringing. Anse laughed and led her on, past a building with a wagon wheel for a sign, and another with a shoe hanging over the door. The cobbler, she realized. Truly, her husband's keep had everything people might need. It wasn't as primitive as she'd first believed. Even with the threat of war and the need for a large, fortified home.

She followed Anse to the end of the lane where she saw a whitewashed building. It featured small, stained-glass windows and its painted door was open wide in welcome to any who passed by. It was beautiful, especially when compared to the other rough stone and thatched buildings she'd seen.

"And this," he said with obvious pride as he pointed, "is the chapel, dedicated to Saint Andrew. It's newly erected and large enough to have Mass there. We are awaiting an appointed clergyman to serve us. Declan's father had commissioned it be built before he passed."

Isabella stood feeling awe and thanks for the chapel. She intended to make good use of it, especially if her absent husband continued to ignore her and his brother continued to pay undesired attention to her. Her knees were sure to be tested because it was probable that she'd spend much time on them praying for her husband. With the Sign of the Cross, she thanked God for such a blessing.

"I see this pleases ye, Milady?"

"This does indeed please me, Anse. Thank you for showing me around. I shall leave you to your duties. If you see..." She ceased in midsentence. Isabella had hoped to have him send Declan to her, but she wouldn't be so forward. If Declan wanted to see her, he would search her out for himself.

"Shall I walk you back to the laird's home?" Anse asked her.

"No. Now that I have the lay of the land, I think I can walk back by myself. Thank you for the tour, Anse. I bid you a good day." She bowed to him.

"Aye, Milady. Ye'll be safe. As long as there are no more runaway horses and carts." His eyes twinkled as he bowed to her in return before he turned and left her standing there.

She made her way back to the cottage, moving slowly so as to avoid Helena and the rest of her husband's unwelcoming family. But before long, she was there at the door and had to go in. Isabella hurried to her room, pleased that no one appeared to see her. Especially, Declan's stepmother who seemed to be haranguing a young maid about something. She didn't stay to listen but made her way to her bedchamber.

Isabella closed the bedchamber door behind her. On her approach to the bed, she saw a bunch of flowers on the pillow. They were tied together with a string. Isabella picked them up, sniffed the floral scent, and smiled. Perhaps her husband wasn't such an oaf after all. She placed the flowers on the bedside table and decided to spend the evening inside her room.

Isabella set about unpacking her valise, musing about her day. She didn't want to think badly about anyone. But Lady MacKendrick wasn't an easy woman to like or befriend. She doubted she'd ever get on with the woman. Helena's face reflected her dislike of her and so it would probably be best if she avoided the woman altogether.

As Declan avoided his son, apparently. She wondered why he hadn't told her about him. And who was the child's mother? Had Declan been married in the past, or was the child a by-blow from some fallen woman? If that was so, where was the woman? Who was she? Whoever she was, Isabella thought, she couldn't be alive. For one thing, Anse had told her it was his grandmother who was supposedly caring for his son. Unfortunately, in Isabella's opinion, she wasn't doing the job well. It wasn't right, she decided, for Declan to act as though the boy didn't exist.

She thought about her own parents. While her mother was overbearing, she at least made sure to care for Isabella, and her father loved her more than words could say. She'd never lacked for care or affection. Unlike now, when it appeared she'd have neither from her husband nor the rest of his family.

It occurred to her that she was lonely. And homesick. What were her mother and father doing at that moment? Probably bickering over something humorous. She briefly stared out the window casement at the darkening sky and withheld the urge to weep. It was a terrible start to the beginning of her life at Declan's home and their marriage. She couldn't help but become sorrowful and sullen.

She emptied her valise and folded her garments. There was nowhere to put them, so she piled them on top of a trunk which she assumed was Declan's. Afterward, she tidied the chamber, washed, and tried to find something to keep her mind from thinking about Declan. She knelt by the bedside and prayed that somehow, she might gain her husband's attention. Isabella's prayers were many and she prayed for Declan's son, her brother in the Holy Land, her mother and father, but mostly for Declan.

It was obvious that he needed her. If only Declan realized that soon. It might save them a bit of trouble because she wasn't about to remain reticent for long.

CHAPTER SEVEN

DECLAN RETURNED WITH the day's sentry just after dusk. He'd wanted to ride close to Campbell's land to spy and learn something to give him the name of the traitorous foe who'd accused him of murder. At one time their clans had been allies, but whatever alliance between them faltered when Leona died. He had married Leona Campbell to maintain peace among their clans and for the years they were together there had been an armistice. When Leona drowned and he'd related the news of her death to her family, they'd accused him of harming her. That they blatantly blamed him for drowning his wife sat most foul in Declan's stomach.

Their rivalry had begun that fateful day. But then to also accuse him of murdering her father went beyond the means of decency. Declan had respected Leona's da and would never have harmed the man. Not only did he need to find out who blamed him for Allan Campbell's murder, but he also sought retribution for his late wife's father. He certainly hadn't killed him, but someone else had. Declan aimed to find out who did the foul deed and why they blamed him. What caused his foe to go against him? He wanted answers and wasn't willing to wait for them.

On his return home, he found Silas in the adjacent woods near their walls. Declan urged his horse into a canter to catch up with his stepbrother. When he reached him, he whistled and his brother slowed his mount, turned, and gave a wave.

"Brother, home at last," Silas said.

"Aye, I heard ye were trekking near Campbell land recently." Declan sidled next to Silas, and they rode together toward the gatehouse.

"'Twas uneventful."

"Were ye trying to find out who murdered Allan?"

Silas bobbed his head. "It was strange that none of the Campbells seemed to be out and about. I found out nothing that would give up the culprit. Their gates and keep are closed. Hardly any of their clansmen were about their fief."

"My thanks, Brother. We will find out who is responsible sooner or later." Declan pressed at his horse's sides, passed his brother, and approached the gate before him.

Returning home, Declan had gained no information that alluded to the cause of his incarceration. He passed the gate, and the guardsman gave the signal that all was well. Lorcan held up his fisted hand and shouted their motto, "Virtue alone ennobles."

Declan raised his fist in response, gave a firm nod, and rode past. He dismounted, grabbed his saddlebag from his horse, and waited for a stable lad to come forth. Silas hadn't come inside the walls yet and Declan wondered what kept him, but as he waited, he saw Anse walking toward him in a purposeful stride. There was a grimness in his expression which was unlike Anse because he had an easygoing nature.

"What goes, Anse? You look like ye are about to expire from grief." His cousin wore a strange look. It wasn't a frown, but he didn't smile either.

"Glory be, what a day," Anse said in a defeated tone. "I am dead on my feet."

He would have laughed at his cousin's disgruntlement, but Anse didn't look as if he was in a teasing manner. "Is there trouble with the soldiers? Is the new training schedule thwarting ye?"

"Nay, 'tis nothing to do with the soldiers."

Declan grunted. "Are ye going to tell me what troubles you or am I going to have to guess?"

"I met your bonny wife. 'Tis the truth, I never seen a fairer lass."

"Aye? And what did ye think of her? Let me hear your praises now. Go on, get it over with. I did well, did I not?" Declan chuckled because although he teased his cousin, he had indeed gained a most pleasing wife.

"And she almost killed herself trying to save your lad."

Declan turned toward him and almost bumped into him. "What say ye?"

"Your lad ran in front of a cart, and she saved him from getting run over. My heart leapt to my throat. Aye, I vow I could not get to her fast enough. God Almighty Himself intervened. If I had allowed her to be harmed on my watch, ye would have been full of wrath and never would have forgiven me. I, ah, well, I did not know ye had yet to tell her about Noah. I opened my big mouth, and she is aware of him now."

"Aye, what else?" Declan sighed, knowing he would have had to tell Isabella about his son eventually. Yet he should have been the one to tell her about him. She shouldn't have found out about the lad on her own.

"She seemed pleased that we have a chapel if that means anything to ye."

He shrugged. "Aye, I supposed she might be a wee bit pious. At least there is that."

"She misses ye."

Declan stopped dead in his tracks. "Did she say that?"

"She did not have to. Ye need to spend some time with her, Declan. Ye needs to come clean and tell her about Leona and Noah. Why do ye not go off for a day or two? Get to know her. And whilst ye are at it, do what ye are avoiding. Remember, 'tis like riding a horse...ye never forget." Anse snickered and shoved his shoulder with a jab of his fingers.

"I need to bathe in the loch, then I will see to her. Can you look after the clan whilst I am gone?" Declan continued onward back toward the gate.

"Don't I always?" Anse said and laughed. "It would be my pleasure, Laird. I am envious of ye. Your wife is bonnier than ye let on and seems sweet-natured. God Almighty himself blessed ye with that woman. I bid ye to get on your knees and thank Him. Not only is she beautiful, but she's courageous and has a tender heart. If ye do not want her, ye know that I would gladly take her off your hands. Hell, any man here in the Highlands would take her."

Declan raised a brow. "Who says I do not want her? Of course, I do. Go on, get back to your duties. Wait, before ye go… Will ye bring her to the loch? I am going to spend the night at my grandda's cabin." He didn't wait for Anse's answer but left his cousin, whose laughter alerted all within hearing distance of his mirth. Declan marched with quick steps toward the loch beyond the wall. As he disrobed, he peered at the water and his chest tightened at remembrances that long plagued him. The day Leona drowned swarmed his mind with dreadful memories, and he could do nothing to shake the images away.

There was nothing to do about it except continue living in spite of her death. With that thought in mind, he dove into the cold loch. The deep water never seemed to warm no matter the time of year. Between the frigid temperature and the memories of Leona's death, Declan only stayed in the water long enough to clean himself. He rushed through washing as if the frigidness was grasping hands trying to pull him into the depths as it had Leona.

Once done, he raced from the water and rummaged through his saddlebag for the clean garments he'd placed there for his sojourn to Campbell land. He redressed and waited for Isabella and hoped she didn't take too long. Declan didn't much like spending time near the loch and only did so to bathe.

Isabella finally came along, guided by Anse. When his cousin saw him, he bowed to Isabella and turned, leaving them alone.

"Wife." He'd been away from her less than a day, and Lord,

how he missed her. She appeared saddened or distraught about something. Then he remembered what Anse had told him. Declan had much to confess to her. He only hoped that he could explain without becoming emotional.

"Good eve, *Husband*. Anse said you wanted to see me?" Isabella stood with her hands by her side. She dressed in a fashionable gown of the type worn by the ladies by the border. Though it looked becoming on her, it was too grand a garment to be worn here in the north. It was elegant but far too impractical. It also did little to warm her and provided no protection from the brisk winds.

"This place…" he began, but his throat grew thick trying to come up with the words to begin explaining what had happened. The memories flooded him, all of them terrible and overwhelming. "This place holds disheartening memories for me."

She stepped toward him. "It's beautiful here. How can such a place hold such memories for you?" Isabella's demeanor seemed cold except for the warmth in her eyes as she beheld the scenery around them and the beauty of his land. He suspected her attitude had more to do with his failures. She was angry, rightly so, and felt deceived, but she was willing to forgive him. "Tell me."

"I shall tell ye, but later. Come, I wish to show ye something." Declan delayed making his confession for the simple reason that he needed more time to reason how to begin. He needed to explain and intended to and hoped the words would come to him. He held out his hand and she took it. Touching her again brought such a sense of peace to him. He couldn't account for it, but his mood lightened, and the horrid remembrances were held at bay for now. He held onto her fingers as if she'd given him the only salvation he needed.

"Where are we going?" She tightened her hold on his hand. Somehow, his beautiful, smart wife had read his mind.

"To the other side of the loch."

They ambled through the trees that touched the edges of the

loch and eventually made their way around to the other side. Birdsong surrounded them, and the breeze that whispered through the branches overhead sounded almost like music as the scent of the pine trees filled his nostrils. His sense of peace grew as the beauty of the area surrounded them.

The stone cottage sat amid the pine trees. A thick layer of the trees' needles sat atop its sloped roof. The windows were covered with wooden shutters and the wooden door had been newly replaced and painted at Declan's direction prior to his arrest. "This was my grandda's cabin. He and my grandmother lived here for a time before he passed. She now lives within the walls, where it is safer for her."

"I see…"

"As a lad, I spent a good bit of time here with my grandda. I come here when I want to be alone, sometimes to ponder decisions, or if something is troubling me. I can think here."

She smiled at him. "It's your sanctuary much like the chapel is mine."

"Aye, I suppose it is. I want you to stay with me here because…" He didn't know how to broach the subject of his dead wife and son. Declan opened the door to the cabin and waved her inside. "There are things we should discuss. Anse told me what happened earlier this day and that you saved my lad." He set his saddlebag near the bed, tossed in a few logs and a hunk of peat into the hearth, and started a fire. The small cabin was chilly but would soon warm.

Isabella crossed the one-room cabin and turned. "Oh, he did. Yes, I met your son. Why didn't you tell me about him?"

"His name is Noah. Come, sit, and I will explain," he said and motioned to her. Declan sat at the small table, and she took the chair near his and faced him. He disliked the furrow of her brow. Hopefully, she would understand.

"You should have told me, Declan. What is there to explain? He is your son. That is all you should have told me. And perhaps why he does not live in your dwelling or with you." Isabella folded her hands and set them on her lap. "A lad should have the guidance of his father. You abandoned him. That tells me much about you." Her tone implied that she'd judged him most dreadfully.

"I did no such thing," Declan said incredulously. He knew enough about women to grasp that she was a wee bit angry with him. Well deserved, he supposed. "I find it difficult to talk about. Years ago, I married a woman named Leona to unite our clans. She was a Campbell. We were happy for a time and had a son. When Leona died... Noah was about to turn four in years... Leona drowned at that spot by the loch, where ye found me. That is why that place holds disheartened memories for me. I lost part of my life that day. I mourned her for a long time—"

"As you should have."

"That day when I found her... I could not believe she'd drowned. The worst part was that our son witnessed her death. Something happened to Noah that day, for he has not spoken since and he has not been able to hear either. It might be a good thing that he cannot speak because I imagine he is troubled by what he saw." Declan sighed about revealing his past when he had only ever wanted to forget the heart-rending situations.

Isabella stood and reached him. She wrapped her arms around his shoulders and held him tightly. "I am so sorry you bore such heartache. You cared for her, your wife?"

"Aye, we got on well after we were married. I thought we would have a good life together. I never understood how it happened."

She smoothed a hand over his cheek. "Worry not because I am a good swimmer."

"So was she. Leona was a good swimmer and grew up near a loch. That spot at the loch is where she would bathe Noah. It made no sense then and even less now." Declan leaned his head on her shoulder and was eased by her compassion.

"What a dreadful happening."

He continued, "When she died... Soon after, my father

passed to the hereafter, and I had many responsibilities calling me. I could not look after Noah because he was a handful, especially when he couldn't and wouldn't speak, an active child who doesn't hear commands. My grandmother offered to keep him with her. He stays with her in her cottage. She makes sure he is fed, clean, and kept out of trouble. Although, he is an energetic whip, and my grandmother is aging. Noah might be too much for her to handle."

Isabella set her hand on his head and petted his hair. "I am sorry, Declan, because I misjudged you. And I am sorry that your wife died and that you mourn her. Your son is young and definitely lively from what I saw."

"Aye," he said and kept her in his embrace. "I worry for him because he cannot hear. There is naught I can do to help him. What kind of life will he have? He cannot be a soldier."

"He can be anything he wants to be. I would be happy to look after him if you will allow me." She caressed his neck and smoothed her hand over his shoulder. The compassion in her touch lightened him.

Declan pulled back from her, looked into her eyes, and noted the sincerity in her gaze. "If ye wish to do so, I will not object. But ye must meet my grandmother first. She will want to know ye will see to him if that is what ye want."

"I do. He is now my son, and I shall make sure he is cared for. It is the least I can do to honor Leona's memory." She paused a moment. "Why do you hide from your family? I met your brothers and sister. Your mother seems to have all in hand though."

"I dislike having to deal with their petty issues when I have the weight of the clan to see to. I have enough to deal with regarding clan matters, soldiers, and protection. And she is my stepmother, not my mother."

"Are you not fond of her?" Isabella asked.

Declan shrugged. "I suppose I am fond of her, but she was my da's second wife. I had little interaction with her and only after my wife died did she come forward to offer her assistance with my siblings. They seem to care for Helena and so I do not involve myself with them too much." It struck him that Isabella's situation was identical to Helena's, but his wife was more warmhearted than his stepmother. Helena had often reproached him when she first married his father. Fortunately, Declan had already begun his training and stayed in the barracks.

"Oh, I understand. I shall try to win their favor even though they seem to dislike me." She lowered her face.

He pressed her chin upward. "Isabella, no one could ever dislike you."

"So you don't dislike me either?" Her pitiful tone alerted him that's what had bothered her.

"Hell, nay. I chose ye, did I not? You are the only woman the king offered who appealed to me." Declan grabbed her hand and pulled her toward him. He settled her on his lap and leaned his head on her shoulder. Her body was tense, and he rubbed his hand over her back to try to ease her. "'Tis the truth, I am far from versed in wooing a woman. I do not want to disappoint ye though. You are so bonny and I—"

"Shhh. Don't say that, Declan. I want you as you are. You do not need to be anything but yourself. I could care less about wooing, courtly ways, or poetic verses. You already have me so there is no point to court me."

"True enough. Then kiss me, Wife, for I want ye like no other."

Isabella set her lips upon his and as soon as their lips met, all the tension ebbed from his shoulders. Declan held her face and continued to kiss her. He liked the way she responded as her tongue gently prodded his. Her hands held onto his shoulders, and he embraced her with his arm around her back. With his free hand, he petted her hair and was awed by the softness of her tresses.

Declan kept his mouth on hers but lifted her in his arms and crossed the small cabin to the bed. He gently placed her in the center and then pulled back his mouth. Her eyes shone with desire and her gaze stayed on him as he removed the outer layer of his tartan. He couldn't disrobe fast enough for her because she knelt beside him and helped him remove his belt and lower tartan.

"You are handsome, Declan. Very pleasing on my eyes," she said huskily.

"Not as bonny as ye are." He set a quick kiss on her lips. "Now let us remove that gown for I know ye will be just as lovely beneath it." His hands fumbled with the ties of the bodice and back. Once he had it loosened enough, he pressed the fabric to fall from her shoulders. She wore a silken shift beneath, but he saw the hue of her nipples under the material. The sight of her full, soft breasts with just enough flesh ceased his breath. He set a hand just below them and caressed the soft skin of her torso.

She gasped. "Your hands are cold."

He found his first smile. "Aye, sorry." Declan rubbed his hands together and breathed on them to warm his palms, and then set his hand back on her breast. "Better?"

Isabella sucked in her breath as she nodded, then began to untie his tunic. She pressed his tunic upward, over the confines of his abdomen and chest, and removed it. With her hands splayed, she roamed them over his skin. Her touch ignited raw passion within him. It had been too long since he had been touched with such affection, and how he missed being with a woman. He let her have ample time to explore his body, but her touches excited him, and his body responded. Neither spoke. Declan couldn't take his gaze from her lovely face as she watched him in return.

"I have never been with a man…"

He shifted her back upon the bed and finished undressing. "As it should be. No other will ever touch ye but me, your husband." He was gladdened by that. "Worry not, Isabella, we will take it slow."

"But I do not want to wait. Tell me what to do."

Declan grinned. He'd married a woman who knew what she

wanted. That she wanted him pleased him more than he could have hoped for. He knelt next to her and slid the rough palm of his hand over her bare leg. Her creamy skin was as soft and delicate as heather petals. His hand meandered up her body, over her curvaceous hip, over her torso, between the valley of her breasts. He leaned forward and set his mouth on her erect nipple. The sensation drew her gasp and his smile. Declan took his sweet time, enjoying the thrill of hopefully filling her with desire.

Isabella stroked his hair and pressed her hands over his back. He liked her touch. With each passing second, his body grew more rigid, and a fervor to take her swarmed within him. His manhood throbbed and he wanted desperately to join with her. But he reminded himself that she was a virgin with no experience. He had to take it slow, mind-numbingly slow.

"This feels nice," she said and pulled his face to look at her.

Declan set his nose next to hers and placed kisses on her face. His breath hastened and he closed his eyes, trying to maintain a little self-control. But it was lost on him as his hand found its way to her center. He pressed his finger inside her sheath and felt the heat of her insides. Lord, she was wet, warm, and probably too tight. The thought of being inside her forced a groan from his lips as lust wove its way through him.

"What are you doing?" she asked breathlessly.

"I am readying ye, lass. I do not want to hurt ye."

"You won't. Promise me you won't. I don't want to be a coward..."

"Never." He stared into her darkening blue eyes and nodded. But damn, he probably would end up hurting her. She was too soft and delicate, and he was too hard and brawny. Declan continued to tease her vagina, delving his fingers and gently caressing her, stroking her with intentional movements. "Can ye not tell how much I want ye?" He shifted her hand to feel his hard length.

Isabella wrapped her fingers around his shaft and gasped. "Your skin is hot."

"Aye, I burn for ye." Declan kissed her hard with a purposeful touch to instigate her passion, and as he did so, she continued to fondle his manhood, further hardening him. He pulled her hand away, certain if he allowed her to continue, he would expire long before he wanted to.

"You are hard everywhere," she said and caressed his arm with her palm.

"Aye, and ye are exquisite." Declan lay on his side and faced her. He took a moment to settle his racing heart. It clashed madly against his chest. Isabella pressed him onto his back and leaned over him. He lifted the locks of her hair and set them behind her shoulder. He closed his eyes and took a deep breath to calm his racing pulse.

"Declan, is it supposed to feel this strange?"

He opened his eyes and grinned. "Aye, lass, and it gets even better."

"I cannot imagine so because this is wonderful." She sighed and placed her lips on his neck, then his face, then his chest.

Declan had hoped to take it slowly, but she was making it damned difficult. He pressed her back and shifted himself between her legs. With as much care as he could maintain, he slid into her. Her warmth surrounded his length and he moaned at the tremendous sensation of being inside her. Isabella's passage tightly encased his erection. Pulses of her desire urged him onward. It took a great will not to thrust hard and give over to the call of his need.

Isabella huffed and pushed at his shoulder. "This doesn't feel so appealing, Declan."

He froze. "I know, lass, but do not move just yet. The pain will ease."

"I think I want you to get off me."

"Not yet, love." He set his forehead on her shoulder and took another deep breath. Everything in that moment stilled, and with them joined, he realized the importance of it. "It will ease, love. I promise ye will enjoy it."

She wrapped her arms around his torso and closed her eyes. "Please…be hasty. I am not afeared of pain if it is over quickly…"

But the last thing Declan wanted was to have it end before it even began. He inched slowly from her and then with as much gentleness as he possessed, he eased into her again. With each thrust, she inhaled and huffed until she lessened her grip on him. He took it as a sign that she was, at last, enjoying their lovemaking.

"Do ye like this, love?" He rasped out, purposely jerking his arse to propel him inside her.

"Declan, it…feels…"

"Wondrous?" he finished for her.

"Oh, yes, wondrous. Keep doing that." She drew in a breath that spurred him to action.

He thrust harder, deliberately, and each time she met him. Their joining swarmed him with lust and her with desire. Declan's control crumbled as he drove into her repeatedly, but she was just as wild and shifted her hips eagerly. He gritted his teeth knowing that he would soon expire from the fervor of their passion. Declan continued to splay kisses on her face as he persuaded her body to give him what he most wanted—her climax. Isabella gripped his arms and pressed her knees against his hips. She cried out as the first wave of pleasure overtook her.

Declan smiled knowing that soon, she'd be completely undone. He kept with the motion of their joining and didn't let up, tauntingly entering her, and withdrawing. As he pressed against her, she moaned and wept. He kissed her lips gently, to let her know she was safe. Isabella opened her eyes and smiled at him, her eyes shimmering with tears.

He released the control he'd enforced upon himself and rammed himself into her. His body had a will of its own, becoming vastly inhibited by his need. There was no controlling his unhinged desire. When his climax came, it immobilized him to the point that every part of him froze. He shouted as he expelled his seed into her, and his legs shook with such intensity, that he couldn't help but growl. The impact of their joining caused his heart to beat so madly that he gasped for breath. He fell next to her, pressed his hands over his face, and groaned.

"Declan? Are you…all right?"

He grinned but couldn't answer, so he nodded. It took many minutes for his body to settle, his breath to lighten, and his mind to accept what had just happened betwixt them. Not only was Isabella beautiful, but she was alluring as hell.

There was more to her than beauty. She was kindhearted in offering to look after Noah. Her generous nature affected him, and she was beginning to matter to him even though she'd been his wife for such little time.

Declan had to wonder if his heart already softened toward her. It had taken less than a sennight for her to wedge her way into his heart. There seemed to be enough room in his heart for vengeance and for Isabella. Perhaps he even loved her. From the moment he had seen her in the king's antechamber, he was awed by her—the outspoken and bonny lass who had teased him. Even so, there was much to learn about her, and he wanted to know every detail: what pleased her, what displeased her, how she spent her days, and what was important to her.

When he glanced at Isabella, he noticed she had her eyes closed. He reached for the saddlebag, pulled out a flask, and took a sip to wet his throat, and then set it on the table by the bed. Relieved the telling was over, the weight of his confessions eased. He should have known Isabella would be accepting because she had such a tender heart.

Declan placed a soft kiss on her lips, yanked the blanket from the end of the bed, and covered them. His sweet wife was already asleep. He settled next to her, threw his arm over her torso possessively, and closed his eyes. Everything would be well now that they'd come together.

CHAPTER EIGHT

SOMEONE TOUCHED HER and Isabella jerked awake. Her startled gasp filled the small cottage. She eased when she remembered where she was and who she was with. Declan moved the tresses of her hair from her face and set a gentle kiss on her cheek. Isabella groaned. She wasn't much of a morning person, and even less of one now, especially after what she had experienced the night before. Every part of her ached. Declan shifted on the bed, and she opened her eyes. He pressed her onto her back and leaned over her.

"Good morn, *Wife*," he said teasingly.

Isabella groaned. "Aye, *Husband*, is it? I feel like a rock has been dropped on me."

Declan stretched over her and grabbed the flask that he'd placed on the table by the bed during the night. He handed it to her. "Drink. It will make ye feel better."

She held the flask at her lips and tilted it up. The brew, or whatever was in it, burned her chest. Isabella blanched and handed it back. "Whatever was that? It was god-awful."

"A spirit Anse makes. He vows 'tis the only thing that wakes him up in the morn. It really gets ye going, does it not?"

Going to hell, she considered as she used her tongue to try to get rid of the foul taste. Isabella shook her head and tried to swallow the aftereffects. "What are your plans for this day?"

Declan lay back and smiled. "To spend it with ye. What do ye want to do?"

She grinned and shifted closer to him. Declan wasn't modest at all about his body. She wished she was as brazen to lay on the bed ungarbed, uncovered, and unabashed. "I have never seen a man unclothed before. You don't know how appealing you look, do you?"

Declan chuckled. He spread his arms wide. "Look your fill, lass. Just do not touch me because I doubt I have the power to resist ye and ye must be tender after last eve."

Isabella shook her head. "Not overly tender." She blushed a little and then careened her hand over his hard thigh and her eyes widened when she took in the size of him. "You…" She couldn't form the words to say that it was a wonder he'd fit her. And as she thought that, and with her gaze, his manhood grew. She gasped and averted her attention to his chest. With her palm, she smoothed it over the coarse fine hairs smattered there. His hard body was riddled with scars, some large and some small. None of the marks detracted from his handsomeness. When she glanced up at his face, he frowned.

"Wife, if ye do not watch out, ye will find yourself flat on your back with me inside ye."

She giggled low because that was her intention. "Do you promise?"

Declan flung himself on top of her and held her face. His lips met hers and he swarmed her with a desirous kiss. Isabella liked the way his tongue meshed with hers. There was something about the way he kissed her that spurred passion within her. His kisses and touches were somewhat possessive, and she couldn't deny that she liked it. She pulled him closer and laughed when he groaned.

"Now see what ye have done to me? I cannot get out of bed now. Ye are going to have to take care of this problem." His eyes crinkled.

She squealed with laughter when he spread her legs and

joined himself to her. Isabella couldn't help but urge him on because he was being too gentle. The effects of her culmination took her by surprise, and she fell into an exquisite array of emotions. How he did that to her, she had to wonder. He had such power over her, and it was intense and wonderfully thrilling. She roamed her hands over his arms and torso, his chest and face.

Isabella kept her gaze on his and watched the myriad of expressions crossing his handsome face. His brows furrowed and he grunted, and then promptly fell to her side. His breath rasped and she leaned over him. She worried briefly that she'd hurt him, but then she noticed his smile.

"If this is the way it is going to be, Wife, I will probably die before we have our first child."

Isabella lay back and was astounded by what he'd said. "You wish to have children?"

"Aye, as many as ye will give me. Do ye want children?" He sidled next to her and pressed his hand on her face, holding her tenderly. "I hope ye do because making them is splendid."

"I always thought I would like to...have children. I am gladdened that you wish for them too. We probably should have spoken of such things when we were at the king's castle." For years she'd dreamed of having her own family, and now, lying in Declan's arms, she realized she could make her dreams come true.

"Aye, but neither of us was readily willing to give such information, were we? We should get dressed. Do ye want to meet my grandmother? I will introduce ye this day." He chuckled.

Isabella didn't move. She watched him as he sat up. The muscles in his shoulders and back twitched from his movement. Lord, he was too pleasing on the eyes. The way his hair fell over his shoulders onto his back beckoned her touch. She reached up and pressed her hand on his hair, smoothing it. She hoped their children had his hair, wavy, shiny with light strands and a little darker shade mixed in. Her hair was too fair, almost white, so light it appeared.

"Did ye hear me, Isabella? Whatever are ye thinking? Ye are leagues away."

She shook herself from her reverie and nodded. "Aye, I would like to meet your grandmother. Will you also introduce me to the rest of your family? Even though I have been in their presence, I think an introduction from you would make me feel more comfortable around them."

"Aye, come and get ready. We will leave. Lord, I am starving. We'll have a morning meal first." Declan finished fixing his tartan and belted it.

She watched him dress and scoffed at herself for ever thinking he was a barbarian. How could anyone who looked like him be a savage? Isabella realized how wrong she'd been in her assumptions of the Highlanders. She'd misjudged everything about him. He was a man with ordinary problems, family, and situations similar to what the men in her family experienced.

He stood by the bed and watched her with a grin. "Lass, get moving. Do ye need aid? I fear though that if I touch ye, we will not make it out of here until suppertime."

She rolled to the side of the bed and sat up. He handed her gown to her. She slipped her feet into the opening and her arms through the sleeves. After, she wrapped her shawl around her shoulders. Once she was fully dressed, she tidied the bed and pulled the covers to each corner. That reminded her of the flowers Declan had left on her pillow.

"I meant to thank you for the flowers," she said as she joined him by the door.

"What flowers?" Declan took her hand and led her outside.

The day had warmed, and she smiled because since arriving in the Highlands, she'd been cold. Perhaps this day, she'd be warm enough to forgo her shawl. "The flowers you left on my pillow yestermorn. I thought that was kind of you."

He shook his head. "I did not leave flowers on your pillow. Perchance it was one of my family, welcoming ye. Ye see? They do not dislike you."

From her viewpoint, she doubted if any of his family welcomed her. They had been rude to her at supper and forced her to avoid them. But she wouldn't discount that one of them might have done such a kindness.

"We need to get ye warmer garments. May approaches and 'tis often one of the warmer months. The fair weather does not last long though. I will have our milliner come and see ye."

"I would like that," she said and took his hand. Wearing her gowns made her fit in with his clan as much as a fox amongst the sheep. Isabella didn't want to appear as an outsider. This was her home now and she wanted to look like everyone else. Simple overdresses with fewer embellishments would help her to do so.

He guided her around the loch, and they reached the walls of his home. Declan kept walking, and they passed all sorts of buildings: cottages, shacks, stone buildings with heavily thatched roofs. Along the lane, hawkers bowed to Declan as he passed. He stopped at a cart that held all sorts of baked goods. The keeper, a thin man with little hair, greeted him and offered him whatever he wanted.

Declan took a round soft roll and handed it to her. For himself, he then took a longer, darker roll. After, he thanked the keeper and motioned her forward. They stood aside near a small elm tree that must have been recently planted. She took a small bite of her roll and murmured a 'mmm' sound at the sweet taste of it. Declan tore a piece of bread and offered it to her. She opened her mouth, and he popped it in. Isabella moaned at the taste of the dark bread which was delicious and mollified her hunger after their night of exertion. It wasn't as sweet as the roll he'd given her. She likewise tore a piece of bread from her roll and offered it to him.

They stood there unaware of the spectacle they created as the clan's men and women passed. All smiled and either waved or bid them a good morning. As soon as they'd finished eating, Declan grabbed her hand and guided her along the lane. He stopped at a building made of logs that had a worn wooden bench beside its door and knocked.

An aged woman opened the door. Long strands of her gray hair fell over her shoulders. She was a hefty woman whose garments were a little snug, and she wore no shoes or slippers on her feet. Her scowl turned to a wide smile when she saw her grandson. "Declan, lad, oh, 'tis good to see ye. Come, lad, come inside." She opened the door wider and allowed him to enter. "I'd heard ye returned."

Isabella followed him inside the cottage. Her gaze shot around the small, one-roomed domain. It appeared unkempt because there was clothing strewn on the floor, cups sitting in a bucket, and a layer of dust covered every surface. It certainly could have done with a tidying. Noah sat in a corner, playing with a string and a rock. The lad needed a bath, his hair trimmed, and perhaps a little joy to bring about a smile on his little face.

When he raised his eyes, he noticed his father, smiled, and waved. He took his rock again and tossed it against the wall and it skidded back to him.

"This is Isabella, my new wife, Gran. She means to help ye with Noah," Declan explained. "Isabella, this is my grandmother, Lady Marian."

She curtseyed to the woman and smiled. "It is good to meet you, My Lady."

Marian's brows furrowed further. She appeared displeased to meet her. "Och, ye bring a Sassenach here to me home? Then ye tell me that ye married her, and she is to help with your son? My heart is paining me, aye 'tis." She set her hand on her heart and feigned her malady.

Declan didn't seem ruffled by her dramatic attitude. "Aye, I do. She might have lived near the Sassenach at one time, Gran, but since I married her, she's now a Highlander. Ye will do well to remember that. Be kind to her and make her welcome because she is my wife and because I bid ye to."

"Of course, I welcome her. I wouldst not disobey my laird." She straightened and gave Isabella a once-over gaze. "Welcome,

Milady. Och, ye married her? When were ye going to tell me?"

So, she wasn't the only person he'd avoided. Isabella almost chuckled because he'd forgone telling her many things and it appeared he hadn't told his grandmother that he was going to be married. That relieved her and Isabella realized that he hadn't meant to purposely ignore her.

"That is why I am here. There was no time before now to bring my news. You have been overworked with caring for Noah and Isabella has kindly offered to help. Let her. That is a direct order," his words weren't spoken harshly, and his eyes showed affection. He seemed to be teasing the elder woman.

Marian swatted his arm. "'Tis pleased I am to accept her help. The lad is too much for this auld woman these days. I vow the older he gets, the more tiresome he is. Before the sun sets, I am plumb worn out and weary."

"I shall begin on the morrow if that suits you, My Lady." Isabella would spend the evening to come up with a plan to keep the lad entertained.

"Och, I hope you have plenty of vigor for that lad is hard to keep up with, and pray, lass, call me Marian. I am no longer the lady of the clan." Her unhappy demeanor turned pleasant.

"Only if you call me Isabella. I will do my best by him."

With that, Isabella approached Noah. He noticed her moving toward him and he scooted on the floor deeper into the corner in response. She smiled at him and waved in a friendly manner. He didn't wave back or respond. She mouthed the word "greetings", picked up his rock, and rolled it to him.

Noah snatched the rock up from the floorboard. He leaned to the side and appeared to want to escape. Indeed, the lad scrambled to his feet and then shot past her. He ran at his father, wrapped his arms around Declan's legs, and held him tightly.

Declan lifted him in his burly arms until he and the lad were face to face. "Noah," he said slowly. He hugged the lad and then set him back on his feet so he could kneel in front of his son. Then he smiled and motioned to her.

Isabella approached with her husband's wave. She knelt next to him and waited to see what Declan intended. The silence in the small cottage made her tense, but she took a deep breath, then let it out slowly to ease herself. With that, she smiled at the small lad.

Declan sighed too. "I talk to him slowly and hope he understands. He spoke well before the accident and so I deem he is aware of what I say to him. I will tell him about ye and explain..."

To Noah, he said, "This is your new mother. She is kind."

Noah nodded and bowed to her. He made sounds in his throat but didn't speak words.

"She will come and spend time with ye. Ye will be kind to her and obey her," Declan continued.

His son swiped his arm over his face and stared at them. Declan tussled his hair and stood. He held out a hand to Isabella, but before she accepted it, she put her hand out to Noah.

The lad clasped her hand and smiled.

Isabella released his hand and accepted Declan's. When she stood, her husband settled his arm around her shoulder and nodded to Noah.

"I shall see you on the morrow then, Milady, and look forward to the rest," Marian said.

Isabella bowed her head to the elder woman. "My thanks for accepting my help, Marian, and please, we shan't be formal. I am certain Noah will have fun and you won't be as worn out."

"Very well. 'Tis gladdened I am that ye are here, Isabella, even though ye look and sound like a Sassenach."

Declan ignored his grandmother's brashness and guided her from the small cottage. They walked hand in hand on the lane in silence until she stopped and turned to him. "Thank you."

He grinned. "For what, Wife?"

"For letting me help Noah and for taking me to meet your grandmother. Now if only the rest of your family accepts me."

Declan frowned slightly. "Were they unkind to you? If that is so—"

"No, they just don't know me yet. Once they do…" Isabella didn't want to speak falsely. She was sure his family didn't want to get to know her. The way they had treated her told her they wanted nothing to do with her. They'd been more than unkind and held disdain for her.

Declan raised her chin. "Come, we will go see them and ye shall see, all will be well." He grabbed her hand and continued onward.

She followed him to the family cottage, and he opened the door for her. Isabella stepped inside. His family appeared to be eating their midday meal. The main area was somewhat dark and there were no candles lit. It was a gloomy cottage but perhaps that had more to do with the people that occupied it and not because it was dark inside.

Lady Helena stopped midstride as she crossed the open area where the family congregated and stared at them. "Declan, have you come to sup with us? And ye brought her with you? I am taken aback because ye never eat with us. This is an…unexpected pleasure."

Declan motioned to his stepbrother to move out of the seat at the head of the table. Then he motioned to his sister to shift down on the bench. Isabella sat at the end of the bench next to Declan's seat. Her husband sat then and looked with a slight frown at his family.

Declan didn't retort to his stepmother but peered at those round the table. "Now that I am back, I intend to see ye more often. It has been a while since I have dined with ye. Tell me about the happenings. What are ye all up to these days?" He took a trencher from the center of the table and filled it with pottage and set it before her. Isabella bowed her head in thanks to him. He then filled another trencher for himself and took a chunk of bread and dipped it in the pottage.

Rhona scoffed. "Oh, Brother, 'tis gladdened I am to see ye. Claude has it in his head to search for Grandda's treasure and says he found a map in his old cottage. Claude is a fool, aye, and a wee wain."

Claude pushed Rhona's hand and made her spill her pottage on the table. "I am not a child, Rhona. Cease speaking untruths. I did find Grandda's map in his cottage. Aye, and I shall find the treasure."

Isabella smiled. Their discussion and the angst in their tones made her happy. It was like being at home when her mother and father bickered. Thinking of them brought on a brief bit of melancholy because she was beginning to miss them terribly.

"Claude, ye will cease this nonsense. I bade ye to take to the training field. Anse tells me when ye do show yourself, ye do not put your whole effort forth. A warrior trains with his heart as well as with his mind. On the morrow, ye will show at sunup and ye will not leave the field until dusk. Is that understood?"

Claude pouted at Declan's reprimand but nodded. "Aye, Laird, understood."

"I have no time to check on you, but Silas will ensure ye follow my command." Declan turned to face his stepbrother. "Silas, ye will make sure the lad is there, training throughout the day? And ye will check with Anse to make sure he trained well before he is permitted to leave the field."

"As ye wish, Laird," Silas said.

Isabella's heart went out to the lad. It was obvious Claude didn't wish to take to arms. Perhaps she might intercede on his behalf and get Declan to relent, but all in good time.

Rhona leaned forward to look past her. "Have ye given thought to what I asked ye the last time you were here, Declan?"

Isabella noted the apprehension in Declan's sister's voice. She wondered briefly what Rhona spoke about, but Declan set his spoon down and gave his sister his full attention.

"I told ye that ye are not old enough to marry. And I am not sure I approve of Willeli."

Rhona pouted much like her brother Claude. "Och, I am six and ten, Brother. Many lassies are married by my age. Ye promised me that ye wouldst think about it. I beg ye to do so."

"Ye are not ready, lass. I will tell ye when I approve. That is my final word on this matter."

Rhona tossed the roll she'd taken onto the table and hastened away.

Isabella watched her flee the room and suspected there were tears in her eyes. The poor lass. Rhona was interested in Willeli and wanted to marry him, whoever he was. But now Isabella knew how to befriend her, and she would do so later this eve.

Declan remained quiet after Rhona left. Isabella didn't want to intrude or interject her thoughts on how he should interact with his family. Surely, they obeyed him because he was their laird and guardian.

Lady Helena snickered and gazed down at the meat she was cutting with her supper dagger. When she glanced up, she smiled. "Now ye see, Declan, how difficult these wains are? Why, my dearest son never gives me a wee bit of trouble. Aye, he listens to his mother. Do ye not, Silas?"

Silas's dark eyes left his mother's, and he slid his gaze to her. The way he peered at her with his wide smile made her focus on Declan. Isabella kept her gaze on her husband so the man wouldn't draw any conclusions or deem she had an interest in him. She needed to make certain Silas was aware of her devotion to Declan before he got the wrong idea. Still, he had the dreamiest blue eyes, and she couldn't help but glance back at him.

"Of course, I do, Ma. Declan, how long do ye plan to stay? Now that ye are married, I expect we shall see more of ye around here. I wanted to speak to ye about the soldiers and some thoughts I had on the training regimen."

Declan raised his brow. "I am unsure at the moment how long I will be here. As far as your thoughts on soldiering that responsibility belongs to Anse. He is the commander-in-arms and is in charge of training. If ye wish to share your thoughts, do so with him."

Silas appeared to disagree and shrugged. "I shall do that." Silas paused and briefly ogled at her with a grin that made her shudder.

"Why did ye not tell us how bonny the women are near the border?"

Declan kept his gaze on his stepbrother and scowled. "If ye travel there, ye might find out." He glanced at her and then reverted his gaze back to his family. "That brings something to mind... I am told you have met Isabella. She is to be respected and treated with kindness and is now your laird's wife. Ye will obey her as you do me. I expect ye all have made her feel welcome."

Her husband waited for their nods, but they sat there blank-faced and stared at him.

"Ye were aware that I was going to Edinburgh to marry as the king bade. Isabella was the most beautiful, kindhearted, and intelligent woman in the king's castle. I vow I was fortunate we got on and that she accepted me."

With his words, his family nodded. Isabella gazed at Declan with affection. His words lightened her heart. Perhaps marrying him wasn't a mistake after all.

Declan continued, "If ye cannot do so, then ye will be asked to leave. That goes for ye all."

Helena gasped. "What speak ye about? We have not been unkind, Laird. Have we, Milady Isabella?"

Isabella, put on the spot, shook her head. She should have spoken the truth, about how disconnected they had made her feel, how they'd practically shunned her, but she would give them more time to adjust to her being amongst them.

"We bid you a good night then." Declan pushed back his chair. He held out his hand.

Isabella took it and rose. She followed him from the room. They reached their bedchamber and Isabella hurried inside. She was gladdened that was over with. How horrid it was to be in his family's company. Declan must have sensed her notion of that idea because his face reflected the grimness they'd spent dining with them.

"Now ye see, Wife, why I spend a wee amount of time here?

They are unpleasant and extremely needful, every one of them."

Isabella knelt by the small hearth and was about to light a fire when Declan approached. "Let me." He put some wood shavings and sticks inside and lit them. As the flames began to rise, he added a small log, and then another, patiently building the fire. Warmth would soon take the chill from the room, but she doubted it would help the coldness that settled within her.

She readied for bed and once she put on her nightdress, she decided to forgo it. Isabella hoped to induce Declan to want to couple with her again. There was no sense in being coy now; nevertheless, she got beneath the covers. With the bed covering tucked beneath her chin, she berated herself for being a coward. She pushed the covers to her waist and tried to appear alluring.

Declan chuckled and removed all his garments. He pulled back the bedcover and joined her. His body was warm, hard, and wonderfully enticing. He pressed her back and gave her a sweet kiss. When he pulled away, he lay back and sighed.

"I did not realize how rude my family was until this eve."

Isabella set her arm over his torso and smiled. "Worry not for me, husband. You forget I am used to dealing with overwrought, emotional people. My parents are the worst sort and if I can handle them, I certainly can deal with your family."

"You are a brave lass. On the morrow, I will need to get back to my duties. I mean to leave the keep for a bit, perhaps for a few days. Ye will be all right whilst I am gone?"

"I'll be well. Don't worry about me. I shall find things to occupy me and will busy myself with dealing with Noah." Isabella petted his chest and felt comfortable speaking so casually with her husband. It was how it should be, she thought, especially now that she didn't feel like an outsider.

Declan leaned his head against hers and whispered, "Right now, all I want to do is pleasure ye."

"That's all I want too."

CHAPTER NINE

FOG ROLLED OVER the far-stretched hills in front of Declan. The morning air warmed but the ground remained damp from overnight rain which swathed the land in obscurity. There was something oddly pleasing about riding in the open areas of grassland amongst the thick fog. Declan always appreciated the serenity of it. It was as if he'd died and roamed the land almost unliving. Riding through the mist lightened him because he eased and didn't give thought to the hefty problems he faced. Soon the sun would rise and chase away the allure.

When he'd left Isabella that morn, he was apprehensive. After the disastrous supper the night before with his family, he didn't wish to leave her. But he had a foe and murderer to find and gain the vengeance he sought.

The score of men he'd brought with him rode ahead. Anse, Trevor, and Lorcan led the procession toward Campbell land. Declan had left Slone home to look after the clan and Isabella. He intended to meet Robbie Campbell head-on to find out if it was he who had made the accusations that put him in the king's dungeon.

Leona's brother wasn't pleased when Declan married his sister. Robbie had spoken harshly about his objections to their alliance. Yet he didn't think Robbie would go to such lengths to have him tried for his father's murder or accuse him of such foulness.

"Laird, I hear the Campbell's sentry ahead," Lorcan said as he dropped back to ride next to him.

"Lead on and let us cut them off at the pass." Declan pressed his horse's sides and passed the soldiers who rode ahead of him. He rode hard, wanting to meet with the Campbell soldiers. As he reached the pass, a trail that meandered betwixt their lands, he stopped. Before him sat at least thirty Campbell soldiers but he didn't spot Robbie amongst them.

"Where is Robbie, your laird?"

One of the soldiers rode forth with his sword drawn. "You're coming close to trespassing on our land, MacKendrick. Tell me why we shouldn't kill ye now?"

"I want a meeting with Robbie."

The soldier laughed. "Do ye now? Well, what if he does not want to meet with ye? Go on home afore we send ye back bloodied."

Declan wasn't about to stand down. He pulled his sword free and gripped it tightly. Though he wanted badly to use it to wipe the smug look off his foe's face, he held back. "Tell your laird that I will be here awaiting him in these woods. I wish to meet with him and only want to talk. He has a sennight to come. If he does not come, I will deem him a coward and shall send the word of his fear throughout the land." There, he'd meant to insult the Campbell laird to entice him to meet with him. Surely his soldier would relate their conversation word for word.

"I'll give him your message, MacKendrick. Och, I do not think it'll do any good." The lead soldier rode off and the other Campbell men followed.

Declan motioned to his comrades to retreat. They turned and rode until they reached a copse of trees where they could take cover and make camp. The rest of the day, Declan surveyed their location and the best route to take should Robbie Campbell actually show himself.

THE WAIT GREW tiresome as the days and nights passed, and Declan began to doubt that Robbie would meet them. He took the same path on his walk each day in hopes that his former brother-in-law would take his message to heart. But Robbie still hadn't come and there hadn't been any sighting of the Campbell sentry since their encounter days before. It was somewhat disappointing, but Declan wouldn't give up hope.

Robbie had one last day to show himself and it began with pouring rain and a wee bit of a hefty breeze. Before long, a storm engulfed them and soaked them through. The sound of the rain hitting the newly sprung leaves and ground was deafening at times and everyone was cold and miserable, though at least the winged insects were kept at bay. Midges were such a nuisance this time of year but fortunately the area where they chose to camp was devoid of the nasty pests. He held his hand out and let it fill with the drops.

"Psst, Laird, someone comes," Trevor said.

Declan hastily returned to his horse and made quick work to ready it. He mounted it and rode in the direction of where the soldiers were said to be. His men rode closely behind him, and they nudged their horses to move faster. At the crossing, they spotted the regimen of Campbell soldiers who were likely out on sentry duty. A shout came from someone amongst their men. Declan took it as a call to arms and so he too called to his men. They raised their swords and rode toward their adversaries with all the fervor of warriors unwilling to back down.

Sword clashes rang in the air. A few fell from their horses into deep puddles made by the heavy rains and trouncing of horse hooves. Declan searched for Robbie among the men, but he didn't see him. He growled fiercely because he'd only wanted to talk to him. Now, however, he was angry, and if it was the last thing he'd ever do, he'd force the Campbells to accept their fate of defeat—their complete desecration.

More clashes sounded and before Declan could put his sword in any of his foes, they called a retreat and absconded. The

Campbells disappeared into the mist and rain. Silence abounded except for the heavy breath of his soldiers and the snorting of horses.

He turned and peered at his men, taking note of who was wounded, who was felled, and who bore the attack. Declan sheathed his sword and was about to dismount to give aid to those who needed it. His feet hit the ground and were soddened when he landed in a deep puddle. He was about to leave the field when four men returned and rode at them.

The attackers came swiftly at him, taking aim. They intended to cut him down. Declan was struck on the thigh with the flat side of a man's broadsword. His leg buckled and he fell to the ground. He groaned and gripped his leg, knowing the wound was severe. When his men saw him lying there, they ran forth. The rest of the men chased after the attackers and forced them back into the mist. Shouts came and more sword strikes and then silence. With a hiss at the pain radiating from his wound, he tried to rise from where he lay.

"Declan, stay still," Anse instructed. "Do not move."

"Someone get the healer," Trevor shouted.

But they hadn't brought the healer with them and hadn't anticipated a clash. Declan removed his upper tartan and grimaced as he wrapped his leg to lessen the blood flow from a thin laceration where the blade penetrated his flesh. Anse helped him onto his horse. They rode back to camp and a large fire was erected between the trees, where the leaves protected the ground, and it wasn't so damp.

Declan lay next to the fire and groaned. "Damnation, I cannot believe I was struck. I was foolish and left myself unprotected. How could I be so inattentive? Was it the Campbells?"

"I am unsure if it was them. You did not have time to defend yourself, Laird," Anse said. "Let us see what happened to ye." He unwrapped Declan's leg and motioned to Trevor, who handed him a cup of water. He poured the water over his leg and Declan drew in a hiss of breath. "Looks horrible, but not grave. 'Tis not deep enough, och it might need a stitch. Your tartan kept the blade from slicing ye too deeply. It will smart though and pain ye for a time. Do ye want a dram of my brew? It'll help ease the pain."

Declan swallowed hard at the intense throb in his leg and nodded. He took the flask from his cousin and gulped more than a dram. He eased instantly and lay back. The pain ebbed slightly and wasn't so excruciating.

"I'll find something better to wrap your leg. Stay still," Anse instructed.

Declan peered up into the darkness of the trees. The sky lightened and the rain dissipated. This was the last thing he needed. He had no time to convalesce or be wounded. With that thought, he growled again in disgust at his inattention. He should have been ready to meet any threat, but instead, he had inadvertently turned his back and left himself open to attack.

Anse returned with a torn tunic. He wrapped the thinner material around his leg and tied it tightly. Declan relaxed and the pain subsided and at least his brows didn't crease so intently. Trevor and a group of men went in hunt for their supper. When they returned, they cooked the hares they had felled, and all were silent. Declan needed to reassure his men that they would defeat their foes, no matter what it took.

"We will defeat our enemy. I vow we will not cease until the attackers are found and dealt with." His voice pitched with his oath.

"Campbell is a coward," Anse said.

"Aye, he and all his followers. I do not understand why he would not come. Mayhap I should have ridden to his keep and forced my way inside." Declan nodded after his spoken thought.

"Are ye maddened?" Anse clipped. "Robbie wouldst have ye killed before ye even breached his gate. Nay, there must be another way to get him to talk with ye."

A whistle sounded from the men on the other side of the fire. Lorcan sprinted toward them. "Looks to be Laird Murray approaching on foot. His men await yonder, a good distance from us. Do ye want to see him, Laird?"

"Aye, allow him to pass through. He's an ally." Declan leaned on his elbow but sat up and used his hands to shift his leg in front of him. He wondered what his comrade was doing, riding in the woods on such a lousy day.

"MacKendrick, what are you doing camped here? 'Tis a long way from your home." Dermot Murray approached and sat next to him. He took the cup offered by Anse and drank. "Ahhh, 'tis tasty brew, Anse. 'Tis like heaven on my tongue. My thanks."

"I wanted to meet with Robbie to discuss what the hell is going on, but like a coward, he did not come to meet me. His men attacked us," Declan explained.

"What ye need is a mediator," Murray said. "Someone to be the go-between ye."

Declan stared at his friend and could have smacked his forehead in disbelief that he hadn't thought of a mediator. "Aye, that is a fair idea, Murray. So, when can ye leave?"

Murray shook his head. "I did not mean me."

"Why not ye?" Declan nodded at his friend and didn't relent. "Who better? If ye go to Robbie, tell him I only wish to speak to him. He has to agree to meet me. We cannot have this hostility betwixt us. Our lands are too close and there will be many skirmishes if we do not come to some accord. Tell him that Leona wouldst be displeased by our discord and that I am not his enemy."

"Very well, but if I come out of this unscathed, ye will owe me."

Declan chuckled. "Aye, I will. Let me know when he wishes to meet. Tell him I shall come alone if that's what he wishes."

"I will and after I speak to him, I'll come and see ye. I want to meet yer bonny wife. She cannot be as unsightly as you described." Murray guffawed with laughter, drawing the gazes of the soldiers who sat nearby.

Anse spit out the gulp of brew he'd taken. "What did ye say?

Laird, you told Murray that Milady Isabella is unsightly?" His cousin shook his head and scoffed. "'Tis the truth, Murray, there be no fairer lass in the land. I vow I have not seen a bonnier woman. Declan is a fortunate man."

"Damn me, och is she as fortunate I wonder? Aye, so he is. Does she have a sister?"

Declan bellowed a laugh. "Nay, unfortunately, for ye, Murray, she does not. At least I do not think she does." When he'd been at the king's residence the morning of the combat, he had taken time to ask questions about her family, her, and their connections. The Forresters were wealthy and somewhat troublesome from what he'd heard, but he appreciated their vigor. He hadn't asked, though, if she'd had any siblings.

Murray grinned. "I cannot wait to meet her then. I shall hasten my travel to the Campbells. Och, before I go, I meant to tell ye... A friar is roaming these parts, his name is Faelan. He is searching for a home, a place to preach."

"Why do ye not take him in?" Declan asked Murray.

"I have no chapel and there is no room for him. You built that chapel, did ye not? Are ye in need of him? He's a Blackfriar clergyman and devout by all accounts. 'Tis the truth he has condemned me for my sins since I will not make my confession." Murray finished his drink and set the cup down next to him. "If ye wish for me to send him on his way, just say so."

Declan didn't want a clergyman on his land because once a friar ingrained himself, he was hard to be rid of. But it wouldn't do harm and he could use all the prayers he could get. Besides that, and probably more importantly, Isabella would welcome a man of the cloth. He nodded to his friend and breathed deeply. "Aye, if ye run across him, send him my way. We will be glad to take him in."

"I shall and am gladdened he'll be gone." Murray stood and bowed to them. "I should get going if I want to find my bed before nightfall." He waved and walked away from the camp into the woods where his mount was probably held by his followers.

Declan tried to stand but his head spun when he got to his knees. He sat back on the ground and held his head. His wound had shaken him more than he thought it had. Anse moved to stand before him and held his hand out to him. He didn't want to take his cousin's hand, but he needed to if he was to get up. Declan gripped it and huffed at the pain that shot through his thigh.

"We got ye, Laird. Lean on me, and we will get ye to your horse."

He appreciated his cousin's help but detested the fact that he had to rely on anyone. A laird should not have to depend on the support of his soldiers. But he was in no condition to argue. By the time he reached his horse, his breath was labored. He used his good leg to help shift him into the saddle. That, and Anse's shove up.

The intense pain wracked every part of him. "I hope I make it home before I..." Declan couldn't get the words out before he pitched forward and retched. He heard the yells of his men and Anse caught him before he fell from his mount. His cousin shifted him back with his forearm and held on to his arm.

"Whoa, steady there, Declan. Do ye need me to tie ye to your horse?" His cousin hooted with laughter and the rest of his men smiled widely. "Or ye can ride with me." He patted the space in front of him and chuckled.

Declan scoffed loudly. "To hell with that. Och, if I fall ye better pick me up."

Anse was in a jesting mood. "Oho, I deem ye have already fallen, Laird. Very hard for a bonny lass, who as we speak, is probably warming your bed."

"A warm bed sounds good to me about now. Let us make haste." Declan clipped the last, but he couldn't help but envision Isabella lying naked in his bed, awaiting him. That was, if he could make it home.

CHAPTER TEN

ISABELLA WOULD NEVER get used to the cold or the cold-hearted clansmen and women of Clan MacKendrick. She missed Declan but tried her best to fit in and find a way to sway the clan to like her. It all seemed futile because most of the people gave her looks of disdain and wouldn't speak to her. And Declan's family still avoided her, even though she tried to be amiable. For nearly a sennight, she ate alone and spent time walking about the walls in reflection of how she found herself so far from home and isolated.

On her morning walk to Marian's, she stopped and picked up a loaf of bread for the aged woman. She'd done so each day for the past sennight in hopes of winning her favor. At least Marian appreciated the kindness and thanked her even if the bread remained uneaten. Isabella suspected Marian wouldn't dare eat anything given to her from a *Sassenach*, as Marian had put it. She knocked on the door to Declan's grandmother's cottage and waited.

"She is not there, Milady," a soldier said as he passed by.

Isabella called after him, "Do you know where she is?"

"Aye, by the loch."

She opened the door to the cottage and set the loaf of bread on the table next to the other uneaten loaves. After she left, she headed toward the loch, and on her approach, she saw Noah trying to yank his arm from his grandmother's hold. He was being an imp, as usual, and she almost smiled.

"Ye needs a bath, lad," Marian said and tried to pull him toward the water, but the lad dug in his heels. He tried to thwart her, but the old woman wasn't having it. "Ye are as filthy as a pig in mud. How long has it been since ye bathed?" Her question went unanswered.

Isabella hurried forward and knelt on the sandy bank in front of Noah. "Cease now."

Noah straightened up and stopped trying to yank his arm from his grandmother's hold.

"I vow he is as hard to bathe as a wily cat. I cannot get him in the water."

"I shall try. Go on and return to your cottage and I'll bring him after I get him to bathe."

Marian snickered. "I doubt ye can, lass. Och, I shall go." She headed back to the trail by the tree line and left them.

Isabella continued to kneel before Noah and took hold of his chin so he would look at her. Fear showed in his gaze, and she was saddened that such an emotion troubled him. What was worse, though, was that Noah couldn't put voice to his troubles. She mouthed her words slowly in hopes that he would understand what she was saying. "There…is…no… reason…to…fear."

Noah bobbed his head and pointed at the water. After what Declan had told her about his wife's death and that the lad had been scarred by the event, she grasped why he feared to be there and why he wouldn't bathe in the loch. Somehow, however, she had to convince him the water wouldn't hurt him.

She pulled him to sit with her on the bank and they faced the water. After a moment, she bade him to look at her again by turning his chin. "Let me get you clean. You won't have to go in the water if you don't want to." Isabella held up her hand to show she promised.

He nodded and Isabella found the bucket Marian must have brought. Inside she discovered a lump of soap, and a larger cloth with which to dry his body, along with some clean, folded clothing. She took a cloth and soap from it and set it by the water's edge. Then she helped Noah to undress. After, she wet the cloth and soaped up his body hastily. He stood silent, watching the water as if it would somehow get him. When she finished washing him, she used the bucket and gently poured water over his head and skin to remove the soap until he was finally clean. How innocent he appeared. Even though he was seven in years, he appeared much more tender of an age.

After, she helped to dry and dress him. When he was fully clothed, she ran her fingers through the long locks of his hair and tickled him. Her playfulness gained a smile from him. If she could find a pair of shears, she would trim his hair, but she would have to ask Marian if she had any. Smiling, she helped him wrap the thin tartan layer over his body and secured it with a small length of rope.

When she finished, she gathered the bathing items into the bucket. Isabella held out her hand and hoped he would take it. Instead, he turned and fled. The lad ran fast and even though she tried to catch up to him, he was nowhere to be seen when she left the tree line that surrounded the loch. Where had he run off to and why so fast?

Isabella muttered to herself, "Well, at least I bathed him, and he's now clean."

She continued onward on the lane and reached Marian's cottage. The door was open, so she stepped inside. Setting the bucket by the door, she approached the woman who sat in an uncomfortable-looking chair by the window. "I was able to bathe Noah, but he fled after."

Marian pointed to the corner. "He came but a moment ago."

"There you are, Noah!" He sat on the floor and played with the string and rocks.

She approached and squatted down to his level and smiled. He didn't look at her. Instead, he shimmied away.

Isabella had hoped he would be used to her by now. For five

days, she had come each morning and tried to persuade him to join her outside. She wanted to spend time with him, but the lad was wary, and with good reason she supposed. Each night she tried to think of fun games to play with him, but he never allowed her to entertain him.

She stood then and noticed Marian had dozed off in her chair. Isabella said nothing as she went about tidying up the cottage. She made their beds, folded clothing, piled the unclean garments by the door, and straightened up the kitchen area, ending the tasks by setting the small kettle on the fire to heat. The whole time, Noah continued to play by himself in the corner.

Her work done, she knelt next to him and hummed a tune she'd learned when she was little. The lad watched her intently with a frown. Isabella placed his small hand on her throat so he could feel the vibration of her voice. Soon, she bellowed the song and Noah's eyes widened and his smile grew.

Marian briefly opened her eyes and scowled at them for their antics before closing them once more.

As the old woman's snores filled the cottage, Isabella finished the song, took hold of his hand, and squeezed it. He smiled at her and for the first time since she arrived, Isabella felt as though she'd made a difference in his life. Since Marian continued to slumber, Isabella took Noah outside. The day had warmed, and it was the perfect time of day to find something fun to do. With the sun overhead, most of the children played outside.

She ambled along the lane toward the merchants and saw Silas, Declan's stepbrother, speaking to one of the soldiers. He made her uncomfortable with his leering smiles, so Isabella turned to avoid him. He called after her. She stopped and turned back because even though he made her skin crawl, she couldn't be rude to her husband's brother. After all, it could just be her imagination that he was looking at her in a less-than-brotherly way. Her primary focus had to be getting along with Declan's family. Silas stepped to them and frowned down at Noah. Isabella felt the tenseness in the little boy's hold before he pulled away and made a strange sound in his throat. With that, Noah sprinted away to race back into his grandmother's cottage. Isabella wanted to go after Noah, but Silas blocked her path and wouldn't let her pass.

"Milady Isabella, you should not encourage the lad. He's naught but a simpleton. Ye have better things to do with your time," he said in a harsh tone. "…like walk with me by yonder loch."

Isabella couldn't help but scowl at the man. "Noah is not a simpleton. You should refrain from speaking so about your laird's son."

Instead of appearing mollified by her scolding, Silas stepped toward her and smiled. "My apologies, Milady. The lad sometimes makes a nuisance of himself, and I detest the thought that ye are spending misguided time with the lad."

Isabella took a step back. "He is now my son, and I will spend every moment of the day with him if that is what I wish. Do you not have training or something with which to occupy yourself?" She hoped her words reminded him that he had duties and walking by the loch wasn't one of them. "Don't you care for your nephew?"

"Aye, I care, mayhap a wee bit more than I should," he declared, but with an indifferent tone. He shrugged and gave a slight, almost mocking bow. "I will leave ye then." He didn't walk off. Instead, he stayed where he was, too close for her comfort and blocking her ability to walk on.

"Good day," Isabella said and turned her back to him. Declan's stepbrother annoyed her. She didn't want to be accusatory toward him, but she read people well. Beneath his overly cordial manner, there was something amiss about him. He wasn't mean toward her like the rest of the family. Instead, he watched her with his startling eyes and their mocking expression.

She'd suspected the moment she'd met him that he was untrustworthy, and she wondered if Declan thought so too. Isabella decided that she would ask him, albeit discretely, what he thought of Silas. She didn't want to insult Declan by declaring her distrust of his stepbrother if he harbored good will toward him. Her instincts were typically correct and she knew a snake when she spotted one, at the same time, she was in a new place with people who lived very differently than where she'd been raised. It was possible she was wrong in her assumption of Silas, just as she'd been wrong about Declan.

Isabella returned to the family cottage and changed her garments. She'd become soddened from bathing Noah and dirty from cleaning Marian's cottage. Now in dry, clean clothes, she entered the main living area and spotted Rhona sitting in a chair by the hearth. It was the perfect time to approach the lass because they were alone, and no others seemed to be inside.

Her sister-in-law appeared pretty in a dark-blue frock and with her blond hair arranged in a bun. There was a stitching of small flowers that bordered the bodice of her dress. Isabella wondered if she'd sewn them.

"Rhona, good day. May I sit with you?" Isabella waited for her sister-in-law to nod, then took the chair closest to her. She placed her hands in her lap and enjoyed the warmth of the hearth's fire for a moment, before she asked, "So, tell me about this Willeli. Have you always known him?"

The lass set aside her sewing. She stared at her with eyes very similar to Declan's. Her golden-brown eyes were almost as light as honey, and yet, not as alluring as her husband's. Rhona shifted forward in her chair. "It is none of your concern."

Isabella lowered her chin, saddened the lass wouldn't speak to her. But she wouldn't give up trying. "I only ask because you seemed upset the other eve when you asked Declan for a decision. You wish to marry this man?"

"It matters not, because my brother will never allow it. There is no sense speaking about it now or ever." Rhona stood and pressed back the long strand of her blond hair that had become loose from the bun.

"Why won't Declan allow it?" Isabella asked and stood to

block her from leaving.

"He deems Willeli too lowly for me to marry but he is one of our clan's devoted soldiers." Her shoulders appeared to sag then as she stared at the floor. "My brother refuses to give a proper reason for his disapproval." Her voice trembled.

"Would it help if I spoke to Declan for you? I can try to convince him to accept your choice." She hoped by offering her support, the lass would become more amiable toward her. It was the only way to win her friendship.

Rhona lifted her face to Isabella's, and she scoffed, "Why would ye do that? I am nothing to ye and ye're nothing to him. He doesn't care about ye, or any of us. All he cares about is his precious feud with the Campbells and seeking war with other clans."

"I don't believe that to be true, Rhona." Isabella reached out to set her hand on the lass's shoulder, but the girl backed away. She let her arm fall by her side. "Since I married your brother, I consider you to be my sister, and I *always* support my family members."

Rhona tossed her head and her eyes flashed, though Isabella thought it might be tears causing the effect, and not anger. "I do not want or need your support. My brother will either give his consent or not. He has made up his mind and there is no changing it." She brushed past her and left the room, her sewing abandoned on her chair.

Isabella stood by the hearth defeated, knowing it would take much more than a short conversation to win over Declan's sister. But she had to keep trying. Isabella had always wished she had a sister. At home, she had been forbidden to play with the lasses from the village. Her mother had proclaimed they would be an inappropriate influence on her and that she was destined to be a lady and marry a great lord or a man of her station. How wrong her mother had been.

She wanted to be accepted by Declan's clan, but she continued to feel like an outsider. As she was about to leave and return to her bedchamber, Helena strolled into the room, carrying a large pot.

"Ye need to keep your nose out of other people's concerns. I heard ye speaking to Rhona. She's a meek lass with simple ideas in her head. Her laird knows what's best for her. Ye have no right to interfere in his matters that do not concern ye and I mean to tell Declan so when he returns," Helena scorned as she passed by.

Isabella shook her head in disbelief at the woman's words. "I don't deem that to be true, Lady MacKendrick. Declan values my input." Though she was unsure if that was true, she wouldn't let her husband's stepmother believe otherwise. "Rhona is an intelligent lass, and she should have a say in who she marries and her future. I certainly didn't."

"Och, well, I suppose your parents were pleased to be rid of ye since you are past the marriage age. Your king did ye a service and ye are fortunate to be married to Declan. 'Tis much like ye are not married at all for the amount of time he spends here. Declan did not want to marry, and now, he is saddled with the likes of ye. Ye are free, lass, to do as ye please. Perhaps ye should take a lover akin to Silas and find yourself some pleasure because ye shall likely get none from my stepson."

She tried to follow along with the woman's harsh ramble and heavy accent. What was she telling her? As if she would be unfaithful to Declan. And with Silas? Why in the world would Helena make such an insinuation? Perhaps Isabella wasn't so off with her assessment of the man.

Either way, Isabella didn't agree with her view at all. She missed Declan and hoped he returned home soon. Even though her husband hadn't wanted or planned to marry her, Isabella was certain he was happy now that the deed was done. He'd practically told her so when they were last together.

"Whilst your husband is gone, I suggest ye make yourself busy if ye do not deem to take a lover. There is much that needs doing here, and I suppose ye will be as good as a scullery maid."

Since she'd been young enough to attend to chores, her

mother had insisted that she learn how to properly clean and tend to household matters to better understand how a home was cared for. Performing such tasks didn't bother Isabella because it had kept her busy and she was able to be around the younger maids.

The woman's haughtiness, though, bothered her. Instead of rebuking her for calling her a scullery maid, she took a deep breath and squeezed her hands closed. "I would be pleased to help in any way you deem so, My Lady."

"See Edith and she shall put ye to work for I am busy enough with my own chores."

Dismissed, Isabella couldn't escape fast enough. She hurried out the back of the cottage and crossed the path to the kitchen and servant quarters. With a knock, she then opened the door and found Edith humming over a large pot, hanging over the fire. She startled as the door opened.

Isabella reached out a comforting hand. "Good day, Edith. Lady MacKendrick said you needed help and bade me to offer my aid to you. I'm here to lend a hand."

Edith gasped and blinked with surprise. "She did? Why in heaven's name would that wretched woman send me help? She never did so afore—and ye are our laird's wife. Ye should not be doing common chores. Oh, that horrid woman is scheming, is she not? Come, rest yourself, we shall enjoy a warm drink of mead, and ye can tell me all about yourself."

A sense of comfort settled over Isabella like a blanket, for it appeared that finally, she'd found a friend. Edith had the softest voice, without a hint of an accent. Her eyes were kind and her smile sure, not at all like most of the women she'd encountered so far in the Highlands. Though the woman had to be at least two score in age, she had no gray hairs mixed in the strands of her light-brown hair that was tied back behind her shoulders. Close enough now to discern, Isabella peered at her ash-brown eyes and smiled at the pleasant woman.

She sat on the stool at the worktable and took the offered cup. The mead tasted sweet and it made her feel as though she was wrapped in the coziness of the kitchen. The maid's kind words also warmed her, bringing tears to her eyes that she hastily blinked away. "There is not much to tell."

"Anse said that the king commanded ye to wed our laird. Is that so?" Edith leaned forward in anticipation. There were deep crinkles in the corners of her sparkling dark eyes; this was a woman who smiled often and enjoyed a good story, Isabella could tell.

She nodded. "It was, but I was fortunate Declan selected me. He was the only man who interested me and now I hardly see him. He keeps to himself, and I wish…" It seemed like ages ago since she had her first conversation with Declan. She should refrain from speaking about him to the maid, but she needed to talk to someone about her feelings and the maid seemed caring.

"Aye, ye might not think so now, but give Declan time and he shall grow on ye."

"He already has. I find him kind—"

Edith chuckled. "He was a much different man when his da and ma were living. Aye, always smiling, always helpful to all. Now he separates himself from everyone except from Anse, but they have been friends since birth. Your marriage is new and ye will love him eventually."

Isabella snorted at that. "I am fond of him, but I doubt I shall ever love him. Love is for fools. I don't mean to sound shrewish, and I will respect him, but shall never be so misguided."

"If ye say so, Milady. Sometimes, lass, a woman has no choice but to give her heart to her man, especially when he needs it." Edith took an instrument from the table and began to beat a heaping piece of meat that had sat on the worktable. She whacked it so hard the table shook and a bowl which held fruit wobbled. "I understand your notion well, for I was married once a very long time ago to a man by the border. I did not love him. Tell me, do ye come from a large family?"

Edith had lived by the border. Isabella had wondered why she spoke English well and why her accent wasn't as thick as most of the MacKendricks. Isabella appeased the woman and spoke of her home and family. Just speaking of them made her miss her parents even more. How wrong she had been to want to escape them. At least her family admired her and appreciated her banter and reprimands. Even her mother—though difficult and disapproving—was fond of her, and Isabella even missed her daily lectures. What she wouldn't give to hear her mother's reproach now.

Edith set the tool she used down on the table and sat on a stool near Isabella. She handed her a knife and a loaf of bread. "Ye can help but cutting this bread." She then took another loaf and began to slice it. "Ye were blessed and shall be so again. Give our laird time, lass, and ye shall see. Declan has been brokenhearted and suffered a great deal of pain when his late wife died. Then shortly after, his da passed. He has been in mourning, but alas, 'tis time for him to shake off the cobwebs and rejoin the living. I deem ye shall do well to enliven him." She smiled and clasped Isabella's hand. "How could ye not when you are so bonny and spirited."

"What do you mean spirited?" Isabella hoped she didn't present a wayward manner.

Edith finished slicing the bread and took an apple from the fruit bowl and began cutting it up. "For the pies I'll bake later." She handed her an apple.

Isabella cut up the apple similarly to the way Edith did and placed the pieces in a bowl. They finished the task and she peered about to see what else she could do to help the woman.

"'Tis not wicked to be spirited. I see the liveliness in your eyes, lass. You seek adventure and merriment. Aye, we should all be young and winsome."

"You are kind, Edith, to say so."

"Go on, lass, supper is ready and I'll bring it in shortly."

Isabella got up from the table and was about to leave when Noah ran through the doorway with tears in his eyes. He rushed to her and sniffled. Isabella noticed the reason for his tears. Noah had a scraped knee, and a thin stream of blood ran down his leg. Isabella lifted him and set him on the stool she had vacated. Edith handed her a cloth which she set over his knee and bade him to hold it by placing his hand there.

With her fingers, she raised his chin and spoke slowly, "Stay here. I will be back." Isabella then asked Edith to watch him whilst she stepped out. She hurried to her bedchamber, retrieved her medicinal pouch from her satchel, and returned to the kitchen. Noah was still on the stool, looking as hurt as ever with fresh tears running down his cheeks.

She knelt near enough to him and gently wiped the blood from his wound. Soon enough, she had the wound tended to with a soothing salve and a thin bandage covering his knee. He appeared gleeful that he wore the proof of his injury, a badge of honor.

"There," she said slowly, watching his face for understanding. "You are all better now." Isabella put the items she'd pulled from her medicinal satchel back inside and pulled the strap over her shoulder.

Edith clasped her hands and raised them to her chest. "Milady, I didn't know ye were knowledgeable about healing matters. That's wonderful because our healer, Lillith, lives afar and we sometimes have to wait for her to come and tend to someone."

"If anyone needs aid, please send for me. I've been trained by an old healer and have done so since I was very young. I'd be happy to help anyone in need."

The maidservant nodded enthusiastically. "I shall, Milady."

Noah hopped off the stool and wrapped his arms around her body. Isabella was taken aback by his show of affection, but her heart felt ready to burst with happiness. Perhaps there was a chance at winning him over after all. Now if only the rest of the clan followed suit, she might find warmhearted happiness there in the freezing cold Highlands.

CHAPTER ELEVEN

THE LAST STRETCH of the ride was the most difficult for Declan. He grimaced at the movement of the horse and groaned as pain throbbed in his thigh. At last, the gate came into view. He was never so happy to see his home. Once through the gates, he kept riding until he reached the front of his cottage. There, he dismounted and Anse quickly caught up to him. His cousin took his arm and was about to lead him inside when Isabella came from around the side of the building with Noah walking beside her.

When she caught sight of him, she sprinted toward them. Declan wasn't prepared for her show of affection when she threw herself into his embrace. He leaned on her, wrapped his arms around her, and took in the bonny scent that was Isabella.

"I am so happy you are home," she said, continuing to embrace him.

"Lass…" His voice came out in a pained whisper.

"There's so much I must tell you. But you must be hungry and tired from your journey."

"Wife…"

"I hope your trek was successful. You must tell me everything." Isabella finally pulled back and looked at his face. Her smile faded and she pressed her hand on the side of his face. "What's wrong? Something troubles you. I see pain in your eyes."

"I am injured."

Anse spoke up then, "Aye, our laird got himself nicked and needs to be tended to. I will get him inside and retrieve the healer."

Isabella helped Anse guide him inside. By the time they reached their bedchamber, Declan huffed. He could barely put any pressure on his leg and groaned with each movement. Once he reached the bed, he fell onto it and rolled to a sitting position.

"There is no need to send for the healer," she said and crossed the chamber.

"But, Milady, his wound might need a stitching, and the healer will aid him. I should go."

"Wait, don't leave. I might need your help, Anse." She returned to his side and his cousin slunk toward the door intent to leave and fetch the healer. "Declan, lay back and let me have a look at what you have done to yourself. Anse, you stay put. You can help me." She pushed Declan back by pressing his chest and he did as she instructed.

"Are ye a healer, Milady?" Anse asked in awe.

"Somewhat, uh, I suppose so. I dabbled most of my life in caring for wounds and injuries. My da, you see... Ah, well he often got hurt and, well, never mind. Let us just say that I have vast experience in caring for injuries he and his men incurred." Her face colored but then she appeared to shake herself into action. She pulled Declan's tartan away from his leg and drew in her breath in a hissing sound.

"Is it as bad as it feels?" Declan asked. He resisted the urge to moan or look at it when she gently prodded the wound with her gentle fingertips.

"It is not good, I'm afraid. Anse, give him something to ease him. Something strong. I've tended to similar wounds and will do what I can to ward off infection. I'll have you mended and patched up as quickly as I can. You are fortunate, Declan, that your leg wasn't sliced deeper. It could've been fatal."

But Declan wouldn't allow his cousin to offer him spirits. He wanted to watch his wife and view her every movement. Not because he mistrusted her, but because he appreciated her take-charge attitude and her healing ability—an ability he was unaware of until now.

"It's going to feel worse before it gets better. I am sorry if I hurt you."

"Worry not, Wife, I can bear the pain. Just do what ye must and be quick about it." Declan prepared himself and gritted his teeth so he wouldn't shout or cause her worry. "Like ye, I can handle the pain if it is over quickly." He grinned at throwing her words back to her. Declan recalled her saying that to him when they were first together, and he was about to join with her.

Isabella retrieved cloths and set them beneath his leg. Declan thought she meant to support his leg, but then she snatched a pitcher of water from the basin area and poured warm water over his thigh. At first, it stung but then eased to a throb. Then he realized the cloth was meant to catch the water.

She continued to wipe the sore, dab at it, and poured more water over the gash. Oddly, the water eased the throbbing.

Isabella rummaged through a satchel, he'd only just noticed, and retrieved items from within and set them on the nearby table. Then she mixed a concoction of herbs and used a pestle to grind them. She made a paste and laved it over the wound.

"This will help you to heal and it will numb the area so I can stitch it closed. I'm always careful not to use too much of this medicinal because henbane can be lethal. The woman who trained me was very specific about the dosage. She'd told me that many could easily perish if one is careless. I try not to use it, but you'll need it to ward off infection."

Isabella was diligent about her task but took overlong to finish. She didn't make a sound the entire time she plied the needle. By the time she dressed his wound with a wrapping, he had almost fallen asleep. He was lulled by her gentleness and the quiet in their bedchamber.

"There. You will have to take it easy for the next few days.

No gallivanting about the lands. Give your leg a little time to heal before you walk too heavily on it. But otherwise, you should be well in no time."

Anse pulled her into his embrace and hugged her with vigor. His burly arms wrapped around her. "I am astounded, Milady, and thank ye for helping him. I could not do anything for him."

"That is enough, Anse," Declan said, disliking his cousin's arms around his wife. "Go on and see to the clan. I want a report before ye seek your bed this eve."

Anse released her and nodded. He left the chamber and closed the door.

Isabella tidied up the herbs and put away her satchel. She returned to him and looked apprehensive. He thought they were through with being awkward around each other.

"Does your husband not get a wee kiss on his return?"

She smiled and sat beside him. He shimmied over to make room for her. "Yes, you certainly do." Isabella pressed her lips on his.

Declan had missed her. He had been gone only a sennight, and it seemed like forever since he'd seen her or held her, or hell, even kissed her. There was something in her gaze, in the darkening depths of her eyes though, that told him something was wrong. He pulled his mouth from hers and shifted her to lay next to him.

"Tell me what ye have been up to whilst I was away. Why do ye look so down, Wife?"

Isabella visibly sighed. "It is nothing to be concerned about."

"I will hear your words." Declan leaned his head against hers, reveling in being next to her. He breathed deeply, enjoying her presence more than he should have.

"I still have not made strides in gaining trust with your siblings. Though I tried, I fear they do not wish to get to know me. It is disheartening and I'm distressed about it."

"Ye should not be distressed. Rhona and Claude were doted on by my father. They have always been difficult even when they were wee. Och, I mean to see they are raised properly and not coddled. Perhaps I should spend more time with them, but I have been busy…since my da died. I will command that they to be kinder to you."

"Oh, no, don't do that. I want to win their friendship on my own without coercion." She paused and pouted prettily before saying, "Why don't you allow Rhona to marry? She is of age, and she has her heart set on Willeli. Surely, he is worthy since he's one of the MacKendrick soldiers."

Declan grimaced. There was much his wife didn't understand. "He *is* worthy. But she thinks she is ready for marriage. I do not. Given time, she will understand. 'Tis best for all involved if she matures a wee bit before she is expected to take care of a husband."

Isabella petted his chest. "Perhaps she will do so, ah… *mature* sooner than you think." She settled against him and picked at the front of his shirt before blurting, "Your stepmother is horrid. I have never met a more obstinate woman in my life. She is even more dominant than my mother, which is saying much. I vow I shall never befriend her."

He lifted his head and glanced at her before settling back against her. "Do ye wish to…befriend her?"

"I do if it is important to you," she said so low he almost didn't hear her.

Declan shrugged. It didn't much matter if Isabella was friendly with Helena. "It is not so important, Wife, but I know not what my da saw in the woman. Unfortunately, we must contend with her presence. Perhaps I will have her moved to her own cottage."

She nodded. "I didn't see much of Claude whilst you were away."

"He was ordered to the training fields. I expect that is why ye did not see him. How is Noah?"

"We made progress this day. He scraped his knee and came to me. I think he will be more agreeable on the morrow. Your grandmother seems to have accepted me. At least, she is cordial and not rude to me."

"Good," he said and yawned. "I find myself overly tired."

"Aye, and well you should."

Declan groaned. "Why, what did you put in that salve?"

"Just the tiniest pinch of henbane for pain and to ward off infection. It should help with the pain and ease you. You might get a good rest whilst you are at it."

"Who was rude to you? Tell me, wife…for I…will not…allow…" He couldn't keep his eyes open, yawned widely, and a drowsiness overtook him. Declan fell into a deep slumber before he finished his thought.

DECLAN OPENED HIS eyes and noted the light in the window casement. He had fallen asleep and the last thing he recalled was talking with Isabella. He wondered how long he'd slept. With a hearty stretch, he allowed his limbs to flex and then he pressed his hands over his face to force his alertness. Strangely, his leg didn't pain him and there was no ache. There was only a wee bit of stiffness.

A knock came at the door, and it opened. Anse stuck his head through the opening and grinned. "Oho, ye are finally awake, are ye? Your bonny wife forbade me from disturbing ye. She said ye needed your rest. Wish I had a tender-hearted woman caring for me. I envy ye." Anse laughed and closed the door. He instantly began relaying his report, the accounting Declan had asked for the night before.

Declan rose and was careful not to put too much weight on his leg. He washed at the basin while his commander spoke incessantly. He scooped water into his cupped hands, then pressed them to his face. Still, the drowsiness persisted, and he yawned. He shifted the items that sat atop his trunk, rummaged through it, and retrieved a fresh tunic and clean tartan. With care, he set Isabella's belongings back atop. His wife could use a trunk of her own, and he thought to see to it as soon as he left the room.

Once he'd dressed, he sat on the bedside. He eyed the comfortable bedding and considered lying back down but shook off his need to rest.

"The soldiers have almost finished the third level of the fortification. They will be working on the roof soon. Once that is done, they can begin to finish the inside."

"I am gladdened to hear that, Anse. Now that I am married, I would like to move in at the soonest. What else?"

"Slone told me that Claude showed up every day for training, but he complained the whole day. I do not think that lad is cut out to be a soldier. Your stepbrother was causing problems too, and Slone said he undermined his authority."

Declan folded his arms over his chest and his eye twitched. Aggravated to no end by his family's behavior, he'd had enough. "Let us go to the field and we shall see what's what." But he knew his brother's adversity with training. Perhaps he should have it out with Claude and take him on the field himself, but with his wound, he shouldn't participate in any strenuous activity. Claude needed to learn how to protect himself before he could protect others.

And his stepbrother definitely needed a talking to. Silas was not skilled enough to interject his view on the training methods his soldiers beheld. It was also time to put Silas in his place. If he wasn't injured, Declan might have challenged him and ground him into the ground, just to show Silas he wasn't as skilled as he thought he was. A wee bit of humility went a long way to bringing about a rambunctious soldier.

Before he left the cottage, he looked but didn't see Isabella. When he finished his duties, he decided, he'd go in search of her. There was something she'd withheld from him the night before, he was sure of it, and he wanted to know what had bothered her. Now, the main living area in the cottage was vacant and it didn't seem as if anyone was inside the dwelling. He left and stepped outside.

The day shone brightly with nary a cloud. It would be a fine summer day, one warmer than most, he suspected. With that thought, he removed the tartan he'd set over his upper body and dropped it on the step outside the cottage. Then he rolled up his tunic sleeves and drew a deep breath. His walk to the training area didn't bother him and his leg only pinched. Isabella had done a fair job at mending him.

At the fields, he sat by a tree and watched as various groups practiced arms, bodily combat, archery, and sword play. He spotted his brother Claude on the field where Slone was instructing the younger soldiers. Claude stood and watched. From his posture and the way he stood by the side, he was disinterested in the activity.

There was shouting and Declan spotted his stepbrother berating two soldiers who used bodily combat. Declan drew his brows together at the sight before him. There was chaos, insubordination, and too much belittling going on for his liking.

Declan got to his feet and gently pressed his hand on his leg. It didn't pain him. It just ached a wee bit but was enough to draw his regard. He whistled and called a halt to the exercise. At once the soldiers ceased their practice and strolled toward him.

"That will be all for this day." His soldiers nodded as they passed by him, respectfully greeting him. When Claude got close enough, he called to him, and his brother approached, his expression sullen.

"Aye, Declan? As ye can see, I am here as ye bade."

He motioned to his brother to follow him. Declan didn't want anyone to overhear their conversation. It was best he said what he wanted to impart privately. "Aye, ye are, but ye are also not. Ye are there on the field bodily, but not emotionally."

"I do not know what more ye want from me."

"Why do ye not want to be a soldier? It is what we have been bred to do. Our da would be disappointed to know ye dislike it.

Give me a reason, brother, and I will consider letting ye take up a different form of service."

Claude stopped in his tracks. "Do ye speak the truth?"

"Aye, 'tis my truth because I mean what I say and always do. Tell me what ye wish to do. What inspires ye?" Declan hadn't ever conversed as intimately with his brother before, and it occurred to him that they didn't know one another well. It was time to lessen the distance betwixt them and gain a better understanding of why his brother balked at soldiering.

"I do not wish to fight with ye or anyone else. My faith forbids me to hurt another. It is a sin against God and all that He stands for."

"Your faith? Ye wish to devote yourself to God?" Declan was shocked to hear his brother profess to such a calling. None in his clan had ever chosen to do so before now.

"Aye, but we have no one hereabouts that I can talk to about it. Are ye angry with me?" Claude scraped his foot in the dirt and kept his eyes averted.

Declan set his hand on his brother's shoulder. "Nay, of course, not. If that is what ye wish to do, then of course I will support you. A friar is coming to stay with us, a Friar Faelan. You can speak with him if ye wish and ask your questions."

Claude raised his face to Declan's, and there was surprise—and unexpectedly—hope in his eyes. "Really? You will not be offended if I ask to follow him and learn from him?"

The sight of his brother's emotions so clearly written on his face made Declan feel a bit ashamed that he hadn't thought to question him sooner. "If that is what ye wish, Claude, I will not oppose ye. In the future, though, ye need to be honest with me. I am your laird and brother. We should not hold back what is in our hearts."

Claude nodded. "And what if I still wish to find Grandda's treasure?"

Declan chuckled. "Are ye still after that?" He shrugged. "If ye want to do so, it will not matter to me. Do ye think there really is a treasure though? Grandda liked to tell tales. I vow he made up some of them."

"Aye, and I mean to find it," Claude said enthusiastically. His voice rose with excitement and his eyes shone with the possibility of it. He was still a lad in many ways, Declan realized.

"Go then. Ye do not have to train with the men going forward. Seek Frair Faelan when he comes, and your duty will be to him. I will speak to him about taking ye under his wing."

"Aye, brother, I shall, and my thanks for...understanding." Claude smiled widely and walked off with a spring in his step.

One down and one to go, Declan thought, as his eyes scanned the men in search of his stepbrother. His conversation with Silas wouldn't be as easy, he was certain of it. He couldn't find his stepbrother amongst the men and decided to wait to search for him.

Before he returned to his own cottage, he stopped at his steward's dwelling and knocked on the door.

Rolly answered and swung the door open wide when he saw him. "Laird, come in." He hastened to the table and cleared a chair for him.

Declan was gladdened because his leg twinged. "Rolly, I have not seen you in a while. Everything going well for the season planting?"

"Oh, aye, Laird. The extra coin helped, and the farmers are diligent at their tasks. Crops should be springing forth soon and be plentiful by harvest time. Our wool trade will bring us more coin than the last two years combined, what with the extra sheep we purchased. What brings ye by?" Rolly set a cup of ale before him and took a seat at the small table.

Declan was gladdened to hear that because he'd instructed Rolly to purchase the extra sheep when he'd returned from Edinburgh. During his recovery from being imprisoned, he was able to meet with the farmers and give them the necessary coins to purchase seed. The coins he'd set aside to pay tax to his king would ensure their livelihood for at least two winters.

"I want to have an ornate domed coffer made for my wife as a gift for her. Will you meet with the carpenter and have him create it as soon as possible?"

"Certainly, Laird. I shall see to it before the day's end."

Declan explained what he wanted and after he'd finished his drink, he left Rolly's cottage. The coffer, along with the other surprises he had in store for his wife. would go a long way to showing her that he valued her. Then Declan scoffed at himself because he more than valued her, he just wasn't ready to admit it yet.

Now, he wanted to see Isabella and find out what had bothered her the day before. Certain that she was saddened, he hoped to find out what troubled her. That, and to give her a wee kiss. Or more.

CHAPTER TWELVE

ISABELLA RUMMAGED THROUGH her satchel and couldn't find her supper dagger. She remembered putting it in there before she left for the king's castle. It was her favorite dagger and had an ivory hilt. She was saddened to lose it. Her brother had given it to her, and she cherished it.

While she was in the bedchamber, she folded her shawl and put it with her belongings. The day had warmed, and she didn't need it. Her things had been moved but nothing was missing. Declan must have moved her garments to get inside his trunk.

She had expected to see Declan still slumbering because henbane was potent and often put one to sleep for days, but he'd risen and had left their chamber. With haste, she tidied up the room and rounded the side of the massive bed. As she reached for the corner of the bedcovering, she noticed a MacKendrick tartan she assumed was Declan's, rumpled in the center. Isabella leaned forward and grabbed it. There was something inside. With a flick of her wrist, she fanned it out and gasped. A bloodied dead rat with her supper dagger sticking in it had been wrapped inside the tartan.

She backed up and almost screamed with fright at seeing the ghastly rat. Who would do such a thing? Someone was pulling a jest on her, she suspected, and her suspicions led her to one of Declan's family members. Isabella grabbed the handle of the dagger she so loved, carefully carried the carcass to the window, and flung it through the opening. The tartan was too soiled, so she rolled it into a ball to be discarded. More importantly, the dagger her brother had given her was soiled forever now; she'd never be able to use it again without thinking of this moment. She saddened at that.

After such a horrid sight, Isabella needed air. She left the cottage and walked toward Declan's gran's home. Noah had to be awake by now and she hoped to spend time with him. On her walk, she saw some of the clan's women and rushed past them. Isabella kept her head down and couldn't bring herself to offer a greeting. Fortunately, she hadn't eaten much morning fare. If she had, she might well be retching by the nearest bush. Her stomach continued to convulse. She couldn't shake the sense of fear that such a loathsome trick brought to her.

At Marian's cottage, she knocked and waited for the door to open. Marian greeted her with an unexpected smile, and that—for a moment, anyway—cleared the clouds of concern from Isabella's mind. "Good morn, Milady. I was wondering when you were going to come by."

Isabella bowed to her. "Please, Marian, I thought we said we wouldn't be formal. Call me Isabella. Is Noah within?"

"Oh, nay, that lad finished his morning fare and sprinted outside early this morn. I have not seen him since. 'Tis such a bonny day. I imagine most are doing their chores outdoors."

She nodded as she stood by the door. "Indeed, it is warm. Is there anything you need of me this morning? Do you have clothing to launder or perhaps you wish me to put on your supper?"

Marian smiled. "Ye are a kind lass to offer, but nay. Helena had a servant stop by this morn and she took our laundry. As to supper, 'tis too warm for anything hot. Mayhap we shall have some cut-up vegetables and I'll cut up a bit of the chicken left from yesterday's supper."

"That sounds good. Would you mind if I joined you?"

"Ye are welcome. I am going to take a mid-morn nap. These old bones tire easily these days. I shall take to my sewing later after my rest." Marian motioned her to the door.

Isabella hesitated. She didn't want to appear hasty to leave, especially since Marian appeared to be friendly this morning. "If you wish, I'll be happy to help. My mother insisted I learn to sew, and I can do fine embroidery too."

"Oh, nay, 'tis only mending I need to tend to."

"Enjoy your rest then. I will go in search of Noah." Isabella closed the door behind her and peered about the lane. Noah was nowhere in sight.

She hurried along the lane and near the wall, she spotted him. He was trying to throw rocks over it. The poor lad was bored. Isabella had thought of a wonderful surprise for him, however, and would see to it later that day. So that she didn't startle him, she approached from the side and smiled as she stepped in front of him so he could see her face and her mouth move when she spoke to him. "Can I join you?"

Noah nodded and handed her a stone. Isabella laughed when she threw the rock up high to try to get it over the tall stone wall. She missed the crest but not by much. Noah tried again and it hit the top, but the stone fell back down to the ground. She laughed and he smiled. They continued tossing the rocks and eventually, Isabella's rock flew over the pinnacle and disappeared. Noah jumped and raised his hand in celebration. She hugged him and if their antics were noticed by the clan's people standing nearby, they likely thought they were being silly.

"Milady," someone called.

She turned hastily and found Silas standing behind her. Isabella hadn't noticed his approach. All her good spirits from playing with Noah and from her encouraging encounter with Marian vanished as quickly as if they'd never been there at all. She bowed her head and bid him a good day.

"What are ye and the dour-faced lad up to?"

"Why must you be so mean?" Isabella frowned at him. For as

handsome as he appeared, he was quite the opposite in his manner. Noah was just a child, and it wasn't his fault he couldn't hear or speak. Even though Noah was deaf didn't mean he was a simpleton as Silas would have everyone believe.

"I apologize, Milady, forgive my brashness. Can we not be allies? 'Tis my fondest wish."

Isabella stared at him with skepticism. He was the last person she wanted to befriend but it occurred to her that this was only because he was mean-hearted toward Noah. "We shall see." She took Noah's hand. "Come." With quick steps, she hastened away.

Silas was by no means what she would consider a friendly sort nor did she want to have him as a friend. Isabella had forgotten to talk to Declan about him. If she saw her husband this day, she would remember to broach the subject.

They walked toward Marian's cottage. There, she opened the door for Noah. Kneeling, she looked him in the eyes and held his chin. "Go inside and rest. I will come for you soon."

He nodded in understanding and walked away from her. Isabella closed the door and hoped he obeyed and stayed put. While he was taking a respite in the afternoon, she thought she'd tend to his surprise. But she'd need Anse's help for that, so she walked along the lane, searching for him. Finally, she saw him talking to a soldier and hesitantly walked toward him. It didn't appear that Anse was reproaching the soldier but speaking confidently to him. She hoped she wasn't interrupting an important discussion.

Anse saw her and ceased his speech with the soldier. "Milady, good day."

"Anse, I was hoping… Ah, I apologize if I interrupted something important."

"Nay, not at all. This is Slone, second-in-command of the MacKendrick soldiers."

"Milady," Slone said. "Pleased to meet ye."

She was in awe of the sheer size of the man. He appeared taller than Declan and just as muscular. But Slone had kindness in his eyes and the way his dark wavy hair fell over his forehead lent him a charming look. Another handsome Highlander. Isabella was appalled that she'd misjudged them before she had arrived in the north.

"What can we do for ye, Milady?"

Isabella smiled. "I am pleased to meet you, Slone. I want to make a swing for Noah by the loch. There is a perfect tree branch for it, but I fear that I cannot climb high enough to tie the rope. Would you have a few moments to help me?"

The men bobbed their heads. Anse walked beside her. "I have the perfect rope for your project, Milady. Slone, go and fetch it. It is under my bunk in the barracks, and hasten to the loch so we can help Milady."

"We will need a flat piece of wood and an awl to make holes in it to attach the rope," she explained.

"Och, why do we not stop by the carpenter's shack? He always has leftover pieces of wood and such. He can make the holes in the wood for you."

Anse quieted on the remainder of their walk. When they reached the building place where the men had set up their work area in erecting the large fortification, he stopped and gazed at the objects strewn about. Finally, he seemed to spot what he sought and went to get it near a corner of the building, returning only moments later.

"Will this do?" Anse held out a piece of wood that appeared a perfectly sized seat for a child or maybe even a small adult.

"It is perfect," she said and waved to one of the workmen. He approached and bowed to her and Anse.

"James, can you make two holes on the ends of this board for me?" Anse asked. "Make sure they are evenly placed."

The workman set off and they waited for him to return.

"Have ye seen the laird this day?" Anse asked her.

"I haven't but I left the bedchamber before he awakened. When I returned later, he was gone. I suppose he is about here somewhere unless…"

"Unless what, Milady?"

"Perhaps he has left the holding again. I don't expect he would tell me that." Lord, she sounded pitiful. Isabella put a smile on her face and explained, "I meant that I am sure Declan has much responsibility to see to, and I am just his wife. Why would he tell me where he is going?"

"Just his wife," Anse said low. "Declan has not had to account for his whereabouts to anyone in years. Give him time to adjust. He will remember his manners eventually."

Isabella laughed and felt it in her stomach. "Really? You jest, Anse. I doubt very much he'll remember me when he has other pressing matters. It is just his way, and I don't expect him to seek me out to tell me where he is going."

"Most wives would expect so."

She shook her head. "I wish he would, but I don't expect it. Oh, here comes James."

The carpenter returned and handed the piece of wood to Anse. He thanked him and they started toward the loch.

Isabella wondered if Declan had left the holding and asked Anse, "Well then…have you seen Declan this day, or did he leave again? I'm not complaining, mind you, but he *should* rest his leg."

Anse slowed his pace. "Aye, I saw him earlier at the training field. You patched him up well, Milady, for he barely limped. I thought he would be laid up for a time. Och, he went off with his brother Claude and then he said something about meeting with Silas."

"I had hoped to inspect the wound this day to ensure it was properly healing." Isabella wondered if she could trust Anse. He had been kind to her since she arrived, and she thought her husband trusted him too since Anse was in command when Declan was away from the holding. She had to talk to someone about the mysterious "gift" left on her bed. It might as well be Anse. Isabella stopped walking and turned to him.

Anse stopped and frowned at her. "What is it?"

"I don't want to burden you with this, but I need to tell

someone, and Declan is never around…" She delayed in speaking the words. Would Anse believe her? She took a deep breath and stared at the ground, too shy to let him see the emotions she knew would cover her face like a mask. "When I was tidying up my…our…*the* bedchamber this morn, I found my—my supper dagger…sticking in a dead rat that had been wrapped in a tartan and left in the middle of my—*our*…bed this morn. It frightened me. I think someone was just trying to scare me or perhaps, they're jesting."

"Ye *what?*" Anse bellowed as his frown turned into a fierce scowl and his brows slanted, furrowing his forehead. Isabella gasped and took a step back from the large, terrifyingly furious warrior. He blinked and appeared to duck his head, shrinking slightly in her gaze. He touched his forehead and his expression turned sheepish. "I do apologize, Milady, because I did not mean to shout."

She found herself unable to speak. These Highland men were frightening when something riled them. She took a deep breath. "It was a rat," she said in a small voice, in case he hadn't understood her. He held up his hand, wide palm out, to signify she need not say more.

"I heard ye, Milady. But my concern is—why would someone do that? Ye should tell Declan about it. He will want to know. That is not a jest, and ye are the laird's wife. No one in our clan would—or should—ever disrespect ye in such a way. I vow someone means to do ye harm."

She nodded and bit her lip. Who? And why? But Anse was right. She needed to tell her husband. "Very well, I will tell him when next I see him. I want to doubt, though, that anyone intends to hurt me. They just mean to scare me. But I am not that easily frightened." She shrugged. "I must admit, it was rather startling though."

He nodded. "Aye, I have no doubt. I will keep my eyes open for this miscreant. It had to be someone who could easily and readily enter your chamber. So, I'll keep my ears open too, for any gossip. Whoever left that message for ye is vile."

"Do you deem it is a message? Why would someone leave such a message, and what do you think it means?"

Anse shrugged. "Hell if I know. Only the foulest of men—or women—would leave a bloodied rat in a tartan on your bed. Ye best tell Declan about it as soon as ye see him. Promise me ye will. He'll want to protect ye."

"Very well, I promise." She nodded but dismissed his overreaction. Probably, she thought, it was just one of Declan's siblings trying to frighten her. They didn't like her, and his order that they be nice to her likely caused this reaction. It made sense, the more she considered the idea.

They reached the loch and found Slone waiting for them. Anse and Slone had the swing set up within a moment. How happy it would make Noah. Isabella couldn't wait to show him. She remembered fondly the swing her father had erected for her and her brother when they were young. They had spent many happy days on it.

After the men tied the swing on the thick branch, Anse grinned. "I think we should test this out, aye, Slone? We do not want the lad to fall off and hurt himself." He sat on the swing and pushed himself until he was flying in the air, grinning like a lad he must have been, bent on trouble instead of battles.

Slone scowled. "'Tis my turn." He stopped Anse from swinging and shoved him off. Anse fell back and landed on the ground.

Slone sat on the swing and shouted as he went higher and higher. Anse stood by, dejected at not having another turn until finally he forced Slone to stop.

Isabella smirked at them and giggled. "Talk about men behaving as boys. I shall see you later. Enjoy the swing for now. I will bring Noah here on the morrow. I am certain no one will get a turn once he gets on it." She left them and walked back toward the keep. With a quick wave, she passed by the gate and continued walking until she came to the chapel. She hadn't yet spent any time inside and wanted to take a moment to pray.

Lady MacKendrick stopped her from entering the chapel. "Oh, there ye be, Isabella. Some things need tending to in the cottage. I left you a pile of mending, and there is a bucket full of spoons and cups that need washing when ye get around to it. Preferably before the evening meal."

Isabella hoped her disdain didn't show on her face. Her impatience with the lady was becoming as worn as an old piece of thread. She'd done nothing but offer kindness to her, and yet Helena continued to be difficult. Obviously, she didn't care that Declan asked her to be nicer to her. Helena was plain rude and an unpleasant person to be around.

"I'll see to it as soon as I finish my prayers." She moved past the woman to make her way into the chapel, but she stopped her.

"Has Declan told ye how he came to be at the king's castle when the king demanded he take a wife?" Lady MacKendrick peered at her with a smug look on her face.

"I don't recall him telling me about it, but I suppose you're going to tell me?"

"Oh, aye. He was accused of murdering his father-in-law, Laird Campbell, and was jailed for it in the king's dungeons. Declan was pardoned when the king was searching for husbands for the border lasses. Yet he got saddled with ye, poor man, but that is the punishment he gets for killing a helpless aged man such as Allan Campbell."

Isabella disbelieved her. Lady MacKendrick had to be lying. Surely Declan would have told her if he was accused of murder and that he'd been imprisoned. That he had been charged with murdering his father-in-law made the lie even more unbelievable. Declan wouldn't hurt someone close to him, or someone aged. He was far too noble to do something so heinous. But Isabella felt the ire burn her cheeks. She was irate that he hadn't told her and that she had to hear it from the wretched woman. She had thought he'd shared all his past with her, but apparently, he'd only shared with her the things he couldn't hide, like his son, and the story of his deceased wife. What else was he hiding from her?

And why?

"Your silence tells me that ye are affronted. Ye see, lass, some men are brutal like Declan, men who take the law into their own hands. Ye would be better off keeping your distance from him." Lady MacKendrick didn't wait for her acknowledgment but strode off.

Isabella shook off the conversation with her stepmother-in-law as she entered the chapel. Now was time to spend with God, not wallow in her dislike for Helena or worry over her husband's duplicity. She could do that later.

The building was sizeable and made of stone. Isabella was surprised Declan had the chapel built before he had his men erect the enormous fortification they'd live in. Lord, she prayed for a delay but then she realized perhaps when it was finished that it wouldn't be so bad. If only his stepmother stayed at the cottage or moved to England or perhaps some other far-off place. Isabella snorted a laugh at the thought of her moving to England. It was far enough away that she'd never have to deal with the harridan.

Her footsteps echoed on the flat stone slabs that led to the altar. When she reached the dais, she smiled at the wooden cross that took up most of the wall in front of her. Isabella knelt and bowed her head. But as she began to pray, she heard someone clear their throat. With a gasp, she turned and found a man standing beside her. She hadn't expected to see anyone there and didn't know they had a clergyman in residence.

"Good day," he said politely.

She rose. "Good day."

"Are ye the laird's wife, Lady Isabella? I am Friar Faelan, newly come to the MacKendrick clan. His lairdship has asked me to oversee the souls of his clan's men and women."

Another thing her absent-minded husband forgot to tell her about. Why hadn't Declan told her that a friar would serve them? It was of little matter, at least for now. Isabella bowed to the man and smiled as she took in the friar, a thin man garbed in a black robe belted by a rope at his waist as was traditional for the garb of a cleric. The length of his brown hair was tapered to his head.

Most of all, she noticed that he had a kind face and blue eyes that showed affection. "It is nice to meet you, Friar Faelan, welcome. I am glad you are here for I often spent time in the chapel where I was raised."

"Are ye devout, Milady?"

She nodded. "I am and pray every day. Will you be performing Mass and Confession?"

"If ye would like me to."

"I'm sure Declan would like that too. Might I make my confession now?"

Friar Faelan waved her onward. "I will sit here with my back to ye and ye can make your confession."

Isabella sat then with her back to him. "I fear, Friar, that I have impure thoughts all the time, especially about my husband."

"Oh, Milady, it is good that ye are attracted to your husband, and I am sure our good Lord would not condone such thoughts."

"I am trying to be a good wife, but honestly, Declan makes it difficult."

Friar Faelan cleared his throat. "Why...ah, how does your husband make it difficult?"

"He is guarded and tells me little about himself or his life. I did not even know he was previously married and had a child until I was here for two whole days. Then there is suspicion about him...Well, I cannot speak of it. He won't tell me what bothers him or what he expects from me. In truth, I am not sure what to do with myself or how to be his wife." She couldn't stop herself from sighing aloud.

"I see. Well, were ye trained on the tasks of being a wife?"

"I was. My mother was thorough and ensured I was taught every aspect of being a wife and lady to a keep. My husband's stepmother is also making it difficult, so I try to stay out of her way when I wish to speak foul words to her. She has said the most atrocious things about him..." Isabella realized suddenly that she was gossiping. Surely the Lord wouldn't be pleased. "I'm sorry, I shouldn't speak so of her, but…" she paused, and then admitted, "I'm not happy. It's difficult here. As much as I try to fit in, I feel as though I never will."

Friar Faelan shifted behind her, then answered with a gentle tone, "Ye will find your way, Milady. Given time, ye will feel more at home. Ye should not listen to suspicions about your husband from others. Instead, seek him out and ask him yourself if what is being said is the truth. Prayer will help settle your spirit and now I am here whenever ye need to speak about your troubles."

"I appreciate that, Friar. I just wish my husband wanted me for his wife. He seems to enjoy being with me at night when… ah, when we are alone." As if she'd conjured him with her confessions, Declan suddenly appeared in the open door of the chapel, a dark silhouette against the daylight. "Oh," she whispered, "He is here."

Friar Faelan rose and peered at the entrance where Declan stood. He made the sign of the cross before her. "I absolve you from your sins, Milady. Say a good Act of Contrition and pray to the Blessed Mother for wisdom. She understands your concerns. And come again soon. Shall we go and greet your husband?"

She dipped her chin, then got up and walked toward him. Before she reached him, she took a deep breath to try to rid her ire. But she was more than angry with Declan, and sooner or later he was going to have to confess to her the deceit he was hiding. "Good day, Declan. Are you here to see the friar to confess your sins as well, perhaps?"

He stared at her and didn't speak. Claude stood next to him and gave him a shove with his elbow. Declan took her hand and squeezed it gently. "Nay, wife. We did not mean to interrupt your confession with the friar…"

"Oh, you didn't. We were finished. I shall leave you to speak with him." Isabella didn't wait for his farewell and hurried through the exit. On her way back to the cottage, she smiled to herself because she hadn't known Declan was pious. With God's help, his sins would be forgiven. At least, she hoped that happened. She also hoped that God would help her win his heart. But then she shook her head. She didn't want him to love her because love was for fools. Isabella only wanted him to want her, to be treated with care as his wife.

With a scoff, she realized with a heavy heart that she was telling herself a falsehood. She wanted far more from him than she was willing to admit—his heart.

Chapter Thirteen

H IS WIFE DISAPPEARED before he could stop her from leaving the chapel. Declan wasn't sure, but he suspected she might be angry with him. Her averted eyes gave her away. He had to find her when he was through at the chapel and figure out what bothered her. Declan didn't like the tension between them and so far, Isabella had been sweet and not the irksome, overbearing wife he'd thought he would be saddled with when he was forced to wed.

He shook off his sentiment and approached the friar. "Friar Faelan, you have arrived, I see."

"Good day, Laird MacKendrick. I am gladdened to be here and thank ye for allowing me to come and serve your clan." Though he was young, more than a score in age, the friar had very little hair but what he did have appeared to be dark in color. Indeed, his face showed nary a whisker. He smiled widely. The clergyman seemed affable.

"Ye are most welcome, Friar. This is my brother, Claude. He aspires to become a priest and to serve God. I hoped ye might guide him and perhaps show him the way…"

Friar Faelan gave Claude a look up and down, and it appeared that his smile grew broader. "Oh, aye, it wouldst be my pleasure, Laird. Come on the morrow, Claude, early, and we'll begin. Ye can help me get settled and figure out what's what. Ye can spread the word that I am here."

Claude bowed. "I would like that, Friar Faelan."

Declan turned and said over his shoulder, "I will leave ye to it then." He hastily left the chapel before the friar suggested he himself attend the confession. Declan wasn't about to confess his sins, not until he figured out who his enemy was. After he sought vengeance, he would make his peace with God, and only then.

On his way back toward his cottage, in his search for Isabella, he came across Silas on the lane walking ahead of him. His stepbrother had disappeared earlier, and Declan hadn't had a chance to speak to him. "Silas, attend me."

His stepbrother stopped in midstride and turned. "Declan, there ye are. I heard ye wanted to speak to me and I have been looking for ye."

"Aye, I did want to talk to ye. Where have ye been all day?"

"I trained earlier and then went to bathe at the loch. What is it ye wanted to talk about?" Silas seemed on edge and his manner off-putting. His hands clenched and his eyes scowled. He seemed to want to flee or acted as if he had somewhere else to be.

"I saw ye on the training field and the way ye spoke to those young soldiers. They are not to be treated disrespectfully. Those men give their arms for the protection of this clan. There is a way to guide them without putting them down and that is not your responsibility. I do not want ye speaking so harshly to them."

Silas peered at him with haughtiness. "They shirked their duty, Laird. I was only trying to spark some fervor in them."

Declan shook his head. "And just so ye know, Slone leads the younger soldiers under Anse's guidance. He is in charge when Anse is not here. Anse is in charge when I am not here. Ye will not go around either of them in the future. Remember, ye are a soldier just like the rest of the men practicing on the field, regardless of your relation to me."

Silas glared at him but nodded. "I was only trying to be helpful."

"When ye learn how to fight with the full use of your sword, ye will be helpful. Ye need more training before ye can teach others." Declan walked away from him and didn't offer any further rebuke. Hopefully, his stepbrother understood.

Anse caught up to him on his approach to the cottage. "Laird, I just spent an hour with your bonny wife this morn." His smile and laughter tensed Declan.

"I just saw her at the chapel."

"Earlier at the loch, she had me help her erect a swing for Noah. Did she speak to ye yet?"

He shook his head. "Nay, she did not. About what? I noticed she was…well, she seemed ireful as if something bothered her. Know ye what troubles her?"

"Aye, I do. I think we should put a guard on her." Anse stopped him from walking forward.

"A guard? Why would Isabella need a guard, Anse? Tell me what happened."

"I promised Milady that she could tell you."

Declan grunted. "When has that ever stopped ye from telling me what is going on? Speak and tell me what troubles her. If she is in danger…"

"I think she is," Anse spoke hastily and told him about what Isabella had found on her bed.

His shoulders tensed at his cousin's telling. Why would anyone want to hurt that winsome lass? His wife! "Someone threatened her."

"I would take that as a threat," Anse said.

"Put Lorcan on her. He will keep guard over her every minute of the day. He goes wherever she goes and tell him to keep his sword handy. Tell him at the soonest so I do not worry about her." Declan would worry regardless, even though Lorcan was a fit soldier and one of the most effective with his sword.

The gate watchman whistled, calling his attention. Declan walked with Anse toward the gate.

Standing on the other side of the iron barred barrier was Dermot Murray, who paced back and forth. His comrade stopped and stood with his legs braced, awaiting entrance. With a nod, Declan told the guards to open the gates.

"Murray, I was not expecting you so soon. Have you met with Campbell then? What says he?" Declan didn't think he had because Dermot didn't appear as if he'd ridden far. Since Murray's lands bordered his, Declan surmised that he only just left his holding.

"Aye, aye. I came to tell ye that Robbie will not meet with you. I tried to persuade him, but the man was adamant and said that he would not meet with a murderer. Even though I swore that ye did not have anything to do with his father's murder. I am sorry, Declan, but it does not appear that Robbie will meet with ye anytime soon."

"Cosh, this is a mess. How am I going to find the culprit when I cannot even meet with Robbie to find out if Allan had any enemies?" Declan waved him off. "Let me think on this and I will come and see ye soon."

"Send word when ye plan to come, so I can make sure I am at my holding," Murray said. He turned and left, walking with quick steps through the gate.

Declan waited for the gates to close before he walked away. Anse had been silent during their conversation. "What think ye about this? Why will Robbie not meet with me? Regardless of how Robbie felt about me marrying Leona, he never showed hatred or animosity toward me."

Anse shrugged his shoulders. "'Tis perplexing, Laird. I thought Robbie respected ye. He might not have been friendly, but there was a level of respect from him after ye married Leona. Surely, he does not believe ye killed his father."

"Who knows what he is thinking? I hope he does not deem me responsible. This matter needs to be handled delicately and cannot wait. I will be leaving the keep again soon. With or without Murray's help, I will find a way to meet with Robbie."

Anse scoffed. "Even if ye put your life in danger by doing so? I say ye wait him out. Eventually, Robbie will come seeking answers."

"He might be willing to wait, but I am not. I want vengeance now. Ye do not know what it was like being in the king's dungeon, Anse. It was a living hell. A recompense needs to be made. Whoever sent me there will pay the price. I will not be appeased until I see it through."

"I have never seen ye so blood-thirsty or ruthless. Being in that dungeon changed ye. Of course, I understand and will lend my sword to help ye achieve it. We will find the miscreant."

"Aye, we will ferret him out and when we do, I vow my sword will meet with his heart."

Anse grunted. "A polecat always leaves his hole and when he does, we will be waiting."

Declan gave a firm nod and walked off toward the cottage. He was intent to see Isabella and find out exactly what happened that morning. Two of his soldiers tried to stop him, but he shook his head and kept walking. Though his leg pained him a little, he ignored it.

The sooner he spoke to Isabella, the better. As he entered his family's cottage, he found Isabella washing utensils at the supper table. Her arms were elbow-deep in the water, and she didn't look up when he cleared his throat to gain her attention.

"Isabella, I need to speak to ye."

"Not now, Declan. Your stepmother wants me to wash these before supper is served." She continued to ignore him.

"Now, Wife," he demanded in a tone that meant she was not to question him, one he used with his men.

His stepmother entered the living area then and he motioned to her. "Ye will wash those, Helena. Isabella and I need to talk." He paid no heed to the glare his stepmother gave him, grabbed Isabella's arm, and forced her to go with him. They reached their bedchamber, and he opened the door, and gestured for her to enter. He followed, then closed the door with a bang.

"Whatever is wrong with you?" she asked, averting him again and dried her hands on the overdress fabric of her gown.

He gestured to the bed and though it appeared she was going to ignore him, after a moment she sat on the edge of the mattress. He sat next to her. Declan took her hand in his and waited for a moment, hoping she would broach the subject of the dead rat, but she remained silent. Finally, he prompted, "Have ye something to tell me?"

She pulled her hand from his and stood. "Have *you* something to tell *me*?" Isabella approached the window and stood gazing through it with her back to him.

Declan sighed. Women were difficult to get through to when they had ire in their hearts. He stood and moved to wrap his arms around her body and pulled her against his chest. She stiffened but didn't pull away. "Anse said something happened this morn… Will ye not tell me what happened?"

He felt her sigh. She kept her gaze at the window. "It was nothing."

"It was more than nothing, wife." Declan took hold of her face and turned it. As soon as her sweet lips came close to his, desire overtook him. He moved to stand in front of her, kissing her, fueled by the passion that sent fervor to his loins. His mouth turned over hers, thoroughly capturing hers with his kiss. Declan moaned when she tensed. He wasn't sure but thought perhaps she wasn't enjoying his affection.

His suspicions proved correct when Isabella pulled away. "Nay." She shoved at his chest and forced him to step back from her.

"Nay?" He was confused by her rejection because her body told him how much she wanted him and yet her words refuted her desire.

"I cannot think when you kiss me so nay, do not. I am ireful with you, Declan, because I'm your wife and yet you keep your secrets close to you. Until you trust me, there will be no more kisses, or anything else for that matter."

He wondered what secrets she thought he held from her. "I only want to protect ye. Ye should tell me—"

She grimaced. "I do not need your protection. What I need is for you to start acting like a husband and be honest with me."

"Ye do need protection, and ye will explain yourself." He glared at her, but she wasn't forthcoming. Angst filled him especially when her beautiful eyes filled with tears.

"You misled me," she whispered.

"About what?" Declan frowned and ran his fingers through his hair as agitation overtook him. He couldn't fathom what she was talking about. His wife was one confusing woman.

"Think about it and it shall come to you."

She was unwilling to tell him what troubled her beyond letting him know she knew he had a secret she'd wanted him to share with her.

There were few people Declan trusted. There was only one thing he hadn't shared with her, and to be honest, he was unsure if he could put his trust in her, yet. His secrets were his to keep; he wondered who among his trusted few had let her know there was something he hadn't shared. It was best that she didn't know what was in his heart—vengeance, mourning, deep sorrow, anger, and the list went on. He wouldn't own to his sentimentality, not now or ever. But now, with her rejection, there was nothing more to say. Declan turned and left the bedchamber.

Outside, Lorcan stood guard with his sword in his hand.

Declan nodded to him. "See that my wife does not leave the cottage without you. Where she goes, ye go. I want her protected."

His soldier bowed his head. "Aye, Laird."

He marched toward the barracks and would seek his sleep there. Then he scoffed aloud because he would get little sleep, trying to figure out why Isabella rejected him, what caused her ire, and what she meant by secrets. Along with being beset by his wife, he probably would ruminate about his quest to seek vengeance. There had to be a way to find his enemy and during the long night, he would give it his extreme consideration.

Anse stood outside the barracks entrance and grunted as he

approached. "What are ye doing here? I thought ye were going to talk to Milady."

"I tried, but to no avail." Declan shrugged and stood by his cousin, hoping to shake off his discontent.

"She did not tell ye about the rat?"

"I forgot to ask her about it," he confessed.

"What the hell were ye doing that ye forgot to ask? That is why ye sought her, was it not?"

Declan grinned. "What do ye think I was doing? She went on about me being honest with her and some such nonsense about a secret. And that she does not need me to protect her. And above all, she was angry."

"Why is she angry?" Anse's brows rose, and he appeared to want to laugh.

"Hell if I know."

Anse muttered an expletive. "I see that I am going to have to take ye in hand. Let me share some wisdom, my friend, that my da told me… A man should understand that he does not protect his woman because she is weak. He protects her because she is *important*."

"Of course, she is important."

Anse hunched his shoulders. "Och, not important enough to be honest with her?"

Declan fisted his hands. He didn't like being answerable to her or for his actions. "There are things that I cannot, should not tell her…"

"She wants ye to include her. Ye do not have to tell her everything but only share your troubles with her. If she thinks she can be helpful to ye, she will feel important."

His words, though unwelcome, had merit. "Ye are the only person who I speak to without being guarded," Declan confessed.

Anse set his hand on his shoulder. "Ye should be gladdened because now ye have someone else to tell your secrets to. And I vow ye will be glad ye did. Just tell her. Let her guide what ye reveal. She may not ask too many questions."

"Aye, but what if she asks questions I am not ready to answer?"

Anse grinned and turned to enter the barracks. "I think ye are beginning to care for the lass. Do not be afeared to admit ye need her."

"I do not want to need her," Declan confessed.

"Aye, ye might not, but ye already do. Finally, ye have the opportunity to love someone without constraint. From what I can tell about her, she is a worthy lass and in need of love. Have ye thought that mayhap she needs the love only ye can give her?" With that, Anse disappeared inside the barracks.

Declan stood there dumbfounded. Since when did his cousin impart such noble wisdom, and about women no less? Still, he couldn't let the thought cross his mind of needing her. Needing anyone weakened him. He wouldn't allow himself to be brought down by a wife, no matter how much he coveted her. Marriage was exasperating.

CHAPTER FOURTEEN

MARRIAGE WAS COMPLICATED. Isabella had a hard time falling asleep because all she could think about were the happenings of the day before. That Declan had been imprisoned in the king's dungeons was kept from her angered her, but only because he hadn't told her about it himself. She'd had to hear it from his stepmother who seemed boastful to be the one to impart such news. Surely the reason for his imprisonment was false because Declan wouldn't kill someone without good cause. At least, that is what she discerned of him.

Along with that troubling thought niggling at her, the rat left on her bed caused her to lock the bedchamber door while she slept. Though she had thought it a prank done by one of his siblings, Anse had made her consider otherwise. What had made whoever it was try such a nasty, vile trick, and what had they hoped to accomplish? She had to admit, if it was to create and fuel fear in her heart, it had worked.

Isabella chose her least favorite gown to wear because it wasn't as heavy as her others. Looking out the window, it appeared to be bright outside and would be hot. She intended to accomplish a good deal, all of which would help her not to think about Declan or the rat left on her bed, her troublesome stepmother-in-law, his obtrusive siblings, or her longing to go home, where her parents were likely sitting down for their morning meal right about now. Isabella had always cherished that quiet moment with them because it was the only time of the day that they didn't berate her.

When she finished her morning chores in the bedchamber, she made her way to the living area. She saw that the only person who remained after the morning meal was Lady MacKendrick.

"Good morn," Isabella greeted her, expecting nothing pleasant in return.

"'Tis naught good. There is too much to do this day."

At least she was beginning to understand the woman. "I'll be glad to help. I need something to distract me." Isabella sat on the bench and helped herself to a roll which had hardened a little. She poured herself a cup of mead and dipped the roll in it to soften it.

"When ye are through wasting time, there is launder to see to. I placed a hefty basket of garments outside the cottage door for cleaning. Then the cottage needs to be swept, trenchers need to be made, and there's mending of garments too. I am off to see the tailor to be fitted for new frocks and then am visiting an old friend and shall not return until this afternoon near supper. See that your chores are completed." With that, the woman set off with a huff.

Isabella wasn't too displeased by the list of chores that needed to be done. At home when her mother rebuked her or wanted to lecture her or if her father was out thieving, she kept herself busy. Cleaning took her mind from her troubles. It was her way of coping with situations she hoped to put aside.

The door opened and she thought Lady MacKendrick had returned. Isabella turned and saw Declan. She hadn't expected to see him. He entered quietly and took the seat next to her. Without a greeting, he helped himself to bread and a fruit smear.

She kept her gaze on her cup and was saddened at the thought that they were at such an impasse. Until he trusted her enough to speak of his troubles, she would keep her mouth shut and be reticent. That was more difficult because Isabella was never one to keep her thoughts to herself.

Declan slid his body on the bench to sidle next to her. He wrapped his arm around her waist and touched his head to hers. Though she wanted to move away, she couldn't help but lean into him.

His voice sounded low in her ear. "Isabella, I want no discord betwixt us. Can we not talk about yesterday?" He set his forearm on the table and watched her closely.

He sat so close that it took all her will not to wrap her arms around him. She raised her chin and saw the hurt in his eyes. That she caused him such dread brought a dawning that she might have been wrong and handled the situation without decorum. "We should discuss it."

He tightened his arm around her waist. "Anse told me about the rat ye found on our bed. Before ye deem to argue with me, until I discern whether that message was meant for ye or me, I will have ye guarded. Lorcan was placed as your guard and will go where you go. I'll take no chances with your safety."

"Yes, I noticed him. He's rather difficult to miss." Isabella nodded and gestured at the imposing, stern man standing on guard by the open door. He was right in wanting to protect her and honestly, perhaps the rat was meant for him as much as her. "I don't need a guard, but if it makes you feel more secure, then I accept that. But Declan, why did you not tell me that you were imprisoned for murder?"

Declan tilted his head and scowled. "How did ye learn about that?" Then he appeared to shrug. "It matters naught. Aye, I was accused of murdering my late wife's da, Allan Campbell, and the sheriff took me to the king's dungeon. It is true, Isabella, not about the murder but that I was imprisoned. I have been trying to meet with Campbell's son, Robbie, to discuss who might have accused me. There is someone out there who betrayed me and murdered Leona's da. I vow to seek vengeance for it and for my late wife's father's murder."

She frowned down at her cup. "You should have told me."

"I did not want to worry ye."

Perhaps. That was something she hadn't considered. She looked back up at his handsome face. "But—Husband—I am worried. There shouldn't be secrets betwixt us. Promise me that you won't keep anything from me again. If we are going to be husband and wife, I want your assurance that you'll trust me. We should share our confidences and we should be able to speak freely to each other. I am not so dimwitted as to reveal things that should be kept between us."

"That is what Anse says, that I should trust ye." He sighed. "And I do. Och, I have been alone for some time, and now that I… I am not used to having someone to speak my problems to. I will try, Wife, but I make no promises, and I know ye are not dimwitted. Until I find out who left that rat and who accused me of murder, let me protect ye. Right now, it is the only thing I can do to make this situation tolerable."

Isabella wrapped her arms around his waist and embraced him. Declan leaned his head against hers again and sighed. Being married was difficult especially when one was married to such an obstinate, headstrong man. She couldn't stay angry with him and in time he would begin to trust her. She had faith that he would.

With him being near, she shifted closer to him and leaned upward to kiss his face. Isabella couldn't hold back her desire for him. She turned his face and set her lips on his. Declan yanked her against him and returned her kiss. Lord, the man knew how to make her melt. She couldn't get enough of him and regretted sending him away the night before. This night, she promised herself, she would make it up to him.

Declan pulled his mouth from hers and leaned his forehead against hers again. "Ye make me want to drag ye back to our bedchamber, Wife."

"That we could, but I promised your stepmother that I would help her this day. Go on about your duties, and I will see you at supper. The wait will make our joining even sweeter."

He kept hold of her and wouldn't let her stand. Declan chuck-led. "If it gets any sweeter, we will likely die from the pleasure. I will give ye an hour or two, wife. Meet me by the loch and if ye wish, bring Noah with you. We should enjoy some time by the water for it is hot enough."

"But the loch holds disheartened memories for you. If it is difficult being there, we should not go." She caressed his face with a gentle hand.

Declan nodded but then shook his head. "It was difficult, but no longer. Lorna loved being by the loch and she wouldn't want us to forgo going there. Besides, we will make new memories."

"Noah is afeared of the water. When I tried to bathe him, he balked. Whatever happened there, on that day…it has a hold on him. Perhaps if you are there, you can get him into the water, and he might enjoy it." Absently, she caressed the bulge of his bicep.

Declan nodded. "I will see if I can coax him into the water. Until later, Wife." He rose and squeezed her shoulder before leaving the cottage.

Isabella spent over an hour by the loch washing the large basket of garments Lady MacKendrick left for her. Her hands were raw from the lye soap and scrubbing. When she came across the tartan the rat had been wrapped in, she took it to the woods and buried it. There was no sense in trying to clean it because the stains were set in. Declan wouldn't wear the garment if it was tainted, she reasoned. Finally, she finished the disgusting task, then moved back to finish the washing.

Lorcan lifted the basket of heavy, wet clothes before she could try to pick it up. "Thank you," she told him, and together they returned to the cottage where she hung them on a line to dry. With that chore done, she quickly mixed the ingredients for an unappealing loaf of wheat bread which she placed in the bread oven to bake. When it was done, she would cut it into trenchers. The scent of it filled the air as she swept the cottage floor, washed the supper ware, put things away, dusted the hearth's mantle, and repositioned the chairs.

She had almost forgotten she promised to meet Declan at the loch. By the slant of the sun's rays over the loch, Isabella was late.

On her way there, with Lorcan following close by, she stopped at Marian's cottage and retrieved Noah. He smiled and jumped about, happy to see her, especially when she took his hand and led him out of the cottage, indicating to him with signs that she had something fun to do in store.

Together, they walked to the loch where they spotted Declan, carousing with several soldiers in the water. There appeared to be some rough play going on. Lorcan looked longingly at the waterplay until she gestured that he should join in while she and the boy sat on the bank and watched for a short while until Isabella stood up to lead him to the swing. At first, he didn't seem to understand what it was, so she lifted him and sat him on the plank of wood, then showed him how to grasp the rope. When she pushed him, Noah gasped.

She stepped to the front of him so she could see his face and was pleased to observe that the lad was smiling. With force, she propelled him higher, and he squealed with what she thought might be laughter. Her heart burst with joy at his pleasure.

Within moments, the soldiers vacated the water and made their way to her. Their interest in the swing came with many questions. She answered and laughed because they all wanted a turn. They stood around and helped her to push Noah. The lad grinned ear to ear as they made such a fuss about pushing him to go as high as the sky.

Isabella left Noah in their good hands and approached Declan. He sat by the loch and watched them. She sat beside him, folded her legs, and clasped her arms around her knees. "He likes the swing. Seeing him smile makes my heart gladdened."

"Ye are good to him. We are fortunate to have ye here with us," Declan said and set his hand on her leg giving it a gentle squeeze. "Since we're not keeping secrets, I'm telling ye now that I am going to leave the keep on the morrow and will be gone most of the day. I do not want ye to worry."

She rested her cheek on her knees and smiled at him. "Thank you for telling me."

He shrugged, almost shyly, a thing she hadn't thought such a fierce warrior laird would feel. "Will ye stay with me at my grandda's cottage this night?"

The thought made her heart beat a little harder. Could it be he was just as affected by her as she was him? "I will if you'll walk me back so I can get a change of garments." Isabella stood and waited for him.

Declan called to the soldiers. "Take Noah back to Marian's when he is finished swinging. Lorcan, ye are relieved of your duty for the moment." The soldiers agreed and he sidled next to her.

They walked hastily in silence back to the family cottage and entered. Declan approached the table and took a hunk of cheese from the tray. "It looks good in here."

Lady MacKendrick came out from one of the chambers and hurried to set a cup in front of Declan. Isabella was about to amble to her chamber to retrieve a change of clothes but heard the woman speak to Declan, and she stopped to listen.

"I vow I spent all day cleaning this cottage. It was a tiresome task, but it needed to be done. Your wife was of naught help. If ye need anything else done, I am happy to oblige."

Isabella's cheeks heated a little. The woman had blatantly lied though because she hadn't lifted a finger to clean the cottage that day. Was she envious of the attention Declan paid to her? She considered that Lady MacKendrick wanted Declan's approval and his regard. Isabella understood how that felt, to be overlooked by someone, so she decided not to make an issue of the woman's duplicity now, here, in front of Declan and anyone else who might overhear them.

Instead, she turned and entered her bedchamber. There, she rummaged through her belongings and retrieved a thin chemise she intended to wear to bed. But as she returned to the living area, she heard Declan's raised voice.

"I know ye did nothing here this day. My wife exhausted herself cleaning this cottage. Why would ye speak falsely? Is it your intent for me to dislike my wife? I remind you, Lady, that the king gave her hand to me, and that I am beholden to make Isabella happy. She deserves no less."

"So, Leona meant so little to you then?" Helena tossed at him.

Declan scoffed. "When I was married to her, she meant everything. But the woman has been dead for three years and I will not mourn her forever. Let her rest in peace. If ye cannot be cordial to my wife, Lady Helena, then ye should seek to live elsewhere."

Lady MacKendrick gasped. "Ye cannot mean that. Your father would turn in his grave to know ye spoke so disrespectfully to me and threatened to turn me out."

"I am the laird now, not he. Ye are no longer the lady of the clan. Your place is not to question me or tell me your opinions. I am the laird. Now, if ye cannot respect my wife, ye will find somewhere to live, another cottage preferably as far from the new keep as possible. I care naught where just as long as it is not here. I will not have my wife disrespected."

"Very well, *Laird*," she said with a huff. "I will be more cordial to your wife but only because I have nowhere to go." Lady MacKendrick turned and left the living area, breezing past her haughtily.

Isabella stood there in complete awe of Declan's conversation with the woman. She was grateful, too, that he'd stood up for her. She let him take her satchel and hand and guided her through the doorway. She felt the tenseness of his hold lessen when they stepped through the threshold.

"This night I am going to show you my appreciation," she vowed.

Declan chuckled. "Appreciation for what?"

"For what you did there, saying what you did to Lady Helena, and sticking up for me. You are not such a wretched husband after all."

Declan laughed. "Nay? Tell me that after ye have been married to me longer than a few months."

"I am sure I shall be just as pleased with you years from now, as I currently am." Isabella wrapped her arm around his waist and smiled. This night she wouldn't hold back and would show him how much he meant to her. "I am going to kiss you everywhere."

Declan stopped in midstride and pulled her into his arms. "Aye, and I am going to kiss ye right now." He set his mouth on hers just as a regiment of soldiers was passing by.

Their calls and banter were ignored by her husband. Declan continued kissing her and Isabella enjoyed every moment of it.

CHAPTER FIFTEEN

ECLAN RODE THROUGH the gate with only two soldiers, Anse and Trevor, on his quest to meet with Robbie Campbell. He didn't want to present a formidable stance when he met with Robbie and hoped that taking only a few men with him would show his unwillingness to instigate the Campbells. The day dawned hot and steamy, much warmer than usual. On the way, they had to stop twice to water the horses and themselves. By the time they reached Campbell land, they were drenched, and their horses labored.

At the Campbell's gate, Declan jumped from his mount and approached to call up to the watchman. "I have come to speak with Robbie Campbell. Tell him I need to talk with him and that it is important."

"If he was not expecting you, I cannot allow you inside."

Declan waved his hand and said, "As ye can see, I come not with an army, only myself and a few followers. I only want to speak to Robbie and I am not leaving until he agrees to see me."

"Wait here and I will see if he wishes to meet with ye. I'll return shortly," the guard said and disappeared.

While he waited for the guard's return, he didn't speak to Anse or Trevor. It was best to keep quiet because the other watchmen stared at them. He found it almost comical that they considered their stares and mien threatening. Declan didn't fear them or being close to Campbell's soldiers. It was one thing to take a man down when warring, but quite another to do so without coercion. And that was true because their swords remained in their scabbards, and they showed no animosity.

The guardsman he'd spoken with returned a short time later. He opened the gate slightly and peered at him. "Laird MacKendrick, my laird said to tell ye that he cannot meet with ye presently. He gave me this missive to give to ye and said for ye to return in a fortnight." The guard stuck the sealed parchment through the unlatched gate.

Declan took the missive and returned to his horse. They left hastily and didn't speak until they were far enough away from Campbell's holding.

Anse was the first to speak, "What does his message say?"

"I will read it when we make camp."

The sun was nearly setting by the time they reached the dense woods at the edge of Campbell land. There, they found a clearing and set up a small camp. Trevor started a fire and Anse pulled out a helping of foodstuff from his saddlebag. After the horses were settled, they sat around the fire even though it was warm enough to forgo it. Declan removed the parchment from inside his tunic and cracked the wax seal on the parchment. He leaned toward the fire to gain enough light to read the words.

Declan, I know why ye wish to see me. I am unavoidably una-vailable at present due to a family matter. Come in a fortnight and we will discuss this disparaging dilemma. With your aid, we will find my father's murderer for I know ye were not re-sponsible. ~RC

He gripped the parchment so tightly, he had to take a breath to ease himself. Though Declan was pleased by his brother-in-law's invitation, he was unsettled because he'd hoped Robbie might give him news of who the culprit might be. "Robbie does not believe I murdered his father."

Anse grunted. "That is good news, aye."

"He wants my help to find the culprit."

"Aye, we should help him. Robbie was your wife's brother, and we are speaking of seeking justice for your former father-in-law. I have been thinking about this and I deem the murderer wanted you to take the blame and probably spread the tale. Let us discuss what this foe would gain if ye were put to death for murdering Allan Campbell because apparently that was his intent." Anse took a cup of ale offered to him by Trevor.

Declan appreciated his cousin's skill at comprehending the politics between the clans. Like his father, Declan's uncle, Anse had the natural ability of diplomacy. His cousin was perhaps the wisest man he knew and he relied on his knowledge and advice. "Who would gain if I am dead? There is ye." He meant to lighten the mood with a jest and hoped his cousin took it as such.

Anse chuckled and scoffed. "Cosh, there is no way in hell I want to be laird. I am satisfied with my lot in life, a lowly commander. I am content, Declan, and do not seek to overthrow ye."

He thought that to be true. Anse had never aspired to want to take the reins and always boasted that he had more free time to enjoy his pursuits, whatever they were. "And I am gladdened to hear that, Anse, but ye are not a lowly commander. We are fortunate to have ye in our clan. Then who else might want to be laird?"

"There is your stepbrother, Silas. He is vindictive enough to go after the lairdship," Trevor said. "I see the way he tries to insert himself with the soldiers."

Declan mulled over Trevor's words. "Aye, that is true. He deems he is better than all the soldiers. But is he intelligent enough to pull off such a ruse? I cannot see him being so crafty."

Trevor scoffed. "Nay, I do not think he is capable of forming such a dubious plan either. He is always speaking but it is from his arse."

Anse bellowed at Trevor's speculation.

"I cannot discount him though. If Silas is my enemy, I vow I will slay him where he stands," Declan said.

Anse shook his head. "What ye need to do is set a trap for him. Trevor, when we return, ye can keep an eye on Silas. Follow him and report back to either me or Declan. If we find proof of his deceit, ye can confront him, Laird."

Declan nodded in agreement. "That is a sound plan, Anse. But let's consider. What if my enemy is not Silas? Who else would gain?"

"Any member of our clan," Trevor said.

Anse rubbed his chin and said, "Nay, none of our brethren would go against Declan. Our family has ruled our clan for generations. They all respect you too much to try to usurp ye. I cannot see any of our men taking such a stance to gain the lairdship, because even if they did attain it, they would lose the following of many, if not all, of our clansmen."

"Whoever it is, is a treasonous knave, and I like not this turmoil." Declan finished his drink and tossed his cup on the ground in front of him.

"Ye best watch your back, Laird, because so far, they have been unable to take from ye what they want. They will become even more diligent in trying to kill ye," Trevor said.

Declan grunted. "They can certainly try, och I will be more watchful."

Anse grimaced. "I will mingle with our clansmen more oft when we return and listen to their conversations. This kind of plan, to overtake the lairdship, is hard to keep secret. Someone will make a mistake and speak of it, and then we'll have our foe."

Declan wasn't sure about that, but he was just as concerned as Anse and Trevor. He would return to the Campbell's keep and speak to Robbie in two weeks. Perhaps he had a suspicion of who their traitor was. Declan felt the heat of vengeance running through his body.

IN THE MORNING, they set out and rode toward home. By mid-morning, they'd reached the pass that abutted their land. The forest thickened and beneath the leaves and branches, the woods darkened. Anse stopped his horse and motioned to him. He and Trevor stopped immediately and searched Anse's expression for a sign of why they had halted.

"Someone is near," Anse whispered.

Anse always had good hearing. Declan hadn't heard anyone riding nearby. His cousin twitched his fingers and indicated both he and Trevor should ride about to find out who trailed them. Declan rode toward the left and Trevor to the right. Anse took the trail back the way they had come. The forest seemed to be still and quiet. No animals or birds scurried or fluttered.

Declan kept his horse silent and at a slow pace as he rode through the dense woodland. He rounded a tree and suddenly, something hit him from the side, hard enough to knock him off his horse. He landed on the rough terrain and his head slammed onto the leaves and loam of the forest floor. When Declan realized that some*thing* was actually a some*one*, he flailed his arms and legs to protect himself from the attacker while avoiding being trampled by his frightened horse. He swung his fisted hand at the foe until he got to his knees and was able to pull his sword from his scabbard.

Shouts came from the woods. Trevor made their war cry. Declan tried to see who it was that ambushed him, but his sight was blurred. All he could make out was the outline of a hooded figure, which stood over him with a dagger gripped in a pale hand, ready to thrust. Too near the ground to use his sword, and in a thwarting position, Declan reached to try and stop the assailant from pushing the blade into his body when he heard Anse shout. Hoofbeats thudded, shaking the ground. Declan wasn't sure whoever approached was friend or foe; he curled into a ball and prayed he wasn't about to be run over by a warhorse, here in the woods. Through slitted eyes he saw his attacker hasten away before the horse reached them.

The hoofbeats stopped and there was a thud as Anse jumped from his mount into view. He knelt next to him. "Are ye struck? Did he harm ye?"

Declan shook his head. "Nay, he did not get a chance and fled thanks to ye."

His cousin held down a hand and helped him to rise. "Let us find Trevor and make haste."

They searched for the MacKendrick soldier for a short time before they found him. Trevor sat on the ground, leaning against a tree. He huffed as if in pain and held his stomach.

Declan hurried toward him, knelt, and pulled back his tartan to see if he was injured. Blood soaked Trevor's tunic and he lifted it enough to see the damage. The soldier had a gash on the left side of his abdomen. He winced when Declan tried to assess if the wound was deep or fatal.

"We need to get him aid," Anse said as he paced near them.

"Did ye see who attacked ye?" Declan asked Trevor. "Was there more than one man?"

Trevor moaned and shook his head. "Did…not see…more than…one." He closed his eyes.

"Trevor," Declan called to him, "Keep your eyes open."

Anse lifted the wounded man and helped him walk toward the waiting horses. "The ride home is too afar. He will succumb if we do not get him aid. Let us stop and have Lillith patch him up?"

They rode out as if the devil himself were after them. Declan worried for Trevor. His wound appeared grave, and he didn't want his soldier to die. Within a league of riding, they approached Lillith's cottage that sat by a copse of trees, at the far-stretched border of their land. Before they reached the worn plot of land before the entrance, Lillith stepped through the doorway.

"Good day, Laird. I was not expecting you." Then she appeared to notice the steely regard on their faces and the slumped over man riding in front of Anse. "Oh, ye are not here for a social visit. Come, get him inside." She turned and entered her cottage.

Declan took Trevor from his cousin's horse and once Anse

dismounted they worked together to carry him inside. The cottage was dark and there were all sorts of scents from various drying plants that hung from rope and on the walls. On a long table, many jars of medicinals lined in rows, along with pestles and the tools of Lillith's trade. She was a renowned healer and many, even those from other clans, sought her aid when needed.

"Lay him there," she said and pointed to a small wooden cot by the long table.

They gently lowered Trevor onto the cot. "He was struck with a dagger. The wound looks grave. I am unsure if ye can save him."

"We shall see." Lillith began removing Trevor's garments with shears and grimaced. Blood covered most of his torso and soaked his garments. "It will be close, Laird. I'll see what I can do to help him, but I am not making any promises. Await outside for I need to focus. I cannot have ye both peering over my shoulder. If I need ye, I will call."

Declan tensed at her words. Apprehensively, he stepped outside and Anse followed him. If his soldier didn't survive, Declan would be devastated. Trevor was not only a good soldier, but a close trusted comrade. They had been raised together, trained, and caroused throughout their lives. Declan wouldn't put a voice to his thoughts. Instead, he prayed, and began to pace.

CHAPTER SIXTEEN

ISABELLA SPENT A good hour in the chapel, praying for Declan's return. He had been gone for over a sennight when he'd told her he was only going to be away a day or two. She repeatedly asked Lorcan if he would send men out to search for him, but he dismissed her worry. Lorcan was like a shadow, never leaving her side or presence. Isabella was glad for his company, but he rarely spoke to her. Instead, he followed her like a shadow, focused on her security.

Lorcan, by the look of him, was more than capable of protecting her. He appeared similar to Slone and she'd begun to wonder if he could be his brother, for they both had the same features of face, body shape, and wavy brown hair.

At least she didn't have to worry about the threat that Declan had insinuated about before he left. Whoever threatened her must have absconded or changed their mind. There had been no further messages—or dead rats—left for her and that relieved her.

The clan seemed docile what with the heat of summer affecting everyone. Most tended to stay inside during the hottest part of the day. For days, nary a person walked on the lane in the mid-afternoons. Isabella knocked on various cottage doors and invited the women and children to the loch. She hoped to give everyone time to speak to her since she wasn't introduced as Declan's wife, a slight she had hoped he would remedy, but with him away, she took care of it herself. The clan began accepting her and the women spoke to her more frequently, giving her greetings as she passed by.

At the loch, the children played by the water. Their light-hearted banter solaced her. Noah seemed in good spirits as he played with some of the lads. He even made sounds from his mouth and ran around, displaying normal boyhood excitement. As the days passed, the women began to set up covers on the bank and some even brought their mid-day meals to share. Isabella joined Marian and Edith on their blanket to listen to the elder women speak of times gone by and reminisced about their children when they were young.

Isabella noticed Rhona sitting by herself. She decided it was a good time to talk to her and perhaps make strides in winning her friendship. She approached the lass and sat on the grass next to her. "Good day, Rhona. Do you mind if I sit with you?"

The lass shook her head. After a moment, she asked, "How did you do it?"

"Do what?" Isabella asked her.

"Silence Lady Helena?"

Isabella would have laughed but didn't, even though the thought of Lady MacKendrick being silenced was somewhat comical. Most of all, she'd realized, it was a blessing, one she wouldn't destroy by poking fun at the woman. "Your brother spoke to her and demanded that she respect me, or that she should seek elsewhere to live." She looked out over the shimmering water of the loch and inhaled the clean fresh air. She hadn't been able to enjoy her new surroundings as much, until Helena had started to leave her alone.

Beside her, Rhona said softly, "I am sorry…"

Isabella turned and peered at her. "Sorry that Helena now has to respect me?"

Rhona giggled. "Oh, nay, for the way I behaved when ye first arrived. I am sorry, Milady. I was unkind and should not have been. My mother passed away years ago and I have not had a woman to speak to about…certain things. I cannot speak to Helena about anything because she taunts me and calls me a simpleton." Rhona spoke awkwardly, lowering her voice with each word.

"I understand. She made me feel the same way." Isabella leaned to touch the young woman's arm. "Please, Rhona, call me Isabella. You are my sister-in-law now and I want us to be close, friends even. You can trust me because I shall never betray your confidence in me. My mother spoke of nothing but the duties of a wife and I was fortunate to have her to ask questions." Isabella chuckled when Rhona's eyes widened.

"Even about what happens in bed with a man?"

"That was her favorite topic. I mean not to take the place of your mother, Rhona, but I bid you to think of me as an older sister. You can ask me anything and I shall answer you honestly and as best I can."

Rhona nodded. "Well, as ye know…I worry that Declan will not allow me to marry Willeli. I love Willeli and we have been together…you know, like that. I fear if my brother does not come around, I shall likely be heavy with child by the time he does."

"Oh…" Isabella realized what Rhona meant. Whether or not she was ready to be a wife in Declan's opinion, it didn't appear to matter. Willeli and Rhona had made their decision and had already been intimate. "Worry not because I will speak to Declan and get him to agree."

"How will ye be able to do that? Declan is stubborn, I vow, and when he sets his mind to something…there is no changing it."

Isabella smiled. "I shall tell you a secret that my mother passed on to me…" She leaned closer. "When a husband wants to please a wife in that way, it is easy to gain his accord. You just have to time it right."

"You mean withhold yourself unless he agrees?" Rhona giggled.

"I don't mean to actually withhold yourself, but after, when you have exhausted your husband or pleased him beyond sense, you can get him to agree to pretty much anything."

"That is quite sneaky."

"But unfortunately, necessary sometimes, especially when your husband is being bull-headed."

Rhona laughed. "I am gladdened ye are here. We shall talk more." Rhona clasped her hand. "There is Willeli. I must speak to him." She got to her feet and scampered away.

Isabella searched for Noah amongst the children to assure herself that he was well and safe. She rose and walked around the coverings that littered the ground, speaking to some of the women she passed, wishing them a good day.

She noticed Claude, who stood by Friar Faelan; they were looking at an old piece of parchment. Curiosity piqued her interest and she walked toward them.

They didn't cease their conversation when she reached them, but after a moment, the friar looked at her and said, "Oh, Lady Isabella, 'tis a fine day for an outing. I am heartened ye invited all here by the loch. It was a fine suggestion. It is much cooler here. I may even walk in the water a wee bit." Father Faelan grinned. And then, he walked off and removed his sandals by the water. The clergyman wandered along the bank holding the hem of his robe up like a lady wearing a gown, and with the water up to his knees.

She turned to her brother-in-law. "I have seen you at the chapel every day this week, Claude. Are you apprenticing with Friar Faelan? I heard the friar speak of sacraments."

The lad shook the hair from his eyes. "Aye, my brother gave me permission to learn from the friar. In time, God willing, I will be able to take the orders and then I will be a friar. Or a priest." He smiled and ducked his chin.

Isabella clapped her hands. "That is wonderful news. I thought you were rather passionate about it when you spoke of it at supper that one time. Are you learning much from him, from Friar Faelan, that is?"

"I am. He can go on and on sometimes, but I like listening to him speak of God and our duty to serve Him. It is what I was meant to do."

She smiled and was happy for him. Declan had actually listened to his brother and allowed his pursuit of the clergy. "What have you got there?" She pointed to the parchment.

"Oh, this is my grandda's treasure map. I found it in his cottage hidden beneath a floorboard. It is hard to decipher for it is written in Latin—so Friar Faelan says—and some other language he doesn't know."

"Maybe you can still figure out what it means by the images drawn," she suggested.

Claude peered at the parchment he held open and nodded. "I will study it further and maybe ask some of the elders what they think."

"That's a great idea.

"I would be pleased to help you. Why don't I meet you tomorrow after morning Mass and we'll look at it again and try to follow the markings."

As she finished speaking, Isabella heard the call of the gate watchmen. She turned and saw Declan riding through the keep's gate. Relief overwhelmed her and she was pleased he was safely home. She would give him a little time to get his reports before she hunted him down.

"I'll do that, Milady."

"Please, Claude, you are my brother-in-law. Call me Isabella. It'll be fun helping you search for your grandda's treasure. It will be an adventure. Perhaps Noah and I can help you. A lad his age would love the quest."

He smiled, bowed to her, turned, and walked away.

Isabella's heart lightened that she'd been able to befriend Declan's siblings. She thought about it as she retook her position on the blanket where Marian and Edith sat, discussing various methods of what stitch to use on a tapestry Edith was making. She listened as she snatched an apple from the trencher that sat in the center of the cloth and set about eating it. A commotion sounded from afar and she turned to see what was happening.

Declan stood before Willeli and Rhona. He didn't look pleased by any account, as his voice rose and his face reddened. Quite suddenly, she saw him grip the lad's tunic before shoving him away with great force. Willeli fell to the ground onto his backside.

She heard Declan yelling from where she sat. "I told ye nay, Willeli. Now, get back to your duties. And you, Sister, will return to the cottage and stay there. I will speak with ye later about your blatant disobedience."

Willeli bowed his dark head to Declan and Rhona stomped her foot. They marched off in different directions. It was only a matter of moments before the lass lifted her hem in both fists and began to run, her hair streaming behind her as she sobbed.

Isabella took a deep breath. Her husband had just returned and already his homecoming was rife with problems. She waited for him to approach and when he stood before her, he threw down his hand to help her rise.

"Wife, there ye are. It is good to see ye." The red-faced yelling man suddenly appeared pleasant and calm.

She would focus on that and not what had just occurred in front of practically the whole clan. "Declan, you are home, finally. What took you so long? I worried that something happened to you." Isabella held tightly to his hand.

"Trevor was injured, and we had to hold up at the healer's cottage whilst she tended him."

"Is he well now?" she asked and hoped the soldier wasn't permanently injured, or—God forbid—had perished.

"Trevor is still there, but he is out of danger. Still, the lad cannot be moved yet and will need to convalesce for some time."

Isabella began walking, leading him away from the others, seeking privacy while they discussed how he'd just treated the young lovers. "I must ask, Husband. What were you yelling about over there? Everyone could hear you."

Declan scowled. "My sister… I caught her and Willeli kissing. She knows my feelings on the matter of her marrying Willeli. I will probably have to send him away if she does not listen to me."

She stopped, released his hand, and stepped back. "How could you? You don't realize what you have done. I spoke to your sister and she—"

"Lower your voice, Wife. Dare ye tell me how to handle my family matters?" he clipped, cutting her off from explaining.

She wouldn't allow him to shut her down. "I do when Rhona's heart is involved. And I am your wife, for heaven's sake. I should be able to speak to you about such matters anyway I please." Isabella glared at him. He was in a mood, but she wasn't about to allow him to belittle her in front of their clan.

Declan frowned fiercely, grabbed her arm, and forced her to walk with him. She huffed as he made her sprint behind him. They continued walking, more like running, until they reached his grandda's cottage. After he opened the door, he gestured her inside, entered, and slammed the door closed.

Isabella stared at him with her mouth agape. She hadn't realized she would instigate his rage when she spoke out about his reaction to Rhona's relationship with Willeli. As she peered at him, she remained silent. She'd never seen him so riled. Declan took two steps in one direction and then two back before her. He didn't appear to know what he wanted to say but sent a glare at her.

The wait for his reprimand became unbearable and the silence in the cottage deafening. She wasn't about to remain silent and Isabella's ire raised her voice. "You have little patience for your siblings, Declan, and for me. I think you need to consider our feelings—"

"Feelings? I forbid ye from speaking to me in this tone," he said and continued to march back and forth as if he were inspecting his soldiers. He wouldn't meet her gaze either after he reproached her.

"You knew I was outspoken when you married me, so don't

tell me you forbid me from speaking my mind now. And I am your wife, lest you forget, and I am telling you that you are acting like a brutish fool when it concerns your sister. If you'll only—"

Declan pressed his hands over his face and his shoulders moved from his heavy sigh. "This is not what I had hoped for on my return. I do not mean to be cross, Wife, but my siblings are my responsibility, and I won't discuss them with ye."

"We are married. What concerns you, concerns me. Let me help you, Declan. Explain to me why you are so distant toward Rhona and Claude. They only seek your approval, surely you must know that."

Declan rushed at her, scooped her in his arms and set her on the small table near the hearth. His eyes darkened with passion. "All I wanted to do on my return was this," he said and set his mouth on hers and crushed her lips. His hands fumbled with her garments as he tried to undress her.

Isabella in turn unfastened his tunic and splayed her hands over his warm skin, until she was finally able to lift it over his head. She'd never tire of the sight of him ungarbed with his muscles taut from her caresses. She then moved her hands to his waist and tried to unlatch his belt, but her hands shook. Desire swarmed her heart and body now and all she wanted was for him to hurry and take her.

"Declan, please…I need you."

He pressed his mouth back on hers, growled low in his throat, and dislodged his mouth from hers. "I want you badly, Wife."

Isabella watched him intently when he released her briefly to finish undressing her. She stood before him naked, peering at him in wonder at what he was going to do.

Declan shed the rest of his garments within seconds. He moved her back to the table and pressed her back upon it. His hand stroked her hair and the side of her face. With hooded eyes, he peered at her with such longing. She'd never seen him appear so hungry for passion. Isabella too had missed him, and her desire was as strong. He pressed her head to the side and set his mouth on the tender skin below her ear. She gasped at the sound of his rasped breath. Declan suckled the skin and glided his lips along the base of her neck. He fondled her breasts roughly as he continued to press his mouth on her neck and shoulder.

Isabella held her breath. With each of his kisses, desire dampened the curls between her legs. A yearning to have him inside her overtook her and she was impatient for him to enter her. She thought he would because he groaned and pressed his hard erection against her. His movements were wild and erratic. He used his body to caress her, keeping her still with his hand flattened on her torso.

"Declan, please…" She moaned, swarmed with the need for him. Isabella leaned upward and stared at his handsome face. Her fingers perused his cheek, and she told him with her eyes that she needed him.

"Shhh…" He lifted her leg and bade her to hold it by pressing her hand there. "Don't let go."

Isabella shrieked when he entered her. She fell back against the tabletop as he propelled her back upon it, driving into her with such force that she couldn't catch her breath. The table shifted a little and she almost shrieked thinking it might crash to the floor. His movements were rushed, and he had his eyes closed but his brows furrowed.

He grunted with each thrust and pulled her back against him when he drove her forward. Declan wouldn't release her, and she held onto the table to support herself and to keep herself from falling off. He continued his sensual assault with effectual strokes to cause her culmination. The intensity of his forcefulness sent her reeling. Isabella cried out, not with pain, but with intense pleasure. Her body exploded with bliss and torment, sending her to an exquisite place she never knew existed.

Declan pulled out of her, lifted her off her feet, and carried her to the bed. There, he said nothing but instructed her to lay back. Impatiently, he drove into her again. His body thrust forcefully against hers unrelentingly. Isabella marveled at the severity of their lovemaking. Declan was wild with his need, and she was as needful of his fierce love play.

"Do ye like this, Wife? Do ye want it hard?"

"Please," she whispered. "Yes, harder."

He was almost brutal in his measured strokes. As he entered and pulled out of her, her vagina twinged and she couldn't hold back the climax that shook her legs and caused her to cry out, surrendering once again to his vigorous treatment. His hands grabbed and caressed her so physically, she huffed and took hold of them.

Declan moaned and rasped from his exertion. He guided himself back into her and thrashed madly until his shout passed his manly lips. It seemed to go on for a long time until he slowed his thrusts and pulled out of her.

Isabella breathed through her nose to try to settle her breath. Yet she'd enjoyed their intense, rough lovemaking, and he hadn't hurt her.

Now, he didn't seem to want to talk so she lay back on the bed and stared at the ceiling of the cottage. It seemed to her that Declan needed release and not the sweet-wifely lovemaking that she offered. That he'd been somewhat fervent with her fueled her need for him to be rougher. She was amazed at her response.

Declan sat on the side of the bed, leaned his elbows on his knees. His head lowered and his breath sounded labored. A long moment passed before he spoke, "I have never taken a woman so roughly before," his voice came quietly. "I acted without honor, and I apologize."

"I should not have been so angry with you... But you knew before you married me that I was outspoken. Perhaps you should have chosen another bride." She wanted to weep as she spoke those words because she hoped with all her heart that he wasn't completely displeased with her. Though she was doing her best, it saddened her to think that he was unhappy to have married her. Isabella placed her hand on his bicep, hoping to calm him.

"Ye know as well as I do that the choice was yours, Wife. I had no say in who I was to marry." Declan set his hand atop hers but kept his face averted.

"What do you mean by that?"

Declan shrugged. "Aye, I got to tell the king who I wanted to marry after the brawl, but it meant nothing because the choice was already made for me, was it not?"

"Perhaps. I'll grant you that I did tell the queen that I hoped you would offer for me." She leaned up on her elbow and wanted to reach out to touch him, but she held back. Declan needed time to calm and not her pawing at him. Besides, Isabella didn't know how to respond to his declaration. "Are you so displeased with me as a wife?"

"Nay, of course not. I am more appalled by my actions. If I hurt ye…that is the last thing I would ever do, Isabella. Ye must believe me." Declan turned to look at her. The discomfort in his eyes spoke volumes.

"You didn't hurt me. I am not a feeble woman, Declan," she said and wiped at her unabashed tears that gathered and fell one by one over her cheeks.

"I have never touched a woman like that before, Isabella. I vow that to be true. Why I lost control sits poorly in my chest. Say ye forgive me," he implored.

"Of course, I forgive you. Come, lay beside me. We will not speak if you don't want to." She opened her arms and he lay back. She clasped his body and enjoyed the feeling of him against her. His hard body, still rigid with his taut muscles, enthralled her. It dawned on her that he could have easily hurt her or worse, killed her with his strength.

"I do not know what came over me, Isabella. Never would I hurt ye intentionally."

"I am not hurt, Declan, and confess I might have enjoyed it. Worry not." She pressed her hands through his hair and sighed. He worried for her and that relieved her.

"What ye said… 'Tis true…what ye said about Rhona and

Claude. I should speak to Rhona soon."

Isabella sat up and shifted to kneel beside him. "Declan, you were right because it is not my place to tell you how to act with your siblings. I understand you have been acting like her father for some years now. But Rhona is a grown woman, though young, and if she wants to marry, you should let her. What is the real reason you won't give your consent?"

He pulled her to lay beside him and she set her arm over his torso. "I...I do not want to lose her yet. She will be gone and living her own life and I fear I will be unable to protect her."

"That is what must be, though. You cannot keep her with you forever. She loves Willeli and they want to have a family. Just as you and I want to have a family. Willeli will protect her now. Let her go. Besides, she is not leaving the clan. Imagine how my parents felt when I left them. I probably won't ever see them again."

Declan grunted. "Ye always speak so frankly, but sensibly. I will give her my consent on the morrow to marry Willeli."

"Oh, Declan, that makes me happy." Isabella practically rolled on top of him and squeezed him in an embrace. There was always a way to make a husband agree and she had proved it to be so. Her husband easily conformed to her idea. She smiled to herself and suspected she might, in the future, have to use such wiles to gain his accord.

"I will make ye even happier in a moment."

Isabella laughed when he pressed her back and set his mouth on hers. Their lovemaking was gentle as Declan tried to make up for his mistreatment of her. Yet deep down, Isabella had to admit that his rough lovemaking stirred something inside her.

CHAPTER SEVENTEEN

DECLAN STOOD OUTSIDE his grandda's cottage and waited for Isabella. She closed the door behind her and stepped beside him. They'd spent the morning enjoying each other but eventually, Declan reminded himself that clan matters and duty needed to be seen to. He hoped that spending the morning with his wife would allay his actions of the previous night. Guilt plagued him and he fiercely scolded himself for ever laying a rough hand on her.

As they walked back to the keep, he remained quiet, not wishing to apologize to her once again. There weren't enough words to convey his regret. Passing the gates, Declan raised his fist to the guardsman and noted all appeared quiet. Anse approached but he was far off and down the lane.

"Can we do that again?"

Declan peered at her with his dubious gaze. "Do what, Wife?"

"You know... What you did...yestereve, before you were gentle. The second time. And the third." She giggled.

He was aghast at her suggestion. "Do ye mean that you'd like me to...take you roughly?"

She nodded but her grin told him she was honest in her request.

Declan shook his head. "Nay."

Isabella pouted. "Why not?"

He set his arm around her back and guided her on the lane. "It is unseemly, Wife, to take ye like that and I will not ever touch ye in such a way again. I will hear no more about it."

"Why did you? Was it because you—"

Declan cut her off with a kiss on her lips. "Shhh, Anse comes."

"Laird, ye finally returned. I thought I might have to come and fetch ye."

"All is well?" Declan searched his cousin's expression for trouble but noted none.

"Aye, but we have duties… The farmers are ready to begin harvesting some of the early crops. I thought we could speak to the troops and forgo their training until the harvest is through," Anse said. "Unless ye want to select certain men to attend to it."

"Aye, I will meet with the soldiers with ye. Some guards have not mastered certain tactics and I want all our warriors to be ready in case we…" Declan ceased his thought when he noticed Isabella peering at him with concern. "We should always be prepared."

"The fief is almost done. There are only minor items left before the dwelling is ready to be lived in. I thought ye might want to take a walk-through in case you wanted anything changed."

Isabella drew a deep breath. "You mean that monstrosity of a home? Must we live there?"

Declan chuckled at his wife's disgruntlement. "Aye, we must. I want our children protected, Isabella. We will move inside the fief at the soonest. Would ye like to walk through it with me when the builders say 'tis safe?"

"I suppose I should."

Anse looked at them oddly. "What is it that I am seeing betwixt ye both? Did something happen? Ye are both acting strangely."

Declan shook his head and Isabella nodded.

"Hell, I am never getting married. Ye two make it seem odious. When ye are ready, Laird, find me and we will get started on the matters at hand." Anse bowed to them, turned, and marched away with haste.

"I mean it, Isabella. I will not touch ye like that again."

She lowered her gaze to the dirt path of the lane. "Very well. Oh, and don't forget, you said you would speak to Rhona to give her your consent to marry Willeli."

"I will not forget." Declan kissed her cheek before he left her at the family cottage. He walked with spry steps toward the training field.

Two hundred men stood facing Anse when he called their attention. Declan raised his hand, and all ceased talking. He proudly surveyed his warriors. There was much he wanted to say to them, and it was time he addressed them about a few pertinent matters.

"MacKendrick soldiers, you know I was accused of murdering Allan Campbell."

His men's voices rose and bellowed their objection at hearing his words.

"No murder was committed by me. I seek the truth and will find the knave who betrayed me. When I find him, we shall prevail. With your arms, we will take on whatever clan dared to insult us with such blatant lies."

His men clamored and their cheers rose. Declan raised his hand calling for silence once again. "Ye also know that I recently married by the king's order. I cannot say I am displeased with my bonny wife. Lady MacKendrick is now your lady, and ye will all protect her with your life. Any slight done to her is done to me."

His men bowed their heads and placed their fisted hands over their hearts indicating their acceptance and vow.

"You have all trained hard these past months and your swords are ready to take up the fight against our foe. While I ferret out this miscreant, I bid ye to help the farmers. Reap the harvest, take time to rest but be ready to be called to arms." Declan would tell those soldiers who needed additional training privately what he wanted them to do.

Anse raised his fist in the air and shouted, "Virtue alone ennobles."

His men repeated their motto, and all bowed their heads when they passed by him.

Declan was pleased by their loyalty. After the men left, he stood with Anse and considered what else he needed to tend to. He thought of Rhona. That discussion would be difficult for him, and so he delayed it.

"What is wrong with ye? I asked ye two times when we are going to leave to meet with Robbie Campbell. The fortnight has almost passed. We should make plans to secure the keep and make ready to head out." Anse shoved him.

"I...my apologies, Anse. My mind is elsewhere."

"What plagues ye?"

"I did an unbecoming thing last eve to Isabella." Declan never kept anything from his cousin and that he confessed to such a grievous sin to Anse tensed his shoulders. "I do not know how to make amends with her over it, och she does not seem as angry as she should be."

"Women are a wonder, Laird. Mayhap she is not angry at all. I say leave it be. If ye apologized and she accepted it, then there is naught more to make amends over."

He supposed what Anse said was true and yet Declan was angry with himself for letting his ire get the better of him. "We should leave for Campbell's fief in two days. We will take about ten men with us. Select them and ensure they are ready. Whilst I am gone, I want Isabella protected. Whoever put that rat in our bed has not been found."

Anse nodded. "Lorcan will continue to watch her while we are gone, and I will leave Slone to look after the clan."

"Nay, you should stay here. Slone should come with me, and you should stay here. I want someone here I completely trust." He set his hand on his commander's shoulder. "With ye here, I can focus on the matter at hand."

Anse scowled and appeared displeased until he praised him. "Aye, very well then, Laird. Just promise me, if ye find our foe, ye will not attack without me. I want to be there when ye stick your sword in him, whoever the hell he is."

His cousin spoke so fervently that it fueled Declan's desire to settle the discord. He liked not that his clan was on alert, that someone threatened his sweet wife, or falsely accused him of foul deeds. Impatience caused him to be irate with everyone. Declan wasn't usually so difficult or demanding and now it was worse because he was being so with Isabella. His irascible behavior was inexcusable.

Declan nodded to Anse and walked toward the keep. It was time to get his conversation with Rhona over and done with. On his walk toward his cottage, he spotted Isabella standing with Claude. His brother seemed much happier since he allowed his withdrawal from the army. Whatever they discussed made them laugh. Noah played at their feet on the ground, but happily. Isabella affected everyone around her. All seemed merrier since she'd come and a joyous mien had settled amongst his clan.

He gave a nod to Isabella as he passed and entered the cottage. It was quiet. He expected to find Helena in the living area, but she wasn't there. Declan knocked on Rhona's door and she bade him entry. He opened the door and found her sitting in a chair by the window.

"Sister…"

"I have not left the cottage," she said in a low tone.

"Nay? I should not have punished ye so harshly." When she didn't retort to him, he sighed. "I have come to tell ye that I give my permission for ye to marry Willeli. I will speak to him and tell him of my decision."

Rhona stood so quickly that the chair slid back. "Why…? What made ye change your mind?"

"My wife. She is far more intelligent about these matters than I am. She told me that ye are a grown woman now and that I should not refute your happiness. Will marrying Willeli make you happy?"

Rhona rushed at him and clasped her arms around him. "Aye, brother, more than ye know. When can we have the wedding?"

He set his hands gently on her shoulders and pressed her away. "I must go to the Campbells and am not certain when I shall return. Perhaps when we have the harvest festival. That would be a good time to take your vows, since all the clan will be called together. We can have the gathering by the loch where we used to have such celebrations."

"I cannot tell you how pleased I am."

"I only rejected your pursuit because…well, I was not ready to admit that ye were grown up and that ye did not need me."

Rhona shook her head. "I will always need ye, Declan. Never forget that."

"I hope ye do. Since da passed, I have had many regrets. That I left ye and Claude with Helena is one of them. I should have paid more attention to both of ye."

"Claude and I understood that ye were pulled away for the clan. We did not mind so much."

He clasped her hand and squeezed. Declan left her and hastened to find Isabella. A great relief eased his chest and he wanted to tell his wife that he'd spoken to his sister. He approached where he had last seen her with Claude, but they weren't there.

His grandmother called to him. Declan hadn't seen her and turned to greet her. "Good day, Gran. Have you seen Isabella?"

"Oh, aye, she is probably at the loch with most of the ladies in the clan. They take a respite there in the afternoons when 'tis hottest."

He stuck out his arm and offered it to her. "Will ye join me?"

"I shall like that." His gran latched her arm with his and they walked to the loch. "Never thought I would see ye this happy again, not since Leona… It does this auld heart good to see ye getting back to your life. I was wary of Isabella when she first came, but now, I cannot see our clan without her. She is most selfless in her demands and giving."

"She is a force, is she not?" Declan chuckled. "But aye, Gran, she has awakened in me many things. My wife is tenderhearted and generous."

"Isabella is well deserved of your praise for which I hope ye do so. It has not been easy for her to come to our clan and be an outsider. Many are finally beginning to accept her, even me, for she is so caring."

He patted his grandmother's arm and released her when they reached the loch. Declan was surprised to see the number of people by the water. When he'd arrived home and fought with Rhona, he hadn't taken time to notice that his clan gathered. He was noticing now. His clan appeared joyful. Around him, his clan's women laughed and mingled in small groups. Seeing their comradery delighted him. It had been too long since his clan beheld togetherness. All it had taken was Isabella.

He left his gran when she gave a wave and walked off to see Edith. On his approach to join his wife, son, and brother, he couldn't help but overhear their conversation.

"This is a symbol for a cave. Is there a cave near here?" Isabella asked.

"There are a few of them, most by the glen on the edge of our land."

"Is that far though?"

Claude scrunched his mouth before answering, "A wee bit, but I know of one that is on the other side of the loch."

"We should search that one first. Oh, how exciting. Do you think the treasure will be there?"

"My grandda spoke of it when I was younger. He used to tell me stories about his ancestors and that a man called MacBeth, who was our king at one time, visited the clan, and was a good friend of his grandda's."

"What do you think the treasure will be? Gold, jewels, or likely it'll be something with no worth but still a treasure?"

Declan found himself smiling at their excitement. "If ye go to the cave, ye must take Lorcan with you. I will not have ye unprotected outside the walls, Wife." He meant to insert his concern, but it came out more of an order.

"We might need Lorcan for he is strong and could easily lift the treasure if it is large," Isabella said. "What a fair idea, Husband."

Declan chuckled to himself because his wife was as caught up in the mysterious treasure hunt as his brother was. He envied their passion for it, but since he'd grown and become laird, he had no time for such frivolities.

They spent the rest of the afternoon at the loch. Declan was unable to get Noah into the water and he despaired that the lad would ever get over what he'd seen the day his mother died. For that reason, he wouldn't force his son into the water. Instead, he sat with him beside it as Isabella swam with the other women.

The sun sank behind the trees, and all vacated the loch. Declan joined Isabella for their supper and stayed at home in the family cottage. He was getting used to having a wife again, being home, surrounded by his family. The mood that night reminded him of when he was young and sat beside his father as he ate his nightly supper. There were always laughter and revelry inside their home—until the day Leona was found floating in the loch.

With each day, Declan found it easier to put the past behind him. Yet until he found his foe, he wouldn't let himself be content. His foe was out there, and he would leave the day after next to find out what Campbell had to say about his father's death. Then he would immerse himself into fleshing out the traitorous miscreant. He'd give himself one day more to enjoy the peacefulness that had overtaken them. One last day until he might learn the name of his foe. One more day before he could seek vengeance.

CHAPTER EIGHTEEN

A S DAWN TOUCHED the horizon, mist grayed the sky. A new day sent night birds to their slumber, their songs lessening as the sky remained dismal. Declan assembled his men and rode out to meet with Robbie. Anse wasn't pleased to be left behind, but Declan wanted assurance that his home was protected whilst he was gone. Hard rain pelted them on the trek to Campbell's holding. It took overlong and they didn't reach the fief until the next afternoon. The rain continued and had soaked them through, but none of his men complained. They too were impatient to gain answers.

At the gate, Declan told the guard that he was expected. Within moments, several Campbell guards came and lined the lane toward the keep. Declan took their show of force as a display of protection of their clan. If he were in Campbell's position, he would probably have commanded his men to do the same.

At the castle, Declan dismounted and directed his men to await him there. "I do not need protection but stay vigilant," he told them and handed the reins of his horse to Slone. Grumbles came from his clansmen, but they dismounted and moved away from the entrance. Declan took the steps to the keep and waited for the door to open.

A manservant nodded to him and opened the door wider. "Ye be welcome here, Laird MacKendrick," the aged man said. "Laird

Campbell is expecting you. He is in the great hall meeting with the commander."

Declan found his way there and entered. The chamber was cozy, quiet, and dark. Campbell sat in a chair with an overstuffed cushion. He appeared relaxed and held a cup in his hand. As soon as Robbie saw him, he dismissed his commander, Micah.

He nodded to Micah as he passed; he'd known the man for years. Micah was as valuable to Robbie as a commander as Anse was to Declan. Laird Campbell had praised him often when he visited the keep before his marriage to Leona.

"Declan, I expected you sooner and thought you would be banging on my door long before now. Ye never were known for your patience, and I thought it strange ye had not come before now. Come, and we will discuss this troubling matter."

He approached and stood beside a vacant chair, but then Robbie motioned to him to sit. Declan did so and his former brother-in-law reached for a cask of ale that sat on a table beside him. His dark hair fell over his shoulders as he poured himself a drink. Declan considered how much Robbie resembled his sister, Leona. They had the same color hair and eyes. He recognized the disparaging expression in Robbie's eyes; it was the same off-putting look Leona's eyes had held when she was annoyed. Now, Declan wondered if he'd caused Robbie's annoyance or if it was his typical mien. Probably the latter because the Campbells were of a surly nature.

"Drink?"

Declan nodded. "Aye, I could use a drink."

Robbie filled a cup and handed it to him. "My wife recently bore our first son. That is why I could not meet with ye sooner. I would not have kept ye waiting but she was having a difficult time delivering the bairn. Thankfully, both survived. It was close."

Declan raised his cup. "That must have been a difficult time. A toast then, to your wife and son. My congratulations, Robbie."

Robbie drank down a large gulp of ale from his cup. "Aye, it was a frightening situation there, but all is well now, and my son thrives." He paused and appeared to be gathering his thoughts before he said, "I want ye to know that I never accused ye of murdering my da. When I heard the rumor of ye being the man who killed him, I disbelieved it right off."

"I vow I did not kill your father."

"But someone did. He was found near your border, hanging in a tree with cuts to his body. His blood was drained from him, and his heart torn from him. Who would do such a thing? Why would someone kill my father and then blame ye? It makes no sense. Who the hell have ye made an enemy of?"

Declan was just as perplexed and shrugged. "That he was so brutally murdered…sickens me, Robbie. I cared for your sister, you know that to be true. I tried to be a good husband to her, and father to our son, and I would never harm anyone in your family. Your da beheld a place of honor in my heart. I revered him as if he were my own da."

"My da revered ye as well and never had a bad word to speak of ye. There has been talk…" Robbie sat forward and kept his gaze direct. "One of my soldiers came to me in private and told me that he overheard talk betwixt two of my men. They were offered prestigious positions by a man if they vacated the clan and joined his army."

"So, this man is trying to pilfer your soldiers?"

"Aye, so it seems," Robbie said and nodded. "My soldiers told the man they would think about it and would consider his request. Request, bah. He dangled enough incentives for my men to agree."

"Who is the man?"

Robbie shrugged. "They had not seen him before or know who he is, or if they did, they would not say. Believe me, my men threatened them, but they kept his name to themselves."

"Where are your traitors now? Have them brought here. I want to question them myself." Declan set his cup down and scowled at his comrade.

"Ye cannot question them."

"Why the hell not?"

"Because they no longer exist. I will not have anyone who entertains abandoning my clan be amongst my soldiers. My men will be loyal, or they will answer to me. Och, before I could question them, the sentry who apprehended them was overzealous in their retaliation and dispatched them. The traitors no longer live."

Declan grunted in agreement. There was no room for disloyalty amongst soldiers. "Damnation, if only we could have found out more information before they killed them."

"I did find out more from the man who overheard them, and he confessed much before being done in. He was approached by a man who wore the MacKendrick tartan, someone from your clan. He spoke no name but said the man hoped the king had ye hung for murdering my da but that ye thwarted his plans when ye were pardoned."

"Aye, Alexander released me from the dungeon and bade me to marry a lass from the border region. He gave other incentives too, for which I was grateful because now I can seek the knave who put me there."

"I would caution ye because Alexander only seeks his gain, not yours."

Declan grunted. "That is true, but I must profess I gained much by accepting his offer. What else did he say?"

"I heard your foe recently tried to do away with ye, but ye foiled his attack. That must've transpired before your knave approached my soldiers."

Declan's breath increased as rage heated him. "That had to be when I was attacked in the woods on my way home from when I first came to speak with ye."

"Whoever the knave is knows ye survived, for he is still intent to overtake your clan. He told my men that when ye were dead, he would align our clans—the MacKendricks and the Campbells. That my clan would be easy to overtake once he had your men-at-arms on his side. He promised them prestigious positions within his army. My soldiers, the ones who were approached by the traitor, went missing without permission. I sent my seasoned sentry after them. The defectors confessed much before they killed them."

Declan grunted again because Robbie was a force to be reckoned with. He supposed Robbie's men would rather confess to the higher-ranking soldiers than confess to their laird. Nevertheless, they received their due with their execution.

"What I want to know is, who is your enemy? Ye have no suspicion of who it might be?" Robbie pressed his face as the aggravating conversation continued.

"I cannot think of any man within my clan that would be so traitorous. I have trusted men mingling with my clansmen. If anyone speaks of the deeds, they'll find out."

Robbie scoffed. "So that is none then? There are always one or two men who deem themselves better than their laird. Is there not someone whom ye suspect might want to usurp ye?"

Declan sat back and held his chin, thinking. Only one man occurred to him, but it was inconceivable. "There is my stepbrother, Silas. But honestly, I believe him to be too weak or feckless to come up with such a plan. And none of my soldiers would follow him because they are all loyal to me."

"Ye think they are loyal, but are they? Still, I would not ignore your stepbrother. He could very well be playing ye for a fool and means to deceive ye. Why would your soldiers not follow him?" Robbie belched and reached to pour himself more ale.

"He demeans them. I recently reprimanded Silas for his treatment of my soldiers during training. Nay, it cannot be he who goes against me."

"Well, comrade, someone means to overtake us. I have placed a few spies amongst my clansmen too in hopes of finding out if any others intend to follow this traitor. They'll listen for any word of such an uprising."

"I did the same, but so far, there has been no talk amongst my soldiers. We will not let this interloper try to overtake both our clans. I am certain this miscreant will make a mistake. I should leave ye to your wife and son." Declan rose and was about to take his leave when Robbie stopped him.

"Do not go. Stay the night and journey in the morn. We will have a good supper and we can talk about Leona. I miss my sister and I was saddened to hear of her passing. Now that ye are here, ye can tell me what really happened."

Declan retook his seat. "Aye, I will be gladdened to stay."

"I know it has been years since her passing, but do ye deem this has anything to do with Leona's death? It is strange that she would die from drowning," Robbie said, "My sister was not careless."

"I always thought her death odd but cannot see how this discord is related to her. Our son does well, though he is still affected by what happened that day. Something dreadful happened but nothing has ever come to light about it."

Robbie poured more ale in his cup. "And tell me of my nephew, Noah. Is he of good health and grows well?"

Declan sighed at the woeful telling about his son. "Noah was a clever lad, but I fear he will not become the man I'd hoped he'd be. He cannot hear and hasn't spoken a word since the day his mother died. I think something happened to him that day, but he's been unable to tell me what. For three years, he's lived in silence."

"That's dreadful, Declan, and I'm sorry to hear that. He saw her drown?"

"Aye, he was with her. I suspect he was in shock at what happened. I prayed he'd come out of it and speak, but so far that hasn't happened." He lifted his cup and drank down the ale, quenching his thirst and mollifying his thoughts.

Throughout the evening, Declan spoke of his relations with Leona, how she died, and how Noah was affected by what happened at the loch that day. The only person he had ever professed his deep sorrow to was Anse, but he let his emotions show when he spoke to Robbie about his sister. He confessed how pleased he was with the marriage that Alexander had arranged and told Robbie about his wife.

That dark time had passed but lighter days were ahead of him. How could they not be when he was married to such a woman as Isabella?

CHAPTER NINETEEN

THE RAIN FINALLY ceased. Isabella had to forgo meeting Claude to hunt for his treasure the day before because the rain came so heavily and forced them to stay inside. After taking care of her morning chores, she readied to spend the day outside once the sun returned. Now, it appeared to be getting hotter by the minute. Isabella loved being outside and had often spent much of her day outdoors—or as many as her mother had allowed—when she lived at home.

With a quick bite of her morning fare, she hastened through the door. Lorcan, as always, waited outside for her. He shadowed her but kept five paces behind. On her way to morning Mass, she greeted the clan's men and women. They now smiled at her, which was such a change from when she'd first arrived. Isabella was beginning to feel welcomed and a part of the MacKendrick clan. She thought of home less and less as each day passed.

During Mass, she prayed for Declan and that he received the solace he desperately needed, for Noah that he would someday hear again, for Rhona's happy marriage, and that Claude would find his treasure sooner rather than later. She prayed that her mother and father were well and happy and that her mother found something to occupy her and her father wasn't thieving and putting himself in danger. Then she thought about Christopher and the perils he must be witnessing in the crusade. She offered up more than one prayer for him.

When Mass ended, she met Claude outside. Friar Faelan bid them farewell and muttered something about a man needing last rites at a neighboring clan's holding. He set off before they could ask who was dying.

Claude waved him off. "I wanted to go with the friar, but I cannot leave MacKendrick land without Declan's permission. Since he's not here, I told the friar to go on without me. At least that will give me time to search for the treasure."

Isabella walked beside Claude. "Shall we go in search of the cave?"

"I have nothing else to do," Claude said, "And I'm prepared for a trip to the cave this day." He indicated such by pulling at his satchel. "I have a torch, flint, a small spade, and the map."

"Let us stop and get Noah. He will want to come and needs a little adventure." Isabella wasn't in much of a rush because they had all day to seek the treasure. At Marian's cottage, she knocked lightly on the opened door. "Marian?"

Marian gasped. "Oh, Isabella, ye frightened me."

"Why are you startled so easily? Is something wrong?" She stood next to the elder woman and was concerned.

"Nay, nothing is wrong. I just was not expecting anyone to be there. And I just finished the surprise I made for ye. Here," she said and handed her a folded cloth.

"So that is why you didn't want my help with your sewing the other day." Isabella pressed her hand over the soft material. "What is it?"

Marian smiled widely. "I know ye lost the tartan that Declan gave ye, for he told me so. He said he suspected ye discarded it. I wanted to make ye a shawl with our clan's plaid on it because ye have been so kind to Noah and to me. Here, put it around your shoulders. Ye are slighter than me and so I made sure it was not overly large." She opened the fabric and then spread it over her back.

Isabella took hold of the fabric and pulled it together at the front of her. The shawl was perfectly stitched and would keep her warm when the weather got colder, which from what she'd heard, tended to happen much sooner in the north than it did by the border. "It is perfect." She wanted to weep at the woman's kindness. "My thanks."

"Wear it, lass, in good health," Marian said and smiled.

"I shall. Might I leave it here? I will pick it up when we return from our sojourn. We are off on an adventure this morn. Is it all right if we take Noah with us?"

Marian chuckled. "He has been itching to get outside. Aye, go on, lads and lassie. Enjoy your adventure. I shall make a wee bit of stew for the midday meal, so come back when ye gets hungry."

Isabella took hold of Noah's hand when they exited the cottage. On the way to the cave, they veered around the loch. It was peaceful at the loch as if everything stopped. The water was still, no wind or breeze stirred the trees, and no birds chirped. She wondered briefly at the silence, and Lorcan seemed irritated that they wanted to go afar, but she kept walking as Claude guided them to where he thought the cave was located.

On the other side of the loch, the forest grew thicker. They traipsed through the tall oaks, pines, and the elms whose leaves shaded and darkened the forest floor. It was much cooler beneath the canopy of the trees. Isabella breathed in and smelled the thick permeation of sand and soil. The outdoors engulfed her senses and she smiled.

"I think the cave should be yonder, there near that huge rock." Claude marched forward and turned. "There is a mark on the map that looks about right. I see an entrance."

Isabella took the parchment from him and nodded. "There is an indication that alludes to an entrance." She had searched through the pamphlets she had but found nothing to help her discern some of the language used on the map.

Lorcan called them to halt. "We will go no farther than that cave."

"We don't plan to, Lorcan." Isabella hurried forward and

stopped before the entrance. "It looks deep and dark inside."

"Be cautious, I warn ye, because we know not if any animals have made this cave their home. The last thing we want to come across is a pack of wolves taking their slumber," Lorcan said and walked ahead of her, but Isabella didn't mind because the darkened cave was daunting. It was best to allow the brawny soldier to enter first.

Claude pulled the wooden torch from his satchel and used the flint to light it. Lorcan took the torch from him and waved it inside the cave. Within moments, the bright flame lit up the confines of the cave. The ceiling moved and shimmered from the torchlight. A bat left its perch and made screeching noises. Isabella jumped back and almost knocked poor Noah to the ground. She disliked the vile creatures and hoped this one flew back from whence it came.

Farther into the cave they trekked. Isabella held tightly to Noah's hand. She was beginning to become fearful and wanted to suggest they leave the cave when Claude gasped.

"What is it?"

He took a few more steps forward and knelt. "Here is the exact rock that was on the map. It is similar in shape and a good size. It must be the same one."

Isabella remembered that the rock on the map had almost appeared heart-shaped. "Is the treasure there?"

Claude removed the spade from his satchel. "I will dig a little and see if I can find anything."

She moved back and sat on another rock with Noah. Claude dug furiously for a good bit of time until Lorcan insisted he take over. They waited with bated breath until Lorcan stopped digging. Claude turned and grinned at them.

"Have you found something?"

"Aye, there is something wrapped in cloth not too far down." Claude dug a little more and pulled out the cloth-wrapped item. He placed it on the ground and stared up at her. "What do ye think it is?"

She shrugged. "Open the cloth. Let us see."

He did as she suggested, and the glow of gold shone on the cave's ceiling. All four of them, Noah included, drew an awed breath.

"'Tis a chalice and a cross." Claude held up the items which were larger than she thought they would be. Both objects were at least a foot tall. The cross had markings scratched into it and the chalice was rimmed with small red gems.

"They are beautiful and look ancient," she said and ran her finger over the ornate carving of the cross.

"Come, let us return. I don't like being in here," Lorcan said. "We can view them closer later when we get back to the safety of the walls."

Isabella waited for Claude to rewrap the items and put the items in his satchel. They hastily made their way back out of the cave. Lorcan fell behind them and as always was ever watchful. He was being overprotective, but Isabella didn't mind and was thankful Lorcan was there.

Claude spoke with excitement, "I cannot wait to show Friar Faelan what we found. Who do ye think the objects belonged to?"

"Did your grandda ever mention what might be buried?" Isabella let Noah run free. He veered around them, passed Lorcan, and spread his arms as if he were a bird soaring through the sky.

"He told me stories of when King MacBeth ruled the land and brought back relics from Rome. He gifted some to my grandda's relatives and because they were at war, but many of the objects were secreted away or taken when they were invaded." Claude appeared boastful in his ability to recite his family history.

"They are beautiful objects."

Before they walked past the gate, Claude stopped and said, "I am going to show these to Friar Faelan. Maybe he's returned from his duty. We should keep the relics in the chapel. I will ask Declan when he returns if we might keep them in a place of honor there."

"I think that is a splendid idea, Claude." She glanced at the dust covering her garments and noted how dirty Noah appeared. "Noah and I are going to wash at the loch."

Claude began to walk away but turned back to her. "It is starting to rain. Ye should return to the cottage with me." As he spoke, she noticed several people heading toward their homes.

"It's only a little drizzle. I feel so vile after being in that cave. I pray I don't have a spider or two on me. I shan't be long." Isabella kept hold of Noah's hand and reverted her direction. She headed for the loch and on the approach, the water was still tranquil.

Lorcan followed her, but he kept his distance. When they reached the loch, the soldier remained by the tree line. She hoped to get Noah in the water, but he balked and scurried back on the bank. He sat with his legs folded and skipped rocks that he found near him. She smiled when he celebrated a good throw with a grunt.

Noah was beginning to make more sounds from his throat. She surmised that Noah might even hear a little sound because he'd turned at noises. Of course, he might just be sensing noises from vibrations. Isabella meant to talk to Declan about it, but with him gone so much, she had forgotten. If Noah could hear even the slightest noise, that gave her hope that he would speak when he was ready.

Isabella removed her overdress until she only wore her shift. The water was refreshing and chilly, and she washed herself as best she could without soap. "Milady, ye should not be in these waters by yourself. 'Tis dangerous."

She jumped; she hadn't been paying attention and hadn't noticed Silas coming to stand next to Noah on the loch's bank. She searched for Lorcan by the tree line, but he wasn't there. Chills swept over her but they had nothing to do with the water.

Isabella fixed Silas with a stern look as she crossed her arms over her breasts. She hadn't realized how see-through the thin white material of her shift was when wet. Lorcan had been far enough away, and Noah was just a boy, so it hadn't seemed important. Now, however, she felt exposed to Silas's gaze as if she were completely unclothed. "I am a capable swimmer and besides, I don't intend to go out far. Please, leave me be."

Silas smirked at her modesty, but he didn't listen to her request to leave her alone. Instead, he stepped into the water, fully clothed, and began to progress toward her. A sense of trepidation moved over Isabella as he drew closer. There was a strange look in his gaze.

"Ye are so lovely. Does my stepbrother know how fortunate he is?" He reached out to grab her arm, but she hastened away before he could grasp her.

Isabella sloshed to the bank, her steps slowed by the water and mud sucking at her toes. It felt like forever before she reached Noah, who stood, frozen as a stone statue, with fear in his eyes and terror on his face. "Come…we…should…go." She reached for his hand and her clothing. Even that felt slowed, as if she couldn't move fast enough and couldn't get away.

Before she could collect her overdress from the ground, Silas grabbed her and wrapped his arms around her waist. She gasped and tried to jerk away from him, but he was stronger than he looked.

Noah growled and seemed to suddenly come to life as he ran at Silas and pulled at the man's tunic. Silas shoved the lad and Noah fell back. Isabella heard the thump of his head as he hit the ground, and then he lay on the bank, unmoving. "Noah!" Rage filled her. "Let go of me. Let me get to Noah!" Isabella huffed as she struggled against Silas's grasp, but he gripped her arms and pulled her against him. She could feel his arousal pressed against her bottom.

"Ye are mine now, sweet," he purred in her ear.

"I am not yours. Release me, Silas. Noah is hurt and I need to see to him." Isabella gained her freedom but only briefly, as Silas yanked her off her feet and carried her into the water.

"Let the cretin be. All I want is what ye freely give to your husband. I deserve no less."

No! How could this be happening? She tried to swing out and strike him, or kick him, to no avail. She had nothing with which to protect herself but her words and her voice. "If you hurt me, Declan will never forgive you."

Silas bellowed a laugh. "I care naught. He will be dead soon and then ye will need my protection." He kissed her face and she winced.

She screamed and didn't stop in hopes that someone nearby would hear her. Isabella jerked her body back and Silas lost hold of her. She sank into the water until fully immersed. Kicking, she tried to swim away from the man but when she rose to breathe, he was there, and he pressed her head back under. She couldn't breathe. Panic ensued, and it seemed like a miracle when she was able to get her head above the water. She drew in a deep breath but once again Silas forced her back under. She could hear his laughter reverberating even through the cold, dark water surrounding her.

She was terrified that he wouldn't let her live. When Silas pulled her up from the water and against his chest, Isabella screamed into his face as loud as she could. He grinned sinisterly and gripped her chin in a tight hold. "Never try to keep yourself from me, sweet. I promise I will not be too rough." He kept her lodged against him with his arm around her back and his free hand roaming her body.

Isabella continued to fight him, taking gulps of air, and shouting for help. Silas became angry with her attempts to flee him. He pushed her back under the water and she couldn't take in enough breath when he allowed her to come above the water line.

After a time, as she floated beneath the surface of the water, she began to feel oddly comforted, as if all the peril suddenly vanished. She was dying. It was just her, and God, now. "Please, Lord, don't take me now. Declan needs me. Noah needs me. I cannot leave them..." She prayed, as darkness began to fall over her vision.

CHAPTER TWENTY

A T THE FIRST sighting of his fief's gates in the distance, Declan gave a nod of thanks to God for his safe return. Though he hadn't experienced any threats on his trek home, he was tense from being so vigilant. Confounded to learn that he shared an enemy with Campbell, especially after he'd learned that someone—one of his own men, perhaps—was trying to kill him, Declan sensed danger. He felt peril awaited him behind every tree, beyond every hill, and in every glen. The hair on his neck had prickled so many times, his skin tingled and although he'd kept a keen ear for sounds of followers, he grew watchful. The view of his gate allayed him and the tenseness in his shoulders ebbed. His men rode ahead of him and he waited until they passed the threshold before he too passed.

By the gate, he saw his grandmother who ambled along the lane. She held a wad of cloth in her arms and smiled at him. He dismounted and stood next to her when she reached him.

"Ah, ye have returned. Your sweet lass will be gladdened."

"How is my bonny wife?"

His gran petted his warhorse. "Claude said she's with Noah at the loch and should return shortly. I vow she's the only one who can bathe the lad. I was just taking some clean garments for them to change into."

While he had his grandmother's attention, Declan wanted to

ask her about his parents. "Gran, did something happen years ago to cause a rift with another clan?"

"What do ye mean? We were always at odds with other clans. 'Tis the way of the Highlands."

That was true enough, but it didn't answer his questions. He needed more information. "Were my parents happy? I always thought they were."

His gran shrugged. "At first, they were, but then after ye and your siblings came, there were times when I wondered if they detested each other. By the time your ma passed, they hardly spent any time together."

"Did my da love her?" Declan tensed at asking such questions. He'd always revered his father and thought he was a noble man who cared for his family.

"He did at first, aye, but then I remember their rows. They fought and shouted. None were privy as to why they argued. I recall your da accusing his wife of cuckolding him. After that, my dear son became reserved. I tried to get him to talk to me, och he would not. I suspect your ma had relations with someone else and your da withdrew from much of the clan then."

It couldn't be true. "Who was she with? I disbelieve what ye are telling me."

His gran set her feeble hand on his arm. "Your da never told me who it was. I speak the truth, lad. Your da, from what I sensed at the time, was brokenhearted by her deceit. Then your ma died, and he became even more withdrawn. The day he married that shrew, Helena, was a black day indeed, for she did nothing to bring about his happiness."

Declan scowled hard, trying to recollect his younger years and the happenings then. "I wish I knew what happened betwixt them."

His gran caressed his arm and shook her head. "Ye stayed in the barracks then, aye for your da probably did not want ye to witness their rows. Rarely did ye enter your da's cottage after that."

He dipped his chin, remembering how proud he'd been to be housed with the soldiers. "How did my ma die?"

"No one knows. At the time, the healer spoke of her weak heart, but there was no reason to suspect foul play." His gran made a *tsk*-ing sound. "Why are ye asking such questions?"

"I only realized I did not know much about them." That, at much, was true, and all he was willing to share with Gran until he'd gathered more information.

"'Tis best ye put them out of your mind. Ye are laird now, and our clan prospers." She beamed up at him.

"Aye, my thanks, Gran." Declan stood by the gate and watched his grandmother set off down the lane that would take her to the loch. He wanted to consider what his gran told him, but there was no time for that now. With his horse's reins in his hand, he yanked them to get his horse to follow. But something caught his eye. Declan craned his neck and spotted Noah running toward the gate.

"DA…DA…DA!" Noah shouted.

Declan quickly mounted his horse and rode hell-bent toward his son. That his lad was alone outside the gates told him that something was terribly wrong. That, and the look of terror on his wee face. And the panic in his voice.

His voice! His son had spoken and called to him; Declan only just realized as he reached him. Noah spoke!

When he got to Noah, Declan halted his horse, then bent and lifted his son onto his horse. Noah shook in his arms and cried.

"Noah, lad, what happened? Are ye hurt?"

"Bel…la…Bella…" the boy gasped with panting breaths.

Declan's heart fell to his stomach, which churned with sudden terror as if all of the danger he'd sensed that day had materialized there in one solid mass. "Isabella? Where is she?"

"Hurt…loch. Si…Si…" Noah held him as though if he let go, he'd succumb to the fear that gripped him.

Declan shouted for his men, turned his mount, and rode swiftly toward the loch. Near to the water, he dismounted with his son still in his arms. He placed Noah on the grassy bank. "Stay put, lad."

What he saw sickened him. His stepbrother was holding Isabella under the water. Her long blond tresses floated on the surface, but she was still. Something within him erupted. Rage. Fury. Intense ire. Whatever it was caused Declan to pull his sword free and run at Silas. But his good sense overtook him before he reached the knave and Declan tossed his sword on the bank. Saving Isabella was more important than seeking retribution at this moment.

He raced into the loch, running hard to fight the hold of the water on his legs and feet. It seemed to take forever but probably was only moments—Silas didn't even turn to look at him but continued to concentrate on his grim task.

When Declan reached his stepbrother, he shoved him aside and reached beneath the water for Isabella. He grabbed hold of her garment and pulled her to the surface. She didn't appear to be breathing. It was just like Leona all over again, and for a moment, he saw both of his wives before him, still in the water.

Nay! He lifted her and rushed to the bank where he set her on the grass, spread her arms, and pressed on her chest. Hastily, he pushed aside the strands of her hair and knew only one way to get her breathing again. Declan rolled her onto her side, stuck his finger in her mouth, and forced her to gag. Water spewed out and she began coughing. Declan rubbed her back with forceful strokes to encourage her to inhale and yet expel the water that filled her lungs.

"Ye are going to be all right, lass. Take easy breaths." Declan leaned over her and continued to rub his hand in a circular motion on her back. He couldn't believe what had happened to her. "Where the hell is Lorcan? He was supposed to be protecting you!" Declan scanned the area, but his soldier was nowhere to be seen. Instead, he noticed his grandmother who reached the area and stood by with her hand on her heart, looking forlornly at the scene before her. His men, too, had begun to arrive and were gathered around in a protective ring.

At the same time, he saw Silas, scurrying away like the rat he was. Declan motioned to his men who stood beyond watching and waiting for direction. Four of his men formed a wall and wouldn't let Silas pass them. Two others took hold of his arms and held him forcibly.

Noah pushed past the men, looking tiny next to the fierce warriors. But there was something about him now. The way he seemed to look past them as though everyone was gone, and it was only him and his son. He was present and here, involved in the situation. He reached Declan and touched his face while looking down at Isabella, his small face showing concern. "Da..." he said.

Declan pulled Noah into a hug and caressed his hair. "Noah, lad. Are you harmed? Did he hurt ye?"

"He...He pushed me. I fell and hit my head. I remember now."

He wasn't sure what Noah was trying to tell him. Declan pressed a hand on his son's head again. It was a miracle. "What do ye remember?"

"Mama. I remember he came and..." Noah motioned to Silas. "She said no. But he made her swim. Then she stopped. He is a bad man."

Declan had to clarify what his wee son was telling him. It was inconceivable, and yet he knew in his heart that it was true. "Silas intentionally hurt your mother?"

"Aye. She told me to run, to get ye. But he pushed me. The rock hit my head. I do not remember what happened after that. I think I fell 'sleep. But when I woke up...Mama...she floated in the water." Noah sniffled and looked forlornly at Isabella. "Bella floated." He paused. "Mama died. Is Bella going to die too?"

Isabella groaned and opened her eyes. "No, she is not," she said with a raspy voice and rolled onto her back to give his son a little smile to show she was well, reaching out to take Noah's hand.

"Bella!" Noah flung himself over her body and wept. Isabella wrapped her arms around him, and Declan could hear her sobbing. He wanted to weep as well, but anger had a hold on him, now that he knew his wife was alive.

And knew who had murdered his first wife.

Conflicting emotions—thankfulness and extreme rage—warred within him. Eventually, the knowledge that Isabella survived and that he had his son back made him realize what was truly important. He was grateful, above all. Noah had spoken—in full! And could hear and understand what had been said. God be praised. His son was healed!

"Lorcan," Isabella said, sounding like a frog. Her voice rasped and she spoke so low, he almost hadn't heard her. "He...was...there." She pointed to a copse of trees a short distance from the bank.

Declan turned to look at his men. "Two of ye search for Lorcan. He should be there, by those trees," he said. Then he returned his attention to Isabella. "Are ye all right? I cannot bear to see you like this...harmed."

"Sorry," she said with a small smile. Isabella continued to hold Noah and he continued to hold her. The three of them sat there for a long moment in silence, holding each other.

"Ye have naught to be sorry for, wife. I should apologize to ye for not being here, for protecting ye from that vile piece of cosh." Declan gave her time to recover enough for him to lift her into his arms. "Noah, stand back, lad. I need to get Isabella back to the cottage so Edith can see to her." His son stood aside and waited for him. Declan carried her and walked past his men who continued to hold Silas who struggled and looked sullen but didn't raise his eyes as they moved by. "Have him taken to the pit. I will deal with him later."

Anse appeared then, breathing hard. "I was helping in the fields. But Slone came and got me and told me that... I just heard that Isabella was...attacked. Is she all right? What happened?"

"She is well enough now. I will tell ye about it later. For now, see that Silas is put in the pit. Make sure he does not escape."

Anse nodded. His eyes were hard as he peered over at Declan's stepbrother. He growled, "I will watch the snake myself. Come and find me when ye are able."

"Aye, Anse, I will. I need to make sure Isabella is warmed." Even as he spoke, he felt her shiver in his arms and he tightened his grasp about her. "Then I will see to my…to *him*." He couldn't even bring himself to say *stepbrother*. The man was no kin of his and he would never say so again. He was vile.

Isabella trembled again. Declan tugged at his upper tartan and set it around her. "I am here, love. There is no need to be fearful now."

She set her head on his shoulder and pressed her hand on his neck. "Declan."

In no time, he reached their cottage, Noah trailing close behind. When they arrived, Declan forced the door open with his foot. He did the same to their bedchamber door and gently set Isabella in the center of their bed. His son didn't leave them. Instead, he stood by the bed with wide, watchful eyes.

"Go, lad, and find Edith. Tell her Isabella needs her."

Noah nodded and turned to leave the room. But then the lad spun back, raced to the bed, and jumped up to give Isabella a kiss on the cheek. "I will be right back!" he announced before he raced off to get Edith.

Isabella closed her eyes. Declan watched her chest rising and falling, so he didn't fall apart as he suspected he might, otherwise. As he watched her sleeping and breathing, he couldn't wipe away the thought that that despicable knave murdered his wife, hurt his son, and tried to kill his new wife. Wrath such as he never felt burned his eyes and tensed every part of him.

Edith rushed into the room, Noah on her heels, and her breath heavy from her mad dash. "Noah spoke to me! He told me that Milady was hurt. Laird, is she…?"

"Nay, she breathes. Silas tried to drown her in the loch. I was able to get her to bring up most of the water. I'll have Lillith fetched so she can check her over. It'll take the healer some time to get here. Will ye stay with her? I do not want to leave Isabella alone."

"I shall. Go on, Laird, I'll see to her now. I shall bathe her, make her comfortable, and tend to her. Ye see to your duties." Edith didn't give him another moment's attention when she began removing Isabella's sodden garments.

"Come on, lad." He put his hand on Noah's shoulder and with hesitation on both their parts, they left the room. Together, they stood in the long hallway. Unable to stand still, nevertheless full of anxiety and feelings that made him want to run to confront Silas, but unwilling to leave his wife for long, he began to pace from one end to the other. It didn't escape his notice that his son followed in his footsteps. The poor lad probably had the same feelings running through him. Imagine how he—and everyone, really—had ignored the lad, thinking him beyond sense or communication. Because of Silas. And all those years of thinking that Leona had drowned in a dreadful accident, when in fact she had been murdered.

The poor lass. And their poor son.

Declan couldn't help but hold the culpability for her death. He should have known what was happening and protected her. And this day, if he'd dallied any longer on his trek home from the Campbells, he would likely be burying another wife.

More rage than he'd ever felt spurred him to breathe heavily through his nose so as not to punch a wall and perhaps frighten his son. With that thought in mind, Declan fisted his hands, tried to calm himself, and kept pacing with Noah as his shadow.

The door to his chamber opened and Edith appeared to stand in the opening. "She is not ailing, Laird, just tired from the excitement. Milady just needs a hot bath—not one in the loch— and warm garments. I shall ask one of the girls to heat up some water while I fix her a cup of warm chamomile with honey. That shall soothe her throat. Stay here until I return." She hurried past him and didn't wait for his response.

He looked down at his son, who peered up at him expectantly. "Well, then, lad," he said, and lifted his son in his arms to give him a hug of comfort. As he did so, the lad wrapped his arms around his neck and his legs around his waist. Absurd how the gesture meant to comfort his son comforted him in return.

He peered into the bedchamber to see Isabella curled on the bed, apparently asleep. She wasn't shivering anymore, at least, so he decided to leave her be while he continued to pace the hallway, holding Noah. More questions rankled him. Questions he would soon get the answers to, like was Silas behind the accusation that caused his incarceration? Was he the man behind the threat of trying to overtake his clan and the Campbells? He would question the knave as soon as Edith returned.

Finally, Edith returned with two servants. They carried buckets of warm water and Edith herself held an overlarge tray.

"My thanks, Edith, for your aid."

"Worry naught for her, Laird. Go on with you now. I know ye have things to see to and Milady would not want ye to shirk your duty because of her."

"Noah, stay here with Isabella. I will return as soon as I can." He set the lad down inside the doorway. He brushed his hand over his son's hair. "I will be back, lad. You stay here with my— with Isabella and Edith." With that, he gave a look to Edith. She'd watch his son, he knew, as she nodded at his silent command.

Declan practically sprinted from the cottage to head to the pit. Behind the large stone building that housed the soldiers, it held the clan's criminals. Rarely did they use it, but it was put to good use this day. Declan rounded the barracks and found half the men in his army standing guard. Anse bowed his head to him when he stopped next to him.

"Laird, he is in there but has not spoken," Anse said and handed him his sword. "Ye left this by the loch."

Declan wanted to keep hold of his sword, and his fingers tightened around the hilt. But he needed answers. It was best to conduct his questioning without a formidable mien and he sheathed his sword lest he be tempted to use it.

His men removed the iron grate at the top of the pit and pulled Silas from the deep hole by way of a rope that they had tied around his waist. When Silas reached the top, they dragged him until he lay before Declan's feet. Silas's hands and feet were bound. That wouldn't do. Declan wanted to face his adversary with honor and wouldn't strike down a man who was bound.

"Unbind him," he commanded.

Two of his men used their daggers to cut the ties at Silas's hands and feet. His stepbrother got to his feet to stand before him with hatred burning in his eyes. Declan probably wore the same look, but he tried to maintain a calm exterior. For now, he just wanted answers. He would get his vengeance once everything in the past—and the present—had been explained.

"Silas, ye will tell me truthfully… Why? Why did ye murder Leona? Why did ye try to murder Isabella?"

"Because I wished to hurt ye," Silas ground out with venom in his tone.

"But there are many ways to hurt me. Why take the lives of two innocent women? Are ye that envious? Make me understand." Declan was surprised that his voice didn't falter when he posed his questions. Tears choked his throat like a fist.

Silas's eyes flashed. "Ye do not deserve them," he scoffed. "I saw how ye ignored Leona and now how ye do the same to Isabella. I only wanted their affection since ye cared not about them." He appeared oblivious to the fact that Declan's hand hovered over the handle of his sword. It would only take a false word or movement, Declan realized, before he drew his blade and struck. He took a deep, steadying breath.

"How I am with my wife should not concern ye. Ye, who are vile, willing to hurt a woman akin to the way you did Leona. Ye murdered her, drowning her in the loch, taking her life."

"It could not be helped. She kept screaming. I could not let her call the guard. I had to stop her from screaming." Silas pressed his hands over his ears and his eyes bulged as if even now he could hear her.

Declan felt no pity for him. "Are ye behind the accusation that caused me to be imprisoned in the king's dungeon?"

"Nay," Silas said assuredly.

"Tell me why I should believe ye."

Silas gripped his hair and practically spit when he answered, "I speak the truth. Aye, I would make a better laird than ye, but I was willing to wait for it. I figured that eventually ye would make an enemy ye could not defeat."

Declan scoffed. "Aye, so ye did not plan to do away with me to gain the lairdship? Were ye also intent to overtake the Campbells?"

Silas shook his head vehemently. "Nay, nay, why would I? I have no interest in the Campbell Clan. Never have I hoped to gain anything from the Campbells. I tell ye, I am not the accuser. I did not try to kill ye in the woods, and I am not trying to overtake the MacKendricks. Ye can either believe me, or not. I care naught."

Declan drew his sword, and it sang its vibrant *"shhgging!"* sound, scraping against the sharpener set in the scabbard. His prized weapon would seek his vengeance for him this day. Declan braced his legs and stood in an unmistakable stance with his sword pointed at the miscreant. His body tensed in anticipation of jumping forward to enact the one thrust—ending Silas' life, once and for all.

He would kill the knave, but before he would, he wanted the answer to his last question. "Did ye leave a dead rat in my bedchamber?"

Silas laughed derisively. "Aye, aye. I hoped to frighten your wife enough to seek my embrace, but alas she did not." He shrugged his shoulders. "What does it matter? Now either kill me or set me free."

Declan's hand gripped the hilt of his sword, and he used all the force within him to shove it through Silas's chest. His stepbrother fell backward with a forceful grunt and blood pulsed from the wound with each beat of his dying heart, pooling in a great dark puddle on the ground next to him.

"Good riddance," Anse said and spat on him.

The rest of his clansmen did the same, one by one passing their foe and showing the disrespect Silas deserved.

Declan gave his stepbrother a final stare before he said, "Have him taken to the ravine and tossed into it. He does not deserve a proper burial."

He turned and began to walk slowly away, unsure if he felt vindicated. Had Silas spoken truthfully or not? Even if he hadn't been Declan's accuser or the traitor trying to overtake his clan, his stepbrother deserved to die for taking Leona's life and trying to drown Isabella. Added to the years of difficulty his son endured…

Silas was now at unrest in Hell, where he belonged.

He raised his eyes to the sky. "Ye can rest in peace now, Leona, sweet lass. I have avenged ye." With that, he lowered his head and drew a heavy breath. He heard the mumbles of approval and support from his clansmen and turned to find them nodding. Some had their heads bowed in respect of his words for Leona.

Anse stood with a bowed head and waited until he approached him. "Silas was a sneaky son-of-a-bitch. We did not know what he was up to. I was with the soldiers and because Lorcan guarded Milady, I did not worry for her. I should have put more men on her. God Almighty, what he did to her… I cannot forgive myself."

He set a hand on his cousin's shoulder. "Do not hold yourself in contempt, my friend. None of us knew what Silas did to Leona or what he intended to do to Isabella. Where is Lorcan? I want to question him."

Anse lowered his chin. "He is dead, Laird. Silas killed him with a dagger in his back. Lorcan probably never saw the attack coming."

Another person to grieve, another person lost because of

Silas's envy and evil plans. "We will place him with honor, Anse. See the friar and Claude about burial preparations." He sighed and lifted his chin with an effort. It had been a trying day, almost as difficult as one spent in battle. "Now, I need to see my wife."

"Tell her I am sorry, Laird."

"Nay, if ye want to apologize, Anse, ye should come and do it yourself but there is no need. Ye are not guilty of her attack. Isabella would not want ye to hold yourself accountable."

"Nay, but I should have prevented it."

"As should I have." Declan understood how his cousin felt. The responsibility and safety of their clan's men and women rested on their shoulders. That they had a villainous knave within their midst sat afoul.

By the time Declan had reached his bedchamber, his tension had eased, and he'd shaken off the torment of killing his foe. Quietly, he entered the room where he found Noah sitting next to Isabella on the bed. She was dressed in a clean nightrail and lay back against the pillows with her eyes closed. Edith was in a nearby chair. She, too, appeared to be sleeping. But as he drew closer to the bed, she opened her eyes and got to her feet.

Edith bowed to him. "She is resting now, Laird. I do not deem she suffered much. Ye were in good time to get her from the water. I shall leave ye but there will be a maid in the hallway. Shout if you need anything."

"My thanks, Edith," he said.

With that, Declan removed his boots and upper tartan, discarding both beside the bed. With haste, he washed in the basin, calming even further as the clean water eased him. He crawled onto the bed next to Noah and pressed a hand to his wee face.

"Da, Edith says she is well."

"Aye, we are blessed that she is."

Noah set his small hand in his and Declan peered at it.

"I am sorry, Da."

Declan pulled his son across his chest. "Ye have no reason to be sorry. I think ye were brave, aye. Tell me what happened at the loch that day…the day your mother drowned."

Noah sniffled and began to talk. Slowly at first, with hesitations and fits and starts as he seemed to search for words long denied him. But before long he was speaking freely, recalling in detail everything that had happened from the moment Silas had forced his mother into the water to when Noah was shoved away and fell.

Isabella opened her eyes but was silent. Instead, she watched them.

He returned her gaze. "Silas cannot hurt ye or Isabella anymore."

"Where is Silas?" Isabella asked.

Declan reached across Noah and clasped her hand. "He is gone, love. Ye will never have to lay eyes on him again."

"Gone?"

"He has been removed from MacKendrick land." Declan wasn't sure he should tell her the truth that the man was dead. She was a sensitive lass, with a Christian's forgiving heart, and he wouldn't have her grieving for the knave. If he knew Isabella, he suspected she would be in the chapel praying for the deliverance of the miscreant's soul, and Silas didn't deserve anyone's prayers.

Noah swiped his hand beneath his nose. "There was someone else there, Da, the day mama died. I remember seeing a man standing by the trees watching."

Declan peered at his son and tried to discern what he was saying. "A man? Who was it?"

Noah shrugged. "I do not know. He was not from our clan and wore a different color tartan. He had dark hair though, and I saw him talking to Silas before we walked to the loch, mama and me."

So, the villain hadn't worked alone. Declan wasn't able to enjoy peace then. There was more to do. He nodded to him. "You did good, lad. If you remember anything else…or if you see this man again, you need to come and find me."

"I will, Da."

The need for vengeance would continue to plague him though because there was still one more knave to thwart—the dark-haired man who'd apparently watched Silas murder his wife. If only he knew who it was who wanted to overtake the MacKendricks and the Campbells.

Right now, however, Declan only wanted to hold Isabella and Noah. Vengeance needed to wait.

CHAPTER TWENTY-ONE

ISABELLA OPENED HER eyes and glanced at the window in the bedchamber. It was still dark out. She lay there wondering where Declan was. Last she recalled, he and Noah rested beside her. They weren't there now. She stretched and got up to hurry through her washing and dressing. Before she left the bedchamber, she ran her fingers through her hair. Lord, she probably looked a mess.

In the hallway that led to the main living area, she stopped and listened, but it was quiet. At the massive table by the hearth, she paused to snatch a soft piece of bread from the trencher in its center. Her stomach rumbled because she hadn't eaten a meal since the day before.

"Oh, there ye be," came the familiar cold voice from behind her.

Isabella turned to see Lady MacKendrick standing there. "Good morn."

"Good morn? You mean eve. Ye slept all day. Ye are the laziest harridan. I have been working all day whilst ye have been lazing in your bed."

She knew that couldn't be true because the woman barely lifted a finger to care for the upkeep of the cottage. Isabella quickly swallowed the bit of bread she'd placed in her mouth and rounded the table to put more space between them.

"It is your fault. Why did ye have to come here and lure my son to wanting ye? I hold ye accountable for his death and now ye will pay for it." Helena walked slowly around the table and picked up a supper dagger. She held it in her fist and stared at her.

Isabella's heart raced at the sight of the maddened woman. She continued to move around the table, keeping a good distance from her.

The door slammed and Isabella glanced toward it. Declan stood there with a fierce scowl on his face. He marched to Lady MacKendrick and took her neck in his hand. He squeezed and his jaw flexed with his exertion.

"Ye are the vilest woman alive. I do not know why my da cared for you. Ye are akin to your son, uncaring for anyone but yourself. I told ye if ye cannot respect my wife, I would remove you." Declan wouldn't release the woman. She gasped and clutched at his arm, trying to get him to let her go.

Isabella sidled next to Declan and placed a gentle hand on her husband's arm. "MacKendricks do not kill women."

"There is always a first time," he gritted out.

"No matter how foul the woman is, you shouldn't kill her. Declan, release her. Please." She pulled his arm, and he released Lady MacKendrick.

Helena gasped, bent over, and held her throat. "Ye! Ye are the vile one. I heard ye murdered my son outright. Aye, ye killed him."

Isabella was surprised that Declan remained still. She had never seen him more intense or violent.

"Aye, I killed the miscreant. Your son murdered Leona, hurt my son, and tried to drown Isabella. He was fortunate that I did not slay him at the loch. Ye, Mistress, will be taken to the border of my land and be left there. If ye step a foot on my land in the future, I will not stay my hand. Do ye understand?"

"But I have nowhere to go. Ye cannot make me leave." Helena rasped and straightened. "Your da promised me that I would always have a place here."

"That was before your son killed my first wife and threatened my second. Now my da is dead and his promises with him. I took care of ye out of honor to him, but now I know ye have no decency. He would be ashamed of ye. I care naught where ye go, but ye will be removed from my land before dawn."

Declan shouted "guards" and two men hastened inside the cottage. "Attend this woman while she packs her belongings. She is to be taken to the border of our land and left there. See it done before the sun rises."

The soldiers took Helena's arms even as she continued to complain. Isabella stood by the table, not sure of what to say to Declan. She understood the reasons for his hatred toward Lady MacKendrick. She didn't like the woman much either, but still, to have her banished perhaps was a little too harsh. Yet she knew that in this instance, it wouldn't be right to say so to her husband. They stood in silence until the soldiers passed by with Helena and the door to the cottage closed.

Declan took slow steps toward her. "How are ye? Ye should probably be abed."

Isabella opened her arms to him when he reached her. She thought he'd be tense with ire or shaking from dealing with the horrid woman. But all Isabella sensed from him was his gentle arms holding her. Even his heart beat in a rhythmic lethargy. She kept her cheek pressed against his chest and wanted to stay that way, protected.

"I was hungry," she said when she finally found her voice.

"Ye should return to bed, love." He rested his head on hers and continued to hold her.

"I am well, Declan. Even my throat is returned to normal thanks to Edith's concoction."

Declan pressed her back, then touched her chin with his fingertips and lifted it until she looked into his eyes. "I suppose ye are hungry since ye missed last eve's meal, the morn and mid-day meal too. Come and sit at the table. I will get ye something to eat." Even as he offered, he refused to release her, and she continued to hold him.

Their moment alone was suddenly invaded. Edith strolled into the room, holding a tray of foodstuff on her hip. She set it on the table and smiled at them. Noah followed behind her, skipping into the room, and as soon as he saw Isabella, he rushed forward to wrap his arms around her and Declan both, as far as he could reach. Isabella returned his embrace with her closest arm and after a moment, Declan let her go with one arm and dropped it down to hold onto the lad in their three-way hug.

Anse opened the door to the cottage and marched forward. He bowed to her and then to Declan. "I am here for the meeting, Laird," he said and snatched a roll from the basket.

"Sit first and have your supper with us." Declan let go of them and helped Isabella sit on the closest bench. Noah scrambled to sit beside her as Declan set a trencher in front of her. "Edith, will ye bring a jug of wine to the table?" He sat down beside her as Anse dropped onto the bench on the other side of the table.

"Ye never drink wine. Is this a special occasion?" Isabella hadn't ever seen her husband partake of wine, only mead, ale and whatever was in Anse's flask. But she favored wine, so she was pleased to have it with her supper. She filled her trencher with the delicious-looking bread and stew and peered at the food.

"Aye, we are celebrating the completion of our home. Anse has come to report on the latest and we are going to discuss when we can move in," Declan explained.

Isabella wondered what kind of meat was in the stew. "Is this chicken?"

Edith set a cup of wine before her. "Oh, nay, Milady. Venison. The men hunted yestereve and brought back enough meat to fill our stores for winter."

"But it's only late summer." Isabella almost gagged at the scent. She hastily pushed the trencher away. Never fond of the meat, it was worse now and smelled wretched. Her stomach coiled and she couldn't get the smell out of her nose.

Declan pulled her trencher back to her. "Ye need to eat, love."

"I cannot stomach venison right now. I will just have bread."

When Edith heard her, she returned to the table. "There's leftover pottage from the midday meal. I shall get you some, Milady." She took the trencher away and hurried from the room.

"Are we really going to live in that monstrosity?" she posed the question to Declan.

"That monstrosity is necessary for the protection of my family."

"Da, can I go to Gran's?" Noah asked.

Declan nodded and smiled at him. "Have Slone take ye. Ye will stay there this night and be a good lad for your gran."

Before Noah vacated the room, he approached her. "Milady, I am glad ye wasna hurt. Next time, I will protect ye."

His promise was sweet, but Isabella hoped with all her heart that she didn't need saving again. She took his hand and squeezed it, tears forming in her eyes. His words made her want to bawl with happiness. "You are gallant, Noah, and I'm glad you can hear again."

"Will ye sing to me again?"

"If it pleases you. Perhaps on the morrow, we shall spend the morning together."

He bowed to her. "Milady, I would like that," he said, then turned and fled.

Declan chuckled. "He has been mimicking the soldiers all day. I told him to emulate them, and he has taken it to heart."

Isabella wanted to weep. Her heart burst with joy to see the lad speaking and hearing. She was amazed at how clear his voice sounded. It was remarkable that he hadn't suffered any permanent damage.

"He will be well enough, wife. Do not worry about him. Cease your weeping."

"I am just so…happy." She pressed her eyes to stop tears from gathering. "Now what is this about us moving into the monstrosity?"

Edith returned and placed a small trencher of chopped chicken with chunks of pears and some kind of small bean. "This should help your ailing stomach, Milady."

Isabella drew in the delicious scent of the meal. "It looks tasty." She devoured the meal within a moment. When she had time, she would ask the cook what it was and would ask her to make it for her again.

Anse had remained quiet until now. "The thatchers are putting the last roofs on the outbuildings. On the morrow, they will move the kitchen. That'll take a fortnight at least. But ye will have the small kitchen area at the back of the fief to use until the kitchen is moved."

"Good," Declan said. "And the inside? Are all the doors on the chambers?"

"Aye, the carpenter finished that task this day. He should be putting on the window coverings and finishing up some areas of flooring. All should be ready within the sennight." Anse lifted his cup of wine. "Your new home awaits, Laird."

"On the morrow, love, we can take a walk through it. It might look like a monstrosity, but it will be our home. Ye shall make it so."

She smiled lightly at his compliment. "You have much faith in me, Husband."

"Aye, I do." Declan grinned at her and raised his cup to her before taking a sip.

A soldier peeked his head inside the door. "Laird."

Declan stood. "All stay. I will return."

Alone with Anse, Isabella thought the man was being too quiet and solemn. It wasn't like Anse at all. "What is wrong with you? Why are you being so reserved?"

Anse shrugged. "'Tis the truth I hold a wee bit of guilt for what happened to ye, Milady."

"Oh, Anse, you shouldn't. I should have told Declan that the man was untrustworthy. I sensed it right off, but I wasn't sure if

Declan admired his stepbrother. I didn't want to ruin their relationship if he cared for Silas. It is not your fault and as you can see, I am well."

"I do not deserve your forgiveness, Milady. I must ensure your safety when our laird is not here." Anse's mouth set grimly. "I failed ye."

"My forgiveness is unnecessary. Now, cease this silliness. You did not fail me. You will not be plagued by what that wretched man did. That is the end of it." Isabella raised her voice slightly to effectuate his accord. "Before you go, Anse, I wanted to ask you something…"

"Aye, Milady, what is it?"

"If I wanted to irritate Declan…What would annoy him?"

"Ye want to displease your husband?" he asked with astonishment.

Isabella held in her laughter at the man's shock. "Well, mildly. Tell me, what would annoy him. Is there something that would bother him and raise his ire?"

Anse seemed to ponder her question. "He has a fondness for his family. If someone threatened his family, he would be ireful."

"I know that, Anse. No, I don't mean anything of that sort. Is he possessive of anything?"

Anse chuckled. "Ye."

She laughed and shook her head. "Besides me."

"I do not understand why ye are asking me this but there is his sword. I am the only one who has ever touched it besides him. Declan is superstitious about his sword. A soldier's sword is akin to his woman. He handles it with great care, shows it affection, and depends on it for his well-being. If someone were to move it, touch it, or God forbid, destroy it, he would be full of wrath."

"Oh, that is quite helpful. My thanks."

"Now, now, Milady, do not go and do anything to your husband's sword. It cost him a good bit of coin when he had it made. Aye, he has had it for years and is fond of it."

"I don't plan to do anything with it. Worry not, Anse." Isabella rose and piled the trenchers. She placed them on a smaller table for Edith to discard. As much as she tried to fill her time, Declan hadn't returned. Anse left after a short while, excusing himself with a short bow, and she returned to her bedchamber to await her husband.

Isabella undressed and lay on the bed. She could have laughed at Anse's reaction to her asking him what would anger Declan. Her reasoning was simple: she wanted to irritate him enough to have him be rough with her again. She longed to respond like she had when he was demanding.

In time, she heard Declan's footsteps in the hallway outside of their chamber and in no time, Declan opened the door. His eyes instantly found hers. Quietly, he closed the door and stood rigidly, watching her. Isabella almost read his thoughts because a desirous mien overtook his gaze. He began to approach the bed, and as he did so, he removed his garments. She marveled at the view of his body. Taut muscles, steely arms, strong thighs, and lovely manliness met her gaze.

He pulled back the bedcover and lay next to her. Declan reached to extinguish the candle on the table by the bedside, but she stopped him.

"Leave the candle lit, please."

"Why? I like it dark when we sleep."

She exhaled with a light laugh. "Do you really plan to sleep?"

Declan grunted. "Ye were almost killed yestereve."

"Almost. I am well, truly, Declan. There is nothing wrong with me. I want you."

He groaned and turned on his side. "I do not want to hurt ye."

"Please…" She pleaded in her most teasing tone.

Declan leaned over her and set his mouth on hers. The pleasure of his kiss swarmed through her body. She needed, wanted, and craved his touch. Having him in her arms again thoroughly aroused her. Declan was a sweet lover and easily spurred her lust. Their kiss lingered for a long moment until she pulled away and pushed his body back.

"Let me," she said. "I cannot wait, Declan. I need you now."

Declan eased back and watched her with hooded eyes. "Do ye now?" He spread his arms wide and grinned. "Do as ye will, love."

Isabella straddled his body. She pressed her hands over his rigid torso to his strong neck and caressed him. Purposely, she kept her breasts within his mouth's reach. Declan easily followed her lead and took her hardened nipple in his mouth. Isabella groaned. The exquisite sensation brought on twinges deep within her.

"I am not going to last…" Isabella took hold of his manhood and shifted to help him enter her. She huffed at the intensity of it. With her eyes closed, she propelled her body to take him in, thrusting hard against his erection and within seconds a rush of culmination swarmed her. She couldn't breathe, think, or move, but fell against Declan in a heap of well-pleasured bliss.

He tenderly kissed her shoulder. "Ye are the fairest of lasses, love, when ye come undone."

Isabella breathed hard and kept her head against his shoulder. When she'd calmed enough, she raised her face and kissed him with all the passion coursing through her. He yanked her to him, easing himself from her, and rolled her onto her back. She squealed lightly but instantly wrapped her legs around his hips.

Declan set light kisses over her face, neck, and chest. His rough hands caressed her arms and body. When he entered her the second time, she moaned. He held her legs almost above her body and thrust hard until his breath came heavily.

Isabella couldn't control her desire and another maddening climax overtook her. She cried out at the bliss and tilted her head back. She gripped her calves and kept her position, delighting in the view of him as he neared ecstasy. His handsome face tightened as the first wave of his climax consumed him. Isabella released her legs and set her hand on his face. She roamed her hand over his body but when she reached the pounding of his heart, she stilled and took pleasure in feeling his excitement.

Declan moaned deeply and came undone. She soothed him by whispering how much she liked what he'd done, how her body still twinged. The aftermath of their loving was just as pleasurable as the act itself. Isabella would never tire of him, and she shook the thought of love from her mind. She never believed a person could love another and that it was a senseless emotion. Isabella always thought love was for fools. She now realized she was the biggest fool of them all.

"Good Lord, woman, you are going to slay me."

Isabella giggled. "I like being with you…like this."

He grunted. "And I you, love."

She lay next to him and meandered her fingers over the sparse hairs on his chest. "Can we ever do it like we did that night in the cottage?"

Declan didn't glance at her but pressed his hand over her arm. "A husband does not take his wife that way. Husbands make love to their wives. What ye are suggesting is that we make war."

"Oh, I love the sound of that. Will you make war with me again?"

Declan moaned. "Wife, cease this talk. I will not take ye in anger again, so nay, we will never make war again."

Isabella pouted. Somehow, she had to get Declan to understand that war was exactly what she wanted. She wanted his rough hands on her. Even though he had more than pleasured her by making love to her, she wanted more. She wanted war and Isabella knew exactly how to obtain it. It would take a little cunning on her part and the use of his sword.

CHAPTER TWENTY-TWO

DECLAN WAS UP and at his duties before the sun rose. There was much to accomplish. He met with the seasoned soldiers in his army and directed them to work with the less experienced soldiers. He needed his men ready in case he had to confront his enemy's army.

Anse stood beside him after he dismissed the regiment. "Ye do not think Silas was behind the false accusation then? I swore it was him."

"Noah told me someone else was there when Leona was killed by Silas. Someone with a different tartan than ours. I wonder if this man instigated Silas for his purposes."

Anse grunted. "Ye mean he used Silas to bring ye low by murdering your wife?"

Declan set his hand on his chin. "Aye. Wee by wee he wanted to see me tormented."

"There have been no clashes with other clans currently. The king favored ye by marrying ye to one of the lassies. Who detests ye that much? I cannot think of anyone that hates ye."

Neither could he, but Declan was certain someone wanted his life destroyed before he overtook his and Campbell's clans. He wasn't aware of anything he'd done to warrant such a retribution. He would have to set his mind to thinking about his da. Perhaps his father had wronged someone, and they sought retribution against him through his son. Wars betwixt clans often spanned the life of their leaders and beyond to their heirs.

"Anse, see that triple the guard is posted around our walls. And ensure the sentry is sent out frequently. There is great need and I want us protected."

"The guard has been tripled but I will see to it that the sentry makes more rounds, Laird. Is that why ye wanted to move into the new dwelling? Ye fear we will be besieged?"

Declan shrugged. "Alert the clan to be guarded. If we are besieged, I want my clan safe. I also want Isabella and Noah protected. The fief would do well to protect us. Whoever is out to destroy me could easily use my family to get to me. My wife has suffered enough thanks to Silas and his horrid mother."

"I will go and see to it at once."

Before Anse left, he asked him, "Is Isabella at the new keep?"

His commander nodded. "Aye, she has been there most of the morning. Slone still remains at his post, and I checked in with him earlier. When will Trevor return?"

"Lillith has not said when Trevor will be healed enough to move. I want more men put in position around the keep. See that at least ten men guard my home. And now, I should go and see what my sweet wife is up to."

But before Declan could set off to the keep, a guard shouted his name. He hurried to the gate and met with the lead guardsman.

"This just arrived for Milady, Laird." He handed him a sealed parchment.

Declan studied the writing and discerned that it must be a missive from her parents. He thanked the guard and walked hastily to the new keep. With a nod to Slone, he took the steps and entered. Isabella stood in the great hall and shook out a large tapestry that had been given to them by Marian. It was beautifully sewn with his clan's crest on it.

The two young soldiers whom he had entrusted to help Isabella set the furnishings stood by, listening to her directions.

"It should be placed betwixt those windows there," she said and pointed to the center of the large wall that flanked the room.

"Wife," he called.

She turned to him, and he found his first smile of the day. Lord, she was bonny, and he was enthralled being in her presence. Declan almost scoffed at himself because it was obvious that not only did he care about the woman, but she mattered a great deal to him. He was beginning to realize his heart was fully committed.

"There you are. I wondered where you had gotten to. The great hall is almost finished. Once we get the tapestry hung, the lads will bring in the trestle table and chairs."

"Ye have done well, Wife." He took her hand and brushed a bit of dust from her cheek. "Ye are not working too hard, are ye?"

"Nay, they won't let me lift a finger," she said with disgruntlement. Isabella tilted her head in the direction of the young soldiers.

"Good, they are doing as they were directed. I only stopped in to see ye and to make sure Noah was not being troublesome or in the way."

Isabella smiled at him splendidly. "I sent him off to Marian's. He was bored and I had nothing for him to do. Besides, I could get more done without him underfoot."

"That was a fair idea, love." Declan reached into his tunic and pulled out the missive she'd received. "I almost forgot, this arrived for you." He handed it to her.

"It must be from my parents. I shall read it later." She tucked the missive into the seam of her overdress.

"I should go."

Isabella grabbed his hand before he moved away. "Await. Would it be all right if I gave away a few things we don't need or want?"

"I suppose. If ye do not think we need or want them, then ye can give them away. It matters not to me." Declan gave her a quick peck on her cheek and strolled away.

How sweet was she to think of others? He almost returned to her and would have snatched her hand to lead her to a private place within the keep, but he didn't want to distract her. Instead, he made his way to his cottage. He wanted to speak to Rhona. He hadn't talked to her since his return and there was much to discuss. He found her in the front room working on a bit of sewing. "Lass, I wanted to ask you…"

She got out of her chair in a hurry and stood before him. "Laird, good morn."

"We have not discussed your wedding. I was thinking of having it during the harvest festival. What say ye to this?"

She looked up at him with sparkling, happy eyes. "Willeli would like to do it soon, as would I. The harvest festival is only a fortnight from now. Perhaps we can do it in the morn *before* the celebrations begin?"

It was a fair request. He nodded. "I will speak to the friar and ask him to perform the sacrament."

"You have made me happy, Declan. Da would be so proud of you. It is also nice to see marriage agreeing with you. Marriage is not easy."

Declan's brows drew together at her declaration. "How would ye know about such things?"

Rhona chuckled. "I was always underfoot when Da and Ma argued. They never noticed me, and I overheard every word. Sometimes they shouted fiercely at each other but the next day, they appeared to have made amends. I was young then and do not recall what their arguments were about, but they fought terribly."

He grimaced. "Do ye remember a time when it was heated to the point that it was possible they did not make amends?"

"I was just a lass and didn't understand much of what they argued about. But I recall once that Da accused Ma of being with another man. She denied it, of course, but Da said he had proof. It took almost a month before Da forgave Ma. I remember because that was right before Ma died."

Declan couldn't recall how his mother passed. He had been training with the soldiers and spent little time at home. He'd only been told that his mother had died. "How did she die?"

"The healer could not find the cause and declared that ma's heart gave out."

He shook his head. His mother was a strong woman and hadn't ever shown signs of being ill. Something strange was afoot then. It was too late now to figure out what passed between his parents. Still, it gave him pause because it could be the reason why he now faced an unknown adversary.

Without a farewell, Declan wandered outside and strolled along toward the chapel, perplexed by his conversation with Rhona. He needed to give it more thought. At the chapel, he pulled the door open and entered. He was met by the sound of a harpist playing a beautiful melody and the friar's baritone voice singing words in praise of God.

Declan sat on a bench in front of the altar. When the friar noticed him, he ceased his singing and waved to the musician, who left hastily.

Friar Faelan approached. "Laird MacKendrick, good day to you. Would you like to make a confession, talk, or be alone? I am a good listener and ye appear to have much on your mind. Especially given the events of the past few days. Forgive me for mentioning them, but these are dire times indeed, my Laird, and it's not unusual for even the strongest of men to seek solace in the Lord."

He motioned to the bench and the friar sat beside him. But now, Declan didn't know where to begin. "I think I love my wife."

Faelan grinned. "Well now, 'tis not a sin to love one's wife. That is what should be." He drew his brows down low over the bridge of his nose. "Except...forgive me, Laird, but does the idea of loving your wife distress ye?"

He shrugged. "Nay. Not at all. But my trouble lies in whether or not I should tell her."

"Ye are not the only man who has been confronted with this issue. Do ye deem that it will weaken ye? Or is it the commitment itself that comes with such words that confounds you?"

Declan drew in a deep breath. Confronting this matter was harder than he'd expected. "I am not weakened because I love her, and I do not fear my vows to her. But...what if she does not love me in return? That I could not accept." It would weaken him, in fact.

Faelan chuckled. "I tell ye, Laird, I see the way your wife looks at you and I doubt she harbors anything but love for ye. When ye are ready to declare it, so shall she. I suggest ye not shield your heart for it will do well to be open to her."

Good words, those. Declan nodded. "I will think about that, Friar." He sighed. "Now. There is another worry that troubles me."

Faelan folded his hands and peered at him with his full attention. "Go on."

"I discern there was trouble betwixt my parents before my mother passed. At the time, I was hardly home so I did not notice, but Rhona told me that she oft heard them arguing."

"Does this have a bearing on ye now? Should ye not let their transgressions be kept in the past where it belongs? There is no reason to rehash old wounds, is there?"

"I believe their arguments could be the reason someone is against me now." Declan sighed heavily. "I could be wrong, but what if what happened betwixt them then has caused me to have an unknown foe?"

"Perhaps ye should ask some of the elders who might have been privy to their arguments. They might give ye an insight into their relations."

Declan stood and paced before the altar. "My gran would know some of the elders who were present then. I will ask her again. Perhaps some recollection will shake itself free now that she's had time to think about it." Have ye seen Claude? Is he here?"

"He is in the antechamber reading the *Good Book*," Faelan said. Then he tilted his head back to yell out his brother's name.

Claude popped his head through the door's threshold. "Aye? Oh, Declan, I did not know you were here. I am glad you are. Did Milady Isabella tell ye what we found? About the treasure?"

"Nay, she has not. Much has happened though since I returned... He frowned. Treasure? They'd actually found something from that old map? "What did ye find?"

Claude clapped his hands and disappeared beyond the door but returned a moment later holding a chalice and a cross, both apparently of gold. They glinted in the candlelight from the altar. "Milady came with me when I searched the caves beyond the loch. I found these, buried." He handed the objects to him.

Declan held them, one in each hand. They were heavy, and both were exquisitely etched with embellishments that shone brightly. "I know what these are..."

Claude's eyes widened and he stepped nearer. "What? Do not leave us in the dark."

"Grandda often told stories around the fire about an old king who was given the task of hiding away old relics entrusted to him during the first crusade. He claimed that they, a large regiment from Scotland, traveled with Normans, Flemish, and Germans on a ship from England. They were delayed by a Portuguese army that insisted they aid in capturing Lisbon to expel the Moorish. He boasted about their bravery and that the king was given rewards, which he buried somewhere near here to keep them safe."

"These items appear old enough to be those relics. They must be the objects the old king hid," Faelan said. "Or some of them."

"I suggest we keep the items here in the chapel and allow Friar Faelan to use them in his services," Claude said. "The homage of it will reward us with God's blessing."

"I think that is a fair idea, brother. Ye have my permission to keep them here, Friar. These objects belong to the MacKendricks though and will not leave my land."

The friar bobbed his head. "I am honored, Laird, and will bless these objects at once. Perhaps I will have a special Mass so the clan can participate in the blessing."

His brother and the friar left him and disappeared beyond the door to the antechamber.

Declan sat back on the bench and relished the quiet and solitude of the chapel. Solitary, he was able to fully consider how unaware he had been throughout his life. He'd been unaware of his parent's discord, his wife's troubles with Silas, and whatever animosity forced his foe to take such a stand. Declan opened his eyes and swore he would never be unaware again.

On his return to the keep, he heard the gate watchman shout their call to arms. All MacKendrick soldiers within hearing distance charged to the gate. Declan ran forth and reached the gate at the same time as Anse.

"What goes?" Anse asked.

Declan forged his way through the mass of his soldiers until he reached the watchman.

"There is a band of soldiers riding toward our gates. I saw them in the distance."

He turned and stared, waiting for the riders to come within view. "It looks to be Campbell's soldiers. Open the gate."

His men did as he bade, and the gates were opened. There were at least ten Campbell men on horses. They stopped just inside the gate. Declan recognized Micah, the Campbell's commander-in-arms.

Micah dismounted and approached. "Robbie was on his way to see ye. We were ambushed on the trail, and he was injured."

Declan regarded Robbie's body lying over the back of a horse. "Bring him to the main keep." He rushed to the keep and shouted for Isabella when he got there.

She knelt beside a trunk just inside the hallway. "What is it?"

"There is an injured man…"

"Take him to the first chamber above the stairs. I will get Edith." Isabella hurried away.

Declan directed the men to carry Robbie to the chamber above. Once there, they set him on the bed. He searched his comrade for injuries. "What happened to him?"

His commander paced by the bedside. "Five men rode at us. While we were fending off four of the men, my laird was battling the last. After the four men rode off, I turned back and found Robbie lying on the ground. He was attacked with a dagger that we found still embedded in him. Fortunately for him, he had chainmail on but there are cuts where the chainmail was breached, and he bled a great deal."

"Help me prepare him. We will need to remove his upper garments."

Isabella hastened into the chamber toting a large bucket of hot water. Edith followed her inside, carrying cloths and Isabella's medicinal satchel.

"Tend to him, love. I do not want to lose him."

"Who is he?" she asked.

"Leona's brother." Declan helped Robbie's commander remove the heavy chainmail and the remainder of his garments.

"I will do what I can, Declan, but I make no promises. The wounds look grave. Leave us. Edith and I will tend to him. Edith, we might need Lillith to aid us." She dismissed him and bent over Robbie, prodding his wounds.

He stopped Edith from leaving. "Anse, go and bring Lillith. Edith, stay and help Isabella."

The maidservant returned to his wife's side. Declan tensed. From the sound of Isabella's tone, the odds of Robbie surviving didn't appear to be to his advantage. He motioned to the men to leave the chamber so the women could do their work.

Outside in the hallway, Declan leaned against the wall. Micah took up a similar position next to him.

"Did ye recognize the men who attacked ye?"

Micah shook his head. "It was dark in that part of the forest. We never heard them coming which means—"

"Which means they were lying in wait for you. Why was

Robbie on his way to see me?" Declan hoped he'd had news to impart about their foe.

"He did not say, och only that he needed to see you at the soonest. We rode like hell to get here and took no rest."

Declan detested not knowing why Robbie was intent on seeing him. He growled in frustration and prayed his comrade survived. If he didn't, there was no telling how he'd find his foe then because he sure as hell was in the dark about it.

CHAPTER TWENTY-THREE

ISABELLA WAS DEAD on her feet. She'd tended to Robbie throughout the night and by morning his wounds were stitched, they were soothed with a healing balm, and he was cleaned. The man appeared to rest comfortably though he wasn't out of danger. There was always the risk of infection. Through her ministrations, Isabella prayed he would survive.

Twice he awakened and groaned from the pain of his injuries. He had only settled once she made a tincture which put him to sleep in little time. She was careful to only use the tiniest pinch of henbane to ease him. The man was Declan's brother-in-law and their son's uncle. He was family even though he didn't belong to the MacKendrick clan.

By morning, Isabella's eyes were bleary, and she fell asleep sitting by the man's bedside. She hadn't heard Declan enter the room but awakened and sighed when he lifted her in his arms. It felt too good to rest in his embrace, so she relaxed and let him carry her to their bedchamber in the abutting room. There, he set her gently on the bed and knelt next to it. He pressed his hands over her hair and set a light kiss on her lips.

"Rest, love, ye did well and saved him. I am grateful."

"He is not out of danger, Declan. I should be there in case he needs attention," she said, sitting up. She tried to shimmy from the bed.

Declan pressed her back. "I will have the healer sit with him while you rest. Lillith should be arriving soon. I must tell ye, Robbie was attacked in my woods. Someone awaited him there and ambushed him. I need to go and find the interlopers."

"I understand but you'll be cautious? I will worry for you."

"There will be more than a score of soldiers with me. We are setting a trap for the miscreants. I detest leaving you, love, but I must find out who threatens us."

Isabella pulled him closer and set a gentle kiss on his lips. "Be safe and promise to return to me." She wouldn't release him until he spoke the words.

"I promise to return to ye." Declan gave her a passionate kiss that nearly caused her to swoon. "Ye make it difficult to leave. I placed additional guards around our walls and our home. Ye should be safe, but I would rather ye not go outside the walls until this enemy is found. No traipsing to the loch with Noah."

"I will stay within the walls. Worry not," she vowed. Exhausted, Isabella closed her eyes and drifted to sleep.

WHEN SHE OPENED her eyes, Declan was gone. Isabella blinked and stretched. She must have slept long because it appeared the sun was beginning to rise. With haste, she rushed through her morning routine and hurried to see how Robbie was doing. There were no sounds from within the chamber. She entered and found him sleeping.

The healer likewise slept in a chair. Lillith, she'd been told, had tended to the clan for only a short amount of time. She appeared young, probably the same age as she. Her long blondish-brown hair was braided and pulled to the front of her. Isabella touched her shoulder and startled poor Lillith.

"Do you want me to take over?"

Lillith shook her head. "Ye go on about your day. Edith says she shall come later this morn."

Isabella nodded and left the chamber. There was still much to settle in their new home. Although it was late summer, almost autumn, there was a chill about the fief. She needed to have the lads return and light fires to warm the rooms.

She opened the door and found Slone awaiting her. "Good morn, Slone. I take it Declan has left the holding?"

"Aye, Milady, yestereve. I am to see to your protection. If ye need to leave the keep, ye should tell me so. Our laird told me to keep ye inside, though."

Isabella understood the need for protection since Declan was certain their enemy was close. She wouldn't do anything to cause unnecessary worry for the soldier. "I shall be here within. But might I ask you to bring Noah and Marian here? And tell Rhona and Claude to come as well."

"I will have a soldier give them your messages."

"Good, and please send the lads that were here the other day. There is still plenty to do to situate the rooms and I want to have everything settled by the time Declan returns."

He bowed to her.

Isabella returned to the great hall and repositioned the large table that sat at the end of the long room. It was heavy and she could barely budge it, but finally she got it in place. By the time she had all the chairs reset, Edith had arrived with a tray full of morning foodstuff. She hadn't realized how hungry she was until she smelled the delicious scent wafting from the pottage.

"Sit ye down, Milady, and eat, afore ye fall down from hunger." Edith placed a hardened trencher before her and filled it with the stew.

"Are most of the men gone?"

Edith sat across from her. "Aye, it is eerie having none of the soldiers making noise or taking up the lanes. We should prepare and make ready for their return. There could be injuries to tend to. I have had the maids bring more water from the loch, in case we need to heat it."

"We shall be prepared. I'll make additional bandages and mix some medicinals to have at hand." Isabella hoped none of the MacKendrick soldiers sustained injuries. "Do you suppose they will war with whomever this enemy is?"

"Men like to war. It is their nature to do so. Laird Declan seeks vengeance so I vow the men shall make war." Edith took a roll and broke it into small pieces. As she ate, she regarded Isabella. "Ye look tired, Milady. Do not overdo it this day."

"There is too much to do. I have no time to sit and take rest."

Marian entered with Noah running out from behind her skirts. He didn't stop until he'd reached her. Isabella pulled him into a bear hug and lifted him from the floor. "I vow you have grown since I have come. Soon, you'll be as tall as your da."

That brought forth a wide grin from Noah. "Da says I will be bigger than him one day."

How well he was speaking! Her heart filled with joy. He was so different from the wild lad she'd first encountered. Or the distant child who'd played with a rock and a piece of string in the corner of a cottage, lost in his own world. "I certainly believe that is so. Now, we are all to stay here, inside the fief, until your da returns. Why do you not go and pick out a bedchamber, Noah, and we shall get your things and make a room here for you."

Noah's mouth hung open. "Milady? I shall stay here with you and da?"

"Yes, of course you will. You are now my son too, Noah. We want you to be here with us. That is if you want to be." Isabella wasn't prepared for the tears that gathered in the lad's eyes.

He rushed forth and wrapped his arms around her waist. "I would like that, but only if ye let me call ye 'Mama.'"

Now Isabella's eyes misted. "You can call me whatever you wish. I would love it if you called me 'Mama.'"

Marian sniffled. "Ye have this old woman ready to weep."

"That goes for you too, Marian. You will not live in that lonely old cottage by yourself. There is plenty of room here within the fief and I enjoy your company."

"Since that horrible harridan is gone, I shall be pleased to stay here." Marian smiled and dabbed her eye. "That is the only reason why I left Declan's home."

Rhona and Claude strolled into the great hall. Isabella gazed at those who joined her, and her heart filled with love. Those people were now her family, and she would do whatever it took to make them happy.

"Rhona, have you settled on the day you will wed? Declan promised he would set a day for your wedding." Isabella took her hand and guided her toward Marian.

"Did Declan not tell ye? We are going to do it the morning of the harvest festival."

"You will need a beautiful gown for your special day. Marian, will you help Rhona make an appropriate dress for her wedding? You make the most exquisite garments." Isabella had seen the gowns in Marian's cottage from when she was a young woman. They were simple but elegant.

The two linked arms and removed themselves to the chairs by the hearth. Marian and Rhona were animated as they spoke about what kind of material to use and the finer details of what the dress should entail.

Isabella sat back at the table and tried to finish her pottage. Claude joined her. He was quiet. "How are you this day, Claude?"

"Well, Milady. We are to have a special Mass to bless the relics we found in the cave. Friar Faelan wants to do it soon because he says our prayers will give the relics a special place in our hearts. He means to bless them before he places them on the altar. I shall go and join him if ye do not need me."

"I shall see you later, Claude. Be sure to return for supper."

"Isabella, I am going to help Gran gather her and Noah's belongings and we will bring them here," Rhona said. She motioned to Marian to walk ahead of her. "We shall return before supper."

Isabella nodded to her and took the small trencher that held pottage in her hand. She ate as she assessed the room for anything else that needed doing.

Edith rose and rounded the table. "I am going to see cook about this night's supper and I will have the bedding brought in. It was laundered yestereve. It should be dry by now. We shall get everyone sorted before nightfall."

The maid left her, and Isabella finished her meal. She remembered that Declan had given her a missive the day before. With the chaos of the day, she had forgotten to read it. Isabella practically ran to her bedchamber. She searched for the gown she had worn the day before and rummaged through the seams. Carefully, she pulled out the missive and flattened it. It was a bit rumpled from being creased inside the seam.

She hoped to hear good news from her parents and recognized her mother's writing. With shaking fingers, she cracked the seal and opened the parchment:

Dearest Daughter, I hope this missive finds you happy in your marriage. It is with the sad news that I impart the death of your brother. We received word that he perished in the war against the infidels. Your father has been duly punished by King Alexander for stealing horses, and we must flee our home before the warder comes to imprison him. The lord must have won the king's support for we are now in peril. We shall flee below the border. Worry naught for us. Your ever-loving mother, JF.

Isabella drew a deep breath. She was saddened to hear the news of Christopher's death. Tears trickled over her cheeks at the thought that she would never see him again. Then she thought of her parents. How many times had she warned her father that he would eventually be caught? Her father wouldn't cease his thievery and now he'd probably stolen from a higher-ranking lord who insisted the king take action against him. Now her parents had fled below the border into England. Lord only knew where they would end up but she couldn't worry for them. They had made their bed and now they must lay upon it. Still, she would add them to her prayers when she sought to take Mass.

For the rest of the afternoon, she kept herself busy and tried not to think of Declan out in the woods waiting for his foe to show. She checked on Robbie again and still he slept but Edith told her that Lillith's tinctures were much more powerful than hers. Isabella was always careful not to use too much medicinal in her remedies. She had heard about the effects of what such a tincture could do—end the life of the poor person who needed aid.

Isabella wandered through the keep. She'd finished all that she had planned to do. At the bottom of the stairs, the door opened, and Slone stepped inside. He had a look of concern on his face, one that alerted her that there was trouble. His brows furrowed and his jaw tightened before he addressed her.

"Milady, there is something amiss. I am going to the gate to find out what is happening. Stay inside and lock the door until I return."

She grabbed his arm before he could depart. Her grip tightened in the same manner that clutched her heart. "Have the men returned? Is Declan all right? Oh, I hope it's not the men who attacked Robbie. What is happening?"

Slone shrugged his shoulder and pulled back from her. "There were shouts. I must find out if all is well. Secure the door. I'll return as soon as I can."

After the soldier left, Isabella spotted a beam leaning against the wall which probably secured the door. She set the wooden post in place and jammed the bolt into it with shaky hands. She hurried to the back entrance and noticed the door was open. Footsteps sounded on the back stairs and sent a flutter of nerves to her stomach. Someone had come in through the back. Maybe it was Noah. It would be like a small lad to come in and leave the door ajar. Isabella closed and latched it. Then she hastened to the stairs and reached the first-floor landing.

Noah was enthralled with the bedchamber he had chosen for himself, and she had no doubt that he was there. Of course, Edith still hadn't returned from her meeting with the cook. The men had gone to the gate. That only left the healer inside the fief with her, and Robbie in his bed. A bang sounded as if a door closed. With each step she took in the hallway, her pulse pitched to her ears and a dampness flushed her forehead. She had to make sure no one had entered and approached the chamber where Robbie rested.

Isabella opened the door and saw Lillith staring at her with wide eyes. Her gaze was intent, and Isabella instantly knew there was trouble given the look of fear on the healer's face. She stood at the door unknowing what to do and breathed heavily through her nose. Someone was in the chamber with the healer. Robbie still slumbered from his medicinal-induced tincture. Lillith raised her chin and moved her eyes to the side, once, twice, three times. Isabella took that as a signal to mean she should flee. She gently pulled the door closed, but then it was opened with a force that propelled her forward. A man she didn't recognize took hold of her arm and swung her inside.

The man was young, perhaps the same age as Declan. He was just as tall, muscular, with dark wavy strands of hair falling to his shoulders. She couldn't tell if he smiled or not as his lengthy beard all but covered his mouth. His eyes had darkness in both color and in the way he looked at her.

He motioned to the healer. "Be gone."

Lillith gave her a sorrowful glance as she passed her and fled from the room. The man slammed the door shut and stood before it.

"Who are you?" she asked in awe. "Why are you here?"

"Dermot Murray, Milady MacKendrick."

"You know who I am, but you have me at a disadvantage—"

"Your beauty is spoken of far and wide. I came to speak to Declan, but he is not here?"

She shook her head and wished her husband was home. The man before her appeared dangerous and a tremor of fear stiffened her spine. His voice came in a deep burr mixed with both English and Gaelic words. She understood enough of what he asked. "He is with the soldiers and should return shortly…for the mid-day meal." Isabella purposely lied because she didn't want him to know Declan was gone.

Murray laughed. "'Tis well past sext, Milady, as well ye know. Ye tell a falsehood, do ye not? It matters not because my men even now are cutting him down in his own woods."

Isabella pressed her hands against her chest and drew a fearful breath. "Why…why would you want to hurt Declan? He is your friend, is he not? I have heard him speak of you."

"He is no friend of mine though he deems we are comrades," the man's voice took on a vehemence that spoke volumes of his hatred for Declan. He loomed by the door, blocking her exit.

Would he kill her? He intended to kill Declan? She kept her distance, hoping and praying that someone would soon come to help her. She looked for anything she could use to protect herself, but there was nothing except medicinal jars and cloths that sat on a table behind her. The chamber wasn't overlarge but big enough to fit a large bed, a side table which held a pitcher, a chair, and a basin table. One lone small window provided some light.

"What do you intend to do here?" Isabella backed up against the table where the healer set her items and medicinals. She had to do something to aid herself and with her eyes fastened on the bottle that held the mixture of 'devil's eyes'. The potion was tasteless and odorless. He wouldn't be able to detect it and she made a small unnoticeable nod. If anything, she'd put the man to sleep and could get the guards.

"Declan foiled my plans time and again. It is time to end it."

"He can be quite vexing, can't he? Why don't you sit for a spell? I will get you a drink." She retrieved the pitcher, turned to the table, and with her back to him, she sneakily added a few drops of the tincture. She turned back to him and smiled, held the cup up, and poured a bit of water into a cup. Isabella apprehensively stepped toward the man and handed him the cup. "Drink and tell me why you want to thwart him. What has Declan done to cause your affront?"

Dermot held the cup in his hand but didn't drink from it. He set the cup on his thigh, holding it ever so still. Her heart beat hard in her chest in wait for him to take a swig. "I murdered Laird Campbell. It had to be done so I could accuse Declan of his murder, but then the damned king allowed his freedom. I thought he would be tried and beheaded or at the least, hung, and that would be the end of it."

"Good heavens. Why would you want to accuse Declan of Allan Campbell's murder?" Isabella tried not to glance at the cup and kept her gaze fixed on his face. Lord, she prayed, please let him take a sip or two. She tried to distract him and get him to talk about his problems.

Murray scoffed. "I shouldn't tell ye, but aye, for payment, for his family's debauchery. Your husband was taken to the king's dungeons, and I thought my problem was solved until I heard tell the king released him. The problem was, I did not discern that Declan was friendly with Alexander."

She tried to appear demure and smiled. "The king needed unmarried men to wed to the women he chose by the border."

Murray laughed and the edges of his eyes crinkled. "'Tis humorous, that. When I heard that Declan was released, I tried to end him in the woods, but his men thwarted me, and he got away."

Isabella frowned but then quickly changed her demeanor to humor. She chuckled. "Was that when he returned home with an injured leg?"

Murray leaned to the side and peered at the tables. "Aye, and I suppose that healer fixed him up, or did ye?" He fondled his beard and his eyes changed from mirth to a stern mien.

"Of course, I did. It was my duty to mend my husband."

"Your husband will no longer exist after this day." His eyes glinted with amusement. "Does this distress ye? Aye, I hope it does."

Isabella couldn't let her emotions get the better of her. She had to remain pragmatic and gain his acceptance of her if she was to survive, for she had no doubt he intended to kill her along with Declan and perhaps everyone in their clan. "Not at all. I am not one to become distressed and I don't believe in love. We made a marriage contract to which I have held my part of the bargain. So, you seek revenge against Declan because of what his family did? What did his family do?"

Murray took a sip of the water and then another. "His mother took advantage of my father. They were at a festival, and she lured him into a tent where they had relations."

Isabella held her breath as he looked down at the cup he held and frowned. But then he shook himself and said, "Their affair continued and when my mother found out about it, she killed Declan's mother. Aye, she forced her to take a potion that did her in and killed her almost instantly. That would have sufficed as retribution but then my mother took her own life after because she could not live with the guilt of taking Lady MacKendrick's life."

It was funny how he too was consuming a potion of sorts and yet, was unaware of it. "I am sorry, Dermot, that you suffered. You do know that Declan had nothing to do with his mother's actions and he has suffered too." Isabella took his cup and returned to the table where she kept her back to him. Her heart thudded in her chest as she added a few more drops of "devil's eyes" to the cup. The man was large and apparently needed more medicinal than she'd thought. She turned back to him and held the pitcher, refilled his cup in his view, and handed it back to him.

"It matters not. Before I am through, no one will ever remember the name MacKendrick. I will ensure his clan is abolished and that Campbell's clan is too."

"What has Robbie to do with this?"

Murray grinned. His speech was somewhat slurred when he answered, "He will seek revenge, aye for the murder of his da, his sister, and his comrade. I mean to take care of that before he gets the better of me."

"You mean before Laird Campbell seeks his own justice?"

"Justice will be enacted but only by me," Dermot said and tilted on his chair.

Isabella stayed where she was and stared at the madman. "I hope you don't intend to harm me. I suspect you deem that by harming me, you will hurt Declan. But I assure you he cares not for me."

"Now I know ye speak falsely. Just look at ye. You are a bonny woman, and any man would be pleased to be married to ye. Surely Declan cares for ye. If ye were my wife, I certainly would care." Murray slid from his chair onto the floor and gazed up at her in wonder.

Isabella stepped back waiting for him to succumb. "You compliment me when you don't even know me."

"I...Ye...are...a clever...lass," Murray stammered and pitched to the floor, flat out.

Isabella gasped and jumped back. She breathed heavily at the danger she'd been in. With the man unconscious, she had to ensure he was unable to move if he awakened. She took the ties from the newly hung window coverings and tied the man's hands and feet with them. She checked on Robbie to discover that he watched her through his slitted eyes.

"Stay still, Laird Campbell. You are at the MacKendrick keep. We have tended your wounds, but you must be still, or you will undo the care."

He gestured with his chin and his voice emerged in a whispered rasp. "What is Murray doing here? And why is he tied up?"

Isabella smiled and enlightened him. "He is your enemy. Worry not, he cannot harm you now, at least not for a time. I have rendered him asleep."

"What did ye do to him?" Robbie raised his head to lean toward the side of the bed and scowled at Murray.

"I gave him a drink. Of course, it was laced with a few drops of the 'devil's eyes'. He shall be out for some time." Isabella heard the banging on the keep's door. Shouts came and she glanced out the window casement in the chamber. There were what appeared to be two scores of soldiers ramming the door. "I best go and let them in before they break the door down."

Laird Campbell guffawed and lay back.

"Declan would not like that at all because the door was only recently put on. He's fond of this fief." She opened the door and smiled at him as she passed through the threshold.

Isabella rushed down the stairs and unlatched the beam holding the door closed. Within seconds, the great hall filled with soldiers. She had never felt so protected even though she'd pretty much saved herself.

CHAPTER TWENTY-FOUR

THE FOREST WAS still. Their adversaries were there some-where. Declan signaled to his men to take cover. His plan was simple: he and his men would ambush the ambushers. They would wait in the forest until the interlopers rode through. Whoever attacked Robbie had to be in the forest. He'd brought Campbell's men and thirty of his soldiers. Declan hoped Robbie's clansmen would recognize the men who attacked their laird.

The day dragged by with excruciating slowness. Not one man spoke or made enough movement to alert anyone who traipsed through the woods. Declan grew tired of waiting. He wasn't known for his patience, but to ferret out his enemy, he would wait until heaven met hell.

But then, noise came from afar. He held up his hand to alert the men and to signal to remain where they were.

Six riders on horses rode through the trees at a slow pace. They didn't seem concerned for their safety and spoke to each other as they progressed. Declan continued to hold up his hand. They would pick the perfect moment to intercept them. When the progression of men reached the center of the MacKendrick and Campbell soldiers, Declan lowered his hand. At once his men revealed themselves from their hiding places.

The knaves tried to flee, but swords were drawn and pointed at the foes. They sat still on their horses that were apprehended as some of his men took their reins. Several soldiers grabbed the riders from their horses and tossed them to the ground.

Declan made his way through the circle of men. "Who are ye? What clan do ye hail from?"

None of the men answered.

"They are Murray's men," one of the Campbells said. "I recognize them. They visited our keep only a fortnight ago, but Robbie would not give them entrance beyond our gates."

"Murray. Is your laird here in the forest?" Declan couldn't understand why Dermot's men rode through his woods without their laird or why he'd visited the Campbell fief recently. His comrade had all but said that Robbie wouldn't meet with him. But then a dawning struck Declan as he remembered what Dermot had told him.

"Robbie will not meet with you. I tried to persuade him, but the man was adamant and said that he would not meet with a murderer. Even though I swore that ye did not have anything to do with his father's murder." Yet none of what his supposed ally told him was true because Robbie told him to come. Why had Dermot told him that Robbie wouldn't see him? Dermot lied about his trip to act as mediator. What else had he lied about? Had Dermot offered to be the go-between with Robbie to keep them apart? Why the subterfuge? What did his comrade hope to gain?

Micah, the Campbell commander-in-arms, nudged his way through the crowd. "Laird MacKendrick, I need to speak to ye."

Declan moved aside so the men being held couldn't hear them. "What goes, Micah?"

"They are the men that attacked us. I recognize the man with the torn tunic because I tried to apprehend him and the slippery skelp got away. They tried to murder my laird."

He craned his neck to peer back at the men. "It doesn't make sense, Micah. Why would Murray's clansmen attack your clan or mine? He is a trusted ally."

"He is no ally, Laird MacKendrick. That band of men attacked us, I am certain."

Declan marched back to the men and stood before them. "Where is your laird?"

The men wouldn't answer. Declan had had enough of their silence. His patience was gone, and he grabbed the nearest man and gripped him closely. "Tell me where your laird is, and I will let you live."

The man refused to answer him. Declan tossed him behind him where his awaiting soldiers put the man out of his misery—the misery of awaiting his death. A brief scuffle ensued, and the man existed no longer. He grabbed the next man. "Where is your laird?"

Again, no answer. Declan repeated his motions until the second to the last man answered him.

"He told us to await him here in these woods. That he was going to the MacKendrick keep and would return before nightfall."

Declan tossed the man behind him and moved out of the way of his soldiers. The six men were killed for their involvement in whatever scheme Dermot Murray had planned.

His heart began to pound as it occurred to Declan that Murray was at his keep. This whole thing had been a ruse, and a distraction. While he was down here, waiting to be ambushed, Dermot had probably snuck inside like the polecat he was. And that meant—*Isabella was in danger.*

"Let us make haste. I need to get back to the keep posthaste." Declan ran to his horse, not caring if his men followed. He only had Isabella—and Noah, and Gran, and everyone—on his mind. But Isabella's face was the one he held in his mind's eye as he rode like hell for the walls of his home. At the gate, he raised his hand and shouted, "Virtue alone ennobles."

Behind him, he heard the echoing shouts of his men, and then the calls of those who remained within. As soon as he passed the threshold of the gate, he slid from his horse's back, ready to sprint to his home to find his wife.

But then Anse trotted toward him, holding up his hand.

"Laird, we had a wee bit of trouble. Och, not to worry, though. All is well now."

His knees almost buckled. They—she—Isabella—was safe. "Dermot Murray?" he breathed in response.

"Aye, he is in the pit. Milady did him in. Well, och, nay. She rendered him incapacitated."

Declan scowled at hearing Isabella was involved in apprehending their foe, but then again, knowing his impetuous, bonny, brave wife, he wasn't surprised. "What happened? Tell me on the way to the keep."

Anse sidled next to him and said, "The gate watch didn't know Murray was…our foe. Because of that, Laird, they allowed him through the gate. Once he was through, he fought with the two guards stationed there. The guards called our call to arms and at once the entire keep was put on alert. Not before that damnable man made his way inside the keep. Slone heard the commotion, and he bade Milady to lock the keep doors. She did so, but Murray must have made it inside before she could secure the holding. She says he spoke about your mother and his father. While she kept him talking, she put him out with one of her tonics."

Declan drew a sharp breath. "She could have been killed. Murray could have killed her."

"Och, he did not. Nay, Laird, I do not think he intended to harm her. He was after ye, but your lass, she is clever. When she finally opened the door to the keep, he was passed out. She said she gave him the 'devil's eyes', but unfortunately, not enough to kill him."

"Good, because that privilege belongs to me." Declan reached the keep and entered. Anse followed him inside. He found his family sitting at the table in the great hall as if nothing had happened. Isabella, Noah, Marian, Rhona, Claude, and Friar Faelan were enjoying a lavish supper. He didn't know how to react. Relief didn't come close to the emotions that swarmed him in seeing his wife safe.

"Isabella."

She jumped up when she spotted him, then ran to him. Once she reached him, she pressed her arms around him. He settled his hands on her hips and set his head next to hers. "God, how relieved I am to see ye."

"Och, aye? I was never in danger, Declan. All is well. Your enemy is in the pit behind the garrison, or at least that is what Anse told me. I thought you would like to question him before…"

"Before what, Wife?" He wondered if she'd realized she'd begun spouting Scots a bit. It endeared her to him all the more. Maybe he'd be able to get her to say more, later, when in the throes of passion. He blinked and forced himself to focus on her words. How he loved her…

"I don't imagine you will allow him to live since he confessed to murdering Laird Campbell and that he accused you… He said many things before I got him to drink the tincture," she said, unaware of his thoughts and intentions. But all that was about to change, here and now, in front of his clan and everyone who mattered to him.

"My bonny clever wife. Have I told ye how pleased I am that I married ye?"

"Not recently," she said and giggled. She blinked up at him with her beautiful eyes and her pretty pink lips curved into a smile. "Come, Laird, have some supper."

He shook his head with reluctance. How much he wanted to put his cares aside and focus on her instead of matters of the clan. But her calling him "Laird" like that had reminded him… "There are things I must see to before I can enjoy my supper."

She waved her hand as if brushing his concerns aside. "Robbie is doing well. He was awake for most of the afternoon, but I gave him some more pain medicinal. He will be asleep until morning. I suppose then he will want to talk to you."

"I will wait then to see him until the morrow. Is there anything else, Wife?" Declan grinned. His sweet wife had everything in order, and she didn't appear to have suffered the slightest difficulty.

She pressed her finger to her chin in thought. Then she shook her head. "Nay, Husband. There is nothing else."

He pulled her against him and kissed her hard. "Oh, there is much else, I'm sure ye know," he said in a lowered voice. "I will find my way to our bed this night. Ye can be sure of that."

"I'll take that as a promise." She released him then, and sashayed back to the table in an enticing way that he would find hard to forget. Perhaps that was her intent for Declan found himself smiling as he left the keep.

His men looked at him oddly, but they didn't know that his bonny bride pleased him more than he'd realized she could. Still, it wasn't befitting a laird to be so lovestruck, so he tried to replace his joyful mien with a harsher manner. It didn't take him long to remember that Dermot Murray had invaded his home and might have done in his wife.

That made him fume with ire. Declan motioned to his men to bring up his foe.

Murray reached the surface and was dragged a few feet from the hole. He didn't stand but lay on the ground, still half unconscious from whatever Isabella had drugged him with and waiting for his death.

"Get up, ye miscreant piece of cosh," Declan muttered. He kicked him and commanded him to rise again. "Ye will look me in the eye and tell me to my face that ye planned to do away with me. I want to hear it from your mouth."

Murray groaned and refused to move so Declan grabbed him and forced him to a standing position, but he staggered on his feet. "Why? I considered ye to be my comrade."

"Vengeance is mine," Murray said.

"I did nothing to ye to cause ye to seek vengeance. None of my clansmen affronted ye. Your villainous deeds were misplaced, Dermot."

"Your mother did. She ruined my life."

Declan shoved him back. "My mother?"

"Aye, your harlot of a mother lured my da into a sordid affair. She ruined my family. My mother suffered and killed herself when she learned that my da was with your ma. The guilt of murdering your mother was too much and my mother took her life. For this, you'll all pay."

Declan's stomach tensed. He had heard of such a rumor and the fact that alluded to such an affair, but he wasn't aware that it was between his mother and Dermot's father. That his mother was killed by Dermot's caused him to tighten his grip on the hilt of his sword. Yet he supposed Dermot's mother sought retaliation and couldn't hold the contempt of it. "Ye speak possible truths, but none of that has anything to do with me or Campbell. If indeed my mother was involved with your da, we should not bear the consequences of that."

"Aye, she was. Ask your gran. Ask the elders. There was a time when my clan would have nothing to do with yours because of it. Och, I tried not to hold hatred for the MacKendricks. Alas, I cannot do that now that I know the truth. I hope ye all rot in hell."

Declan's arm shot out and he struck Murray square in the face. His foe fell back but he quickly regained his feet. "Ye are the one going to hell. Even if our parents met and had relations that had nothing to do with me or you. Ye allowed what they did to sully our friendship," his voice beheld a low timbre. Though he wanted to shout and release his ire at the situation, he was more crestfallen that their friendship meant nothing to the man.

"Friendship, bah. There was no comradery betwixt us, per-haps only in your mind," Dermot scoffed. "Ye fell for my ruse. Aye, I befriended ye all to bring ye low." He spread his arms and taunted him, motioning with his fingers for Declan to advance. "I was making progress until ye went and married that woman. If the king had not called ye for the marriage, ye would have perished in that dungeon, or they would have hanged ye."

Declan's face heated with his anger brimming to his eyes. Heat crept around his neck and he fisted his hands. "What then?

Once I was killed, what then?" He'd get his answers and would see to the vengeance that had long plagued him.

"Then I would have thwarted the Campbells and used them to overtake your clan. I could not allow Robbie to live. He would have sought revenge for the murder of his father."

"You are the lowest of miscreants, Dermot. Ye tried to besmirch my good name and have no remorse. I am appalled that ye call yourself a Scot." Declan pulled his sword free. He gripped it tightly knowing exactly where he intended to put it. Though he didn't need the approval of his clansmen, he sought their eyes. There, in the loyal faces of the people of his clan, was all the approval he needed. He swung his sword with all the might he possessed, and practically severed Murray in two.

The soldiers shouted, '*Virtue alone ennobles.*'

He peered at the ground, darkened from the blood of his foe. Declan had never suspected Murray was behind the foul deeds. How had he been so duped by him? He had been far too trusting and took this as a lesson. The MacKendricks would no longer leave their gates open to supposed allies.

"Laird," Anse called.

He turned and frowned at his cousin. "Aye."

"It is over."

"Why do I not feel vindicated then?" Declan's breath rasped from the exertion of his strike and the strain of the day. His heart raced, and his chest rose and fell heavily.

"No one knows what madness induced him to take ye on. He caused his death, not ye. Ye had to seek vengeance for all the pain that he caused you and Robbie. Be appeased by that."

"Mayhap in time I will be solaced with his death."

Anse took his sword from his hand and jammed it into the center of Murray's chest, or what was left of it. Then he purposely shifted his gaze to all the soldiers who stood by. "No one touches this sword. It shall stay there until we are ready to remove it. Let it remain there as a reminder that no one crosses our laird or any MacKendrick."

The soldiers again shouted, '*Virtue alone ennobles.*'

CHAPTER TWENTY-FIVE

THE DAY OF Rhona's wedding and the harvest festival arrived. There was much to celebrate, and Declan stood awaiting his sister's entrance into the chapel. Many crowded within the small place of worship and likewise many more crowded outside the door. A rush of clamor came when Rhona made the procession toward Willeli. His sister looked beautiful but not as bonny as Isabella. Declan was happy that Rhona had found someone to hopefully spend a lifetime with.

Their marriage was sealed with the friar's declaration. Before all left the chapel, he called their attention. "Clan MacKendrick, I bid ye to wait. This day I will marry my bonny wife before ye all as witness of my devotion to her. Ye did not get to witness our marriage and it would please me, Isabella, if ye would again promise to be mine."

Isabella rose from the bench and approached him. Her wide smile told him she was joyful at his surprise. "I would marry you every day if need be, Declan."

"This day would do well enough," he said and took her hands.

The friar began the vows of the Sacrament of Matrimony for a second time that day, and a hush fell over the onlookers. Before the friar announced they had retaken their vows in sickness, health, and especially until parted by death—something that

Declan had determined wouldn't happen for a very long time—he asked if they would like to profess any vow of their own.

Declan turned and glanced at the many soldiers watching them. He hoped to set an example of chivalry for them and turned back to face his wife. "Isabella, from the moment I met ye, I was enamored. I am still enamored and always will be. Ye are kind, outspoken, loyal, courageous, clever and beautiful. Isabella MacKendrick, I love ye."

Isabella smiled and her eyes shimmered with what he hoped were tears of joy. "Declan, I always thought love was for fools, but I have come to understand that love encompasses more than courtly love. It is the giving of oneself to another and on this day as before, I give myself to you completely. I love you."

He couldn't hold back his jubilation at hearing her declaration of love. He leaned forward and kissed her. Declan had intended to kiss her passionately before their clan, but his sweet wife took it to a level that nearly buckled his knees.

Friar Faelan chuckled. "Ahem, ah… Where were we? Ah yes, I proclaim ye husband and wife. Go on to serve each other and God."

Cheers arose. Declan took Isabella's hand and led her from the chapel. Outside, the marriage and harvest fanfare began, as musicians played, fires were lit, and tables were ladened with more foodstuff that would feed an army, as all around he saw the happy faces of his clansmen and women.

He sat with Isabella at a table that had been erected outside their home especially for them. Declan watched as his sister and her new husband danced while Isabella sipped on wine. She appeared as jubilant as his clan. His gaze shifted as he spotted the Campbells arriving.

Robbie strolled toward him along with his wife who held their wee bairn in her arms. His comrade smiled at Isabella. "Milady Isabella, allow me to introduce ye to my wife. This is Mary. And the wee one is our son, Michael."

"Lady MacKendrick," Mary said and smiled. "I am thankful

for your gracious care of Robbie when he was injured. I wish to repay ye for your kindness."

"There is no need to thank me or for repayment. You are family and family always help each other. I am gladdened to see you have mended, Laird Campbell," Isabella said.

Robbie bowed to her. "Declan, I say this now. Our clans are allied for the rest of time. Aye, your wife not only mended my injuries, but she saved me from being killed whilst I recovered. My debt to her is insurmountable."

"I accept your alliance," Declan said with pride. "Join the festivities. There is plenty to drink and eat. Invite your clansmen to partake." The Campbells moved to the next table and intermingled with the rest of the MacKendrick clan. Declan sipped his ale and watched the festivity around him. Perhaps, he thought, there would be more weddings, and intermarriage between the two clans, making their allegiance stronger than ever.

Then he spotted a face he hadn't expected to see. He touched Isabella's arm to get her attention. "Look! There is Trevor. Lillith said she would have him well enough to attend the festival, and so she has."

Isabella waved to the healer and smiled. "Lillith confessed that he might have taken longer to recuperate than he should have. I think he might be smitten with her. Do you see what I see?"

Declan gazed at his soldier and bellowed a laugh. "What I see is a man who definitely took a wee bit longer to recuperate than he should have. I've never seen him smile at a woman like that."

Isabella giggled. "Trevor is a good man, and I am pleased for him. Now we need to find a suitable woman for Slone."

Declan scoffed. "No woman in her right mind would put up with his surliness."

"I accept that challenge, Husband, and will find the prettiest lass for him."

"I doubt that because there is none prettier than ye." Declan bellowed with more laughter but quieted when the musicians ceased, and their leader called for silence.

"What are they doing?" Isabella asked.

"I asked Bang to play a special song for us. Those three men... They are all named Bang because their mother did not know what to call them. She and her husband had no coin for playthings for their lads when they were wee and so she let them play with cauldrons and heavy metal spoons. Watch..."

The three brothers strolled to the center of the gathered clan with their drums hanging on their hips. Children of the clan followed in their wake. Noah joined the lads and lassies. Declan and Isabella stood to better see them. The Bang Brothers, as they were called, started playing. Their beats began softly and wee by wee raised to a rousing sound. Isabella's eyes widened and her lips parted in awe as she watched the innervated affect the beat of the drums had on the people that danced around the brothers. The children, along with Noah, skipped and shouted in glee to the banging. His eyes beheld Noah, who appeared happier than he'd ever seen him. His lad skipped around the Bang Brothers, his face filled with delight.

"I have never heard such music," she yelled loudly enough for him to hear.

Declan grinned for he'd suspected his wife would appreciate the raucous music. She was too excited herself, outspoken, and she took his breath away. Now Isabella spun, jumped, and tried to get him to join her in a maddening dance. But then the intense tempo of the beating of the drums ceased abruptly. Everyone quieted for a moment. The wind whipped at the pennons and Declan waited for the clamor of the crowd. It came in moments as all shouted, roared, and cheered.

"That was incredible," Isabella said. "Do they play like that often?"

"Rarely these days. The Bang Brothers have aged but they have been teaching their sons to play with such vigor. They only played this day as a favor to me."

"I enjoyed it. Thank you for asking them to play. Oh, look, there is Noah. I am pleased to see him playing with the other lads."

Declan shifted his gaze to his son and smiled. "Aye, but he is of age and should begin his warrior training."

Isabella set her hand on his upper arm. "Not yet, Husband. He has missed much of his childhood and needs more time to run and play. Can you not await another year before he begins his training?"

"I do not see the harm in awaiting another year. We'll wait."

She looked at him lovingly. "You are being so agreeable." Isabella gave him a soft peck of a kiss on his cheek. "I am going to talk to Rhona and will return shortly, husband, don't move," she said and walked off toward his sister.

Declan retook his seat and refilled his cup with ale. He hadn't been so relaxed but now that he put behind him the turmoil of Murray's plan to desecrate his clan, he had accepted that the dark days were behind him.

Anse sat next to him and grunted. "I vow those Bang Brothers put on a show, do they not?"

"Ye seem displeased, cousin. What has ye scowling like the devil?" Declan poured a cup of ale for Anse and handed it to him. "Drink and enjoy the fanfare."

Anse chuckled. "I always enjoy it when those men play. 'Tis like my heart is clashing against my chest and that it will erupt."

"Then what has ye so grim?"

"I do not know how to tell ye this…"

Declan frowned at his cousin and shoved his shoulder. "What is it? Speak."

"Your wife…she did the unthinkable. I vow I do not wish to get her in trouble but… She gave me your father's sword and told me to keep it. I don't think she realized it was your da's sword but thought it was yours. Milady said that ye gave her permission to give away your things. I tried to give it back to her and bade her to return it to the keep, but she wouldst not listen. I returned it to the wall in your hall, just so ye know."

Declan rose. "Why would she try to give away my sword, or rather my da's sword?"

"She said she was starting a war."

"Damnation, the confounded woman." Declan didn't bid farewell to Anse but sprinted off to find his wife. He marched through the crowds of his clansmen and spotted her standing with Rhona, by a barrel.

When he reached her, he grinned and grabbed her and lifted her over his shoulder. She gasped and squealed at him to put her down. His clansmen chortled. Near the keep, he set her on her feet, and she ran with him in his sprint inside their home. He chuckled because his wife had the same idea as he had.

She tried to speak to him, but he shushed her. Isabella wanted a war and he'd do his best to give her what she wanted. When he got to their bedchamber, he forced open the door, gently swung her inside, and slammed the door behind him. He paced before her and couldn't find the words to stress how surprised he was that she intended to give away his sword. She stood with her arms folded and peered at him.

Declan grabbed her and ran his fingers through her hair until the strands surrounded his hand. Lord, her hair was soft. He tipped her head back and stared down at her lovely face. Declan set his mouth on hers and gripped her mouth to get her to accept his kiss. His tongue lashed with hers in an urgent, provoked manner. She took hold of his arms and pushed him back, but Declan wasn't deterred.

With his mouth on hers, his free hand roamed her garments until he was able to remove them. She stood naked. His mouth turned over hers repeatedly, determined to keep her busy while he discarded his tunic and tartans. When his skin crushed hers, she moaned. He wouldn't let her speak and kept up the sensual assault. Declan eased her to the bed and gently pushed her back until she fell onto it. He took her legs, each now held in his hands, and set his mouth at her apex. With deliberate strokes of his tongue and mouth, he had her thrashing atop the bedcover within seconds.

"Declan, please…"

He peered at her as her plea stopped him for a moment. Declan wasn't about to give in so easily. "Quiet," he clipped, feigning outrage. He kept up the torment with his mouth teasing and taunting her and wasn't sure how he maintained his ability not to succumb to the rush of blood pulsing to his manhood.

Isabella came undone, crying out as ecstasy had control of her. Declan knelt back and pulled her to her knees. "Do ye want to take me in your mouth?"

Her eyes widened but she did as he asked. She was inept at first, but then her mouth moved over his shaft and Declan tilted his head back and groaned. The warmth of her tongue and mouth heightened the sensation of his need. He allowed her a moment of such play until she licked him. That small gesture caused his legs to shake ferociously. Declan pulled back from her, shifted her back, and fell atop her. He joined them and with all the madness that possessed him now, he jammed his shaft into her. There was no turning back, no gentle touches, no sweet kisses, just maddening torment for them both.

What pleasure it was too, and he followed her commands when she said, "That's it, harder. Hurry, keep going, don't stop. I want all of you."

His control faltered and with the first twinges of his culmination, he shouted at the intense paralyzing force that overtook him.

They came together in bliss that shattered them in a climax unlike any that he'd ever experienced. Declan gently pulled out of her and lay beside her. He rasped for breath which caused his chest to move rapidly. His heart thrummed so hard, he thought that it rivaled the beat of the Bang Brother's drumming.

"Declan…"

He kept his eyes closed and tried to even his breath before he spoke to her. What was she thinking to give his sword away?

That was the first question he intended to ask, but then he couldn't help but take her with unabashed enthusiasm. Hadn't he sworn never to take her roughly again? His promise to her meant nothing, not when she instigated his brashness. He pressed his hands over his face and calmed enough to have a civil conversation with his meddlesome wife.

"Why did ye give my sword to Anse?" his voice was hard, harder than he'd wanted it to be.

She leaned over him and caressed his chest. He suspected she'd intended to soothe him, but it was only making him want to take her again.

"I wanted to make war with you."

He shook his head. "War?"

"You said that husbands make love, not war, with their wives. I wanted you to make war with me. So, I intended to instigate you so that you would…"

"Make war with ye."

"Yes, and I must confess that I enjoy when you are rough. Well, sometimes, but I also like it when you are gentle. There are times though that I want you to make war with me."

Declan laughed so hard that his eyes watered. He pulled her against him and kissed her with a long passionate meshing of their lips. "Ye are the most—"

"Spirited?"

"Aye, spirited woman. In the future, Wife, ye are not to touch any swords. The sword ye gave Anse, by the way, was my da's. It holds a special place on the wall and is never touched. Besides, they are sharp weapons, and I don't want you injured. If ye want to make war with me, just tell me, and I'll oblige." He flashed a smile at her.

"Very well, Husband, I shall do that. I didn't know it was your da's sword and meant no disrespect."

"Nay, if my da were alive, he would've laughed to know ye used it to get your way." Declan pressed his hands over the softness of her hair that fell by her shoulder.

"We should probably rejoin the festival," she said sheepishly.

"Nay, let us lay here for a few moments. I liked hearing ye profess that ye loved me." He hoped she'd say it again.

"I do love you, Declan. How silly was I to think love was foolish? I am grateful to the king for offering me to you and I am happy that you chose me." Isabella rubbed her leg against his.

Declan knew before they left the fief he would take her again, but they would make love, not war. "Ye know very well that ye chose me and I am gladdened that ye did." He pressed a hand on her face and tilted it so he could see her bonny blue eyes. "Ye never told me what was in the missive."

"What missive?"

"The one I gave you before I left to await in the woods… Before…"

"Oh, that missive. It was from my mother. She wrote that my brother died."

Declan leaned up. "Brother? Ye never mentioned you had a brother."

"He volunteered to go on the crusade with the English. Unfortunately, he was killed. I didn't think he'd return and awaited such news. Also, my father was exiled for raiding. He and my mother escaped to England. I suppose some lord gained the king's accord and forced him to bring charges against my father for stealing his horses."

Declan chuckled. "I do like your father. We shall find out where they are and perhaps we can visit them."

"You would go to England for me?"

He shifted his face within an inch of hers. "I would go through the fires of Purgatory for ye, Wife, even to England which is far worse."

"I don't wish to go to England. I warned my father what would happen if he continued to steal from our neighbors. He wouldn't listen. My place is here with you, with the MacKendricks. That's where I wish to be and belong."

"Ah…so that is why ye learned healing methods. Ye had to patch up your father and his men when he returned from thieving?"

Isabella nodded. "Yes, and believe me, my father could be quite emotional when he was injured. When the king bade our attendance, I thought he would weep for a sennight."

That was interesting, Declan thought, for his wife adapted to the situations around her and had many interests. He realized it would take a lifetime to figure her out. Thank God he had the rest of their lives to do so. "Have ye seen the trunk? I meant to present it to ye this morn when we awakened, but ye were gone when I awoke." Declan motioned to the ornate, large trunk that sat next to his.

She pressed her hand over his chest. "I did see it. The trunk is for me? It is beautiful, quite ornate."

"Ye should have a place for your belongings. Ye can keep your things in there until the carpenter makes the wardrobes I commissioned."

Isabella smiled. "That was kind of you."

He stretched and had no intention of leaving their bedchamber until the fires were lit at the festival. That's when the real revelry began.

"I wonder how the other couples are getting on, those that the king bade to marry. Do you think the other brides and grooms are as happy as we are? I hope so because meeting you has changed my life considerably."

"My life was misery before I met ye. Alexander was right. The king said that I wouldn't be disappointed with the ladies he chose as the brides. He also told me that I would have a hard decision to make about which bride to choose. He was wrong about that. That decision was easy because ye were the only bride I wanted." Declan placed a light kiss on her lips. He slunk his hand over her thigh to her bare backside and shifted her against him. "Before we go, Wife..."

She didn't let him continue. Isabella pressed him onto his back and straddled his hips. "Before we leave, we will make slow, sweet love, just how you like it, Husband."

The End

About the Author

Read a Scottish or Medieval Historical Romance book by Kara Griffin and transport yourself to the mystical enchanting realms of the Scottish Highlands and Medieval Britain. Stories of noble swoon-worthy warriors and strong but sweet heroines will have you rooting for them as they encounter dastardly villains, political upheaval, and family dysfunction. Be romanced with sweeping tales of love and honor.

Kara Griffin has always had a vivid imagination and has been an avid romance reader since her early years. Inspired by her grandfather's heritage, she loves all things Scottish. From the captivating land to the ancient mysticism, all inspire her to write tales that make you sigh. With heroes, heroines, villains, and romance, there's always a Happily-Ever-After in her stories.

When Kara is not writing, she enjoys family life with her husband of 34 years, daughters, and five grandchildren. Living in the Pinelands of New Jersey, she spends a lot of time at a nearby lake, the Jersey Shore, and wooded areas of the Pine Barrons. She and her family are huge sports fans and cheer on the teams of the city of Philadelphia.

Website – karagrif66.wixsite.com/authorkaragriffin
Facebook – facebook.com/AuthorKaraGriffin
BookBub – bookbub.com/authors/kara-griffin
Amazon – amazon.com/stores/Kara-
Griffin/author/B006ZCH4PG
Goodreads – goodreads.com/author/show/1428371.Kara_Griffin
IG – authorkaragriffin